A Vacation to Die For

By Lynn Cahoon

The Tourist Trap Mysteries
A Vacation to Die For
Wedding Bell Blues
Picture Perfect Frame
Murder in Waiting
Memories and Murder
Killer Party
Hospitality and Homicide
Tea Cups and Carnage
Murder on Wheels
Killer Run
Dressed to Kill
If the Shoe Kills
Mission to Murder
Guidebook to Murder
Novellas
A Very Mummy Holiday
Mother's Day Mayhem
Corned Beef and Casualties
Santa Puppy
A Deadly Brew
Rockets' Dead Glare

The Survivors' Book Club Mysteries
The Tuesday Night Survivors' Club

The Kitchen Witch Mysteries
One Poison Pie
Two Wicked Desserts
Three Tainted Teas
Novellas
Chili Cauldron Curse
Murder 101
Have a Holly, Haunted Christmas

The Cat Latimer Mysteries

A Story to Kill
Fatality by Firelight
Of Murder and Men
Slay in Character
Sconed to Death
A Field Guide to Murder

The Farm-to-Fork Mysteries
Who Moved My Goat Cheese?
One Potato, Two Potato, Dead
Killer Green Tomatoes
Penned In
Killer Comfort Food
A Fatal Family Feast
Novellas
Have a Deadly New Year
Deep Fried Revenge
A Pumpkin Spice Killing

A Vacation to Die For

A Tourist Trap Mystery

Lynn Cahoon

LYRICAL PRESS
Kensington Publishing Corp.
www.kensingtonbooks.com

LYRICAL PRESS BOOKS are published by

Kensington Publishing Corp.
119 West 40th Street
New York, NY 10018

All Kensington titles, imprints, and distributed lines are available at special quantity discounts for bulk purchases for sales promotion, premiums, fund-raising, educational, or institutional use.

Special book excerpts or customized printings can also be created to fit specific needs. For details, write or phone the office of the Kensington Sales Manager: Kensington Publishing Corp., 119 West 40th Street, New York, NY 10018. Attn. Sales Department. Phone: 1-800-221-2647.

Lyrical Press and Lyrical Press logo Reg. U.S. Pat. & TM Off.

First Electronic Edition: September 2022
ISBN: 978-1-5161-1109-1 (ebook)

First Print Edition: September 2022
ISBN: 978-1-5161-1110-7

Printed in the United States of America

To my high school Home Ec teacher who taught me that a woman do more with her life than just the three jobs my guidance counselor recommended.

Acknowledgments

As the world continues its path to the future, I'm drawn more and more to the past and the what-ifs. As an author, I get to pretend with my characters. Working in fashion was a dream of mine, even though I wasn't the best at sewing or drawing or even putting together the best outfits. I did have one talent: I could pick out the most expensive outfit in any store. I still love clothes but now I choose outfits that provide more function and comfort over fashion.

Thanks to everyone who helped make this book a little better including those I don't know and all the ones I do.

Chapter 1

Mayor Marvin Baylor's excitement made the tone of his voice rise even higher than his normal, birdlike chirp. In fact, the words came out to the business-to-business meeting as more like a squeal. I glanced over at Amy Newman-Cross, my best friend and typically the mayor whisperer, but she just shrugged. Even Bill Sullivan, the City Council chairman and owner of South Cove Bed and Breakfast, frowned. The mayor paused, leaving room for the words to sink in, but no one in the room had heard what he'd actually said.

Bill leaned forward. "I'm sorry, Marvin, but exactly what kind of business is considering moving into South Cove next year?"

Mayor Baylor glared at Bill. Anger dropped the tenor of his voice just a little. This time, the words were clear. "Like I just said, we've had interest from Coastal Investment Properties to do a mini hotel here in South Cove. One with an upscale restaurant. They're all the rage in tourist areas. And all Max has to do is find a suitable property to build on."

This time *I* got the glare from the mayor. Apparently, Max Winter, the sales rep from Coastal Investments, had informed the mayor I had no interest in selling my home. Even for the eight-figure sum the nice man in the expensive suit had offered the last time he sat down at the table with Greg and me. The money would be life changing and we wouldn't have to worry about anything ever again. Except I'd have to buy a new place to live. South Cove property was expensive and hard to come by. And I liked walking to work. And I loved my house.

Greg and I had decided, as our first official decision as an engaged couple, that if we wanted to sell later, like in twenty years, we'd make the decision then. But for now, we loved where we lived. And it was my home.

I shouldn't be made to feel guilty for saying no, even if it meant the mayor wouldn't have his mini hotel and upscale restaurant.

"Uh-oh." Amy whispered. "It looks like you're the fly in his cream pie."

"Yep. His salesman came by the house again last week, thinking that if Greg heard the offer directly, he might make me accept the deal. But what they didn't know is we're both on the same page. We're not selling." I leaned toward her as I filled her in on my part of ruining the mayor's latest expansion plans for South Cove. It wasn't that I didn't like the mayor. Well, I didn't, but that wasn't the problem. The problem was he kept trying to use my property as he courted new businesses to move to South Cove. Well, mine and Esmeralda's house, which sat across the street. But she'd told the mayor to stop sending developers her way or she might do a fortune for him that had bad outcomes.

The mayor's wife, Tina, believed in Esmeralda's psychic talent, so she had put the kibosh on anyone approaching Esmeralda to sell again. Maybe I could ask our local psychic to convince Tina that my property was protected by the spirits as well. I'd chat with her the next time I saw her at the police station. Esmerelda was the part-time police dispatcher for Greg. Oh yeah, and Greg was also South Cove's police detective. In any other town he'd be police chief, but the mayor didn't want to give the title to him because it would come with a raise.

Greg didn't care. He loved his job. And he loved me. So that was all I needed to know.

I tuned back into the discussion that had become a little heated as I tuned out. Bill stood and pointed at the mayor.

"You and your big ideas are going to bring in big companies and ruin South Cove. I've talked to your guy on this mini hotel. He's a snake oil salesman. We don't need some big hotel here. We have the Castle and several bed-and-breakfasts already fighting over the tourist trade. Bringing in a new, fancy hotel would put a lot of us out of business." Bill shook his finger to emphasize his point. "Besides, Diamond Lille's is already having issues finding staffing. You're going to take away all her best employees."

The mayor looked around the room for support. When no one joined his camp, he sighed. "Now Bill, I'm sure you and Mary could deal with a little competition in town. You know it's the American way."

"And so are free and open elections. I wonder how you'd do this October if a viable candidate decided to run against you for mayor. Maybe we need some new blood in City Hall as well." Bill sat down, folding his arms. "It *is* the American way."

"We don't have to turn this thing ugly." The mayor looked around the room frantically. I could see he was trying to add up the support Bill might have in a campaign. "Anyway, the company still needs a viable site to build on and because it's my understanding that Miss Gardner had declined to sell, this might be a moot issue."

Now everyone turned and looked my way.

"Don't make me the bad guy. I don't have a for-sale sign in my yard because I don't want to sell. I like my house," I explained, feeling the weight of the decision on my shoulders.

"But it's a lot of money." Tina Baylor, the mayor's wife, stared at me like I had two heads. "Just think of the trips you and Greg could go on with that kind of money."

"True, but I'd have to buy a new house. And getting him away from the station and work is close to impossible anyway. And you know he won't quit his job just because we have money." I glanced at the clock, praying for a lifeline that would get me out of the hot seat. "Besides, I'd have to find a babysitter for Emma and kick Toby out of the apartment. It's just not going to happen. Anyway, looks like we're at time to close the meeting. Does anyone else have new business before we do? Darla?"

Darla Taylor, the owner/manager of South Cove Winery and our local promotion mastermind, stood up and walked over to the podium, where the mayor was still gripping the microphone. She held out her hand. "Excuse me, can you move?"

"I'll table this discussion until next meeting." The mayor grabbed his papers and walked away, bumping Darla in the shoulder as he passed by.

"You could have said excuse me." She stared at him.

Tina nudged him and he finally looked up. "Sorry to have bumped you."

"Now was that so hard?" Darla went on with her discussion about the Fall Festival that was happening later that month. I was trying not to laugh and Mayor Baylor was sputtering. Finally, he got up and stood by the front door, waiting for the meeting to end. I loved it when someone besides me gave the mayor a hard time. But I worried that Darla and Bill might have caused his heart to rupture or something. The guy was so red, I wondered if he was even breathing. Mayor Baylor might be a tool, but he was *our* tool. And if we had to get a new mayor, it might take a while to train them and break them into the South Cove world.

Darla finished the meeting by reminding everyone that the new digital sign-up sheets for committees were set up at the City Hall website. "Please volunteer. The work you do helps us keep South Cove businesses alive and working together. Even in this challenging atmosphere."

I hated it when Darla appealed to my community spirit. I figured I did my part by managing the cat circus that was the Business-to-Business meeting once a month. I wrote something in my notebook so Darla would think I was writing a reminder, but really, I was listing off dinner plans for the week and what I needed to get at the store. Greg was at a meeting in Bakerstown, so I was in charge of cooking tonight.

I had another task on my list: finish getting us packed for the long weekend trip we were taking. It was to a bed-and-breakfast my aunt Jackie and her husband, Harrold, had recommended just a few hours up the coast. The little town was supposed to be historic, and I was looking forward to the break. We were leaving tomorrow morning and not coming back until Monday. It would have been a week, but I had the Business-to-Business meeting and Greg had his training.

Darla was still answering questions when Max Winter walked into the shop and looked around. Mayor Baylor had returned to his seat at the table, but when he saw Max, he stood and hurried over. I guess he'd been told to come late in case people didn't like the proposal. I'd say that was the case. Max and Marvin talked for a few seconds, then Max met my gaze. He smiled and tipped his hat and turned around and left. Most of the group hadn't even seen him come into the shop.

I wondered what the mayor had in mind. The guy didn't give up easily. And if the minihotel wasn't going to be built on my land, I wondered who he'd talk into selling.

"Jill? Did you have anything else on the agenda? Or can we call it a day?" Darla called from the podium.

Josh Thomas raised his hand but didn't wait to be acknowledged. "We didn't talk about trash collection again. We need a second run after these festivals to keep South Cove from being overrun by rats."

The table did a collective groan.

Josh stood and handed out a flyer. "This goes over the cost of adding a second run for the garbage trucks the day a festival ends. It figures in overtime and the cost of gas and wear and tear on the trucks. And, I've added a second page that describes the problem with rats in a small community like South Cove. If we don't take this seriously, we're going to wind up like New York City."

"Thank you for the well-researched paper, Josh." I handed mine to Amy. "But as we talked about last month, these items are more suited for the City Council meetings. We're supposed to be focused on getting new customers and new businesses into South Cove. Not dealing with the utility issues."

Bill Sullivan sighed and stood. "Jill's right. You should petition the council to look into this. I'm sure Ms. Newman-Cross will be happy to set you up for a slot on the next meeting agenda."

Josh nodded. "I'll stop by City Hall this afternoon and get this set up. Thank you for taking this seriously. I'd hate for South Cove to fall into disrepair." This time Josh shot me a look to kill as he sat down with the leftover leaflets. Like it was my fault this committee didn't deal with his problems.

Darla looked around one more time. "Okay, then, is there any other new business for our group?"

Lille Stanley hurried into the shop, holding a paper over her head. She stopped in front of Mayor Baylor, who had almost made it back to his chair next to his wife. "Are you kidding me? Who was going to tell me that you're setting up a new restaurant in South Cove? Upscale? We already have that with Tiny. He's one of the best chefs on the coast."

Mayor Baylor used his hands to pat down the air in front of him, like that would calm Lille. She was the owner/manager of Diamond Lille's. The diner was the only place you could get a meal, unless you counted the treats I served with coffee as a meal or the limited selection of bar food the winery now served on weekends. "Now Lille, there isn't anything formalized yet. We'll be considering all options for the current businesses that might be affected by a new entry onto the food scene."

"You'll be considering options from your hospital bed." Lille slammed down the paper on the table in front of the mayor. "You need to fix this or there will be consequences."

She stormed out of the shop, knocking over a chair near the entrance as she went.

Amy quietly whistled. "Marvin's having a bad day. I wonder what consequences Lille's talking about."

Whatever it was, I could see it had Marvin worried. He stood and addressed the group. "Sorry for Lille's outburst. I know it's hard to accept change and competition. I hope she sees the error in her thought process sooner rather than later. Max Winter will be coming to our next meeting to talk about the advantages of bringing in a new type of lodging and a five-star restaurant. As good as Tiny is, we all know he's not a Michelin-star chef. Progress is good for the community."

At that he spun on his heel and left the shop. His wife, Tina, followed in his footsteps. Usually, Tina was the one making the grand gestures. But this time the mayor was putting all his eggs in one basket. I hoped it worked out for him.

After the mayor and Tina left, Darla closed out the meeting. As we put the dining room back to normal, Darla came by and wiped off the table I'd just set in the corner with two chairs. "Marvin's painted himself into a corner with this one. I wonder how much money he has invested in the project?"

I dropped the chair I'd just picked up on my foot. "He wouldn't put his own money into a development, would he?"

"Rumor says he has several times." Darla glanced at her watch. "I've got to go. Deliveries are coming to the winery this morning and Matt's going to be swamped."

I thought about what Darla had said as I finished setting up the dining room. Mayor Baylor was acting weirder than ever. And I needed to find out why.

Especially because I wasn't going to give up my home just to make him feel better about a new South Cove business.

Chapter 2

The great thing about starting your vacation on a Wednesday? You don't have the typical weekend visitors clogging up the area. Apple Valley was a sister tourist town to South Cove—just up the highway, still on the coast. We'd checked into the bed-and-breakfast and now we were walking hand in hand to find somewhere to eat dinner. I missed Emma, but she was with her favorite babysitter, Toby. I think he took her to work when he watched her. At least if he thought it was going to be a slow night. I hadn't verified my theory with Greg because I didn't want Toby to get in trouble for letting Emma ride shotgun in a police car, but I trusted Toby. As long as nothing happened to my dog.

"Jill? What about this place? I have a craving for Mexican food and I heard Bill say this place is the best in town." We stood outside the Three Tequilas. Mariachi music flowed out of the small patio that looked like it had tables available. Greg pointed to the menu posted by the door. "The prices are reasonable. For coastal California, that is. My mom had a heart attack the first time she ordered food at Diamond Lille's. She said I should be arresting Lille for charging over ten bucks for a soup and sandwich combo."

"I guess we're used to the prices now." I glanced through the offerings. They served fish tacos, so I was happy with the choice. I just hoped they were as good as Tiny's, or I'd be sad. "And I can have a margarita. I'm sold."

He squeezed me before we went up to the hostess stand. "You can have more than one margarita. We're on vacation."

I liked the sound of that, but I knew if something big came up, we'd be heading back as soon as possible. The good thing was if Greg had a drink, as soon as possible would be the next day. Maybe I should just keep him drinking so we'd at least get a full day of vacation before we had to go back. I wondered what he thought about mimosas with breakfast.

"Dinner for two on the patio, please," Greg said to the young lady at the hostess stand. She couldn't have been over eighteen, but she flipped back her hair and gave Greg a seductive smile, ignoring me, the woman on his left with the rock on her engagement finger big enough to be seen by the Space Shuttle. Okay, maybe it wasn't that big, but it wasn't chicken feed either.

I clung to his arm, suddenly feeling a chill. What was wrong with me? I never let flirty waitresses get under my skin before. Greg was a good-looking man. These types of snide attacks were going to happen. There was just no need for me to react. Even if she still had her hands on an inappropriate spot. Greg held out the chair for me and I slipped in. I swear, the hostess almost sat down on my lap.

When she realized Greg wasn't interested she backed off a little. "Your server will be right with you. Enjoy your evening."

"So, what's the plan for this week? Any chance we can find a sports bar and watch the game on Sunday?" He held up his hands to ward off the blows. When none came he smiled. "I'm only asking because the room doesn't have a television."

"That's because it's not supposed to be a place where you just stay in your room. I guess I could go find a spa while you're watching your team play." Greg didn't get to watch a lot of sports, not when the town was as busy as South Cove. And it was his vacation too. "As long as we've already discussed and have a date and place for the wedding."

He laid down his menu. "You should just have what you want. This is my last wedding, so maybe you should have something pretty."

"Saying 'make it pretty' isn't contributing. Sorry, Charlie, it's time for you to have an opinion on the stuff." I laid my menu down too.

"Well, either the two of you are quick deciders or there's something amazing on the menu I haven't heard about." The waitress was at our table, her notepad out. She wore a traditional Mexican skirt with a white blouse. Her hair was pulled back in a bun. The look matched the atmosphere until she opened her mouth and the New York accent came out. "What can I get you?"

After we'd ordered I leaned back and studied the area. "I know you were talking about going somewhere different from our normal lives, but I love it here. I live on the coast because I want to be here. Of course we can do anything for the honeymoon, but I want something that says sunny California for the wedding."

"Have you thought about having the wedding outside at one of the missions? I don't know if any do outdoor weddings. Or maybe the Castle? But that might not be special enough." He sipped the beer the waitress had just brought from the bar.

"Have you seen the gardens? Or the pool? Although maybe not the pool area because, well, you know." I thought about the place where Greg's best friend had been killed. Maybe we needed to have the wedding somewhere else. So many of the lovely places in South Cove had been murder sites or body dumps. I took a sip of my beer. "Maybe planning this wedding venue in South Cove was going to be harder than I thought. The Castle, the Winery, the beach, even that pretty forest cabin in Oregon, they've all had murder...issues."

"Well, it's not like the murderer in any of the cases is still at large." He laughed as he squeezed my hand. "But I see your point. Which brings me back to having the wedding at a local mission. There's got to be one nearby that doesn't have a sordid past."

"Well, bless my heart. What are the chances I'd run into the two of you here?" Max Winter stood at the edge of our table, smiling down at us.

My stomach clenched. It wasn't that the developer was a bad guy, just one who couldn't take no for an answer. Greg stepped in and greeted him to save Max from whatever I had been going to say.

"Mr. Winter. So nice to see you. Are you here scouting new land opportunities?" Greg squeezed my hand.

"Actually, I'm here on a minivacation. Connie loves these little tourist towns, like South Cove." He waved toward a booth in the back. "Anyway, she just let me know our food is here. Maybe we can get together later. I thought of a different option schedule that might work for your house in case you decide to sell."

"We're not selling." My voice went a little louder than I'd expected, and Mr. Winter took a step backward.

"Well, enjoy your stay anyway. I'd love to buy you both drinks one night. You'd love meeting Connie. She's a firecracker, just like you, Miss Gardner." He nodded, then left the table.

I leaned toward Greg. "I'm not a firecracker and we're not selling."

"You made that perfectly clear. I think even the valet outside heard it." Greg smiled. "Don't let him get you upset. We're here to talk about the wedding and enjoy our newly minted engaged couple status. I was wondering when we should start wearing matching shirts. Or is that only on vacation?"

I couldn't help it—I laughed. "You dork. What are you talking about?"

He pointed to several tables where the wife and husband were in matching T-shirts. One set proclaimed, "I Heart California." Another set said, "Property of Hotel California." "I'd like to petition for a blue color because white makes me look pale. It's obvious I don't spend enough time on the beach."

"I'm not wearing matching shirts on or off vacation unless we're doing a fun run or are on a bowling team." I studied him. "Wait, do you bowl? I've never asked."

"I don't mind bowling. It's just hard to be on a league when I'm on a case. But we could do a fun run. Maybe one that supports the missions. Didn't you sponsor one a few years ago?"

"You know I did. And poor Josh found that woman's body. I swear, I can't hold a Tupperware party without having one of the guests show up dead." I leaned back as the waitress caught the last of my words as she set my plate in front of me. Her eyes widened and she set Greg's meal down, then hurried off.

"Well, either our service is going to be really good the rest of the night or you just scared the poor girl off and we won't be able to get a second drink." Greg took a bite of his enchiladas. "The food's good, though."

"I didn't mean to scare her, but you know what I mean." I picked up a fish taco and ate several bites before looking up at him. He was laughing. At me.

"What?" I pointed my taco at him. "What's so funny?"

"Even out of town we can't get away from discussing murder." He shook his head. "You're the perfect mate for a police detective, do you know that?"

"Maybe I should find one and ask him to marry me?" I sipped my margarita. I did love Greg. And he was right. We were perfect for each other. The only fights we ever got into were about me messing around in his investigations. I wondered what we'd fight about when he retired.

We took a walk down to the beach and my phone rang. I glanced at the display. "It's Toby. Should I ignore it?"

"If he was calling about an issue in town, he would have called my phone." Greg patted the phone on his belt. "I think it's safe to answer."

"Hey, Toby. What's going on?" I held my breath. There were other reasons we could be called back, ones I didn't really want to think about.

"I thought you might want to say hello to my copilot. Change over to video chat."

I did, and when the image came into view, it was Emma grinning at me from the passenger seat of Toby's truck. "Who's a good girl? Are you having fun with Uncle Toby?"

When she barked at the phone in response I laughed, turning the phone so Greg could see her.

"We're on our way to the station." Toby turned the phone back and smiled at us. "I just wanted to let you know your dog's fine."

"You're not going to think everything's fine when the mayor catches you with Emma at the station," Greg warned.

Toby shrugged. "He's never there after three in the afternoon, you know that. Besides, I checked with Amy. She told me Marvin and Tina went out of town yesterday." He reached over to give Emma a rub on the head. "I'll just claim she's an emotional support dog if he does show up. I'm missing the two of you."

"I'm sure you are. Not." Greg took my hand and started walking. "Tell Toby to stop horning in on our vacation."

"I guess that's my cue. Have a great week. Bring us a souvenir." Toby focused the phone camera on Emma. Then he raised his voice to a falsetto. "Bye, Mom and Dad. Emma loves you."

I started laughing, but Toby had hung up before we could respond. "The babysitter is running amok with our dog."

"He's going to teach her bad habits," Greg groused, but I could tell he was amused as well. "You ready to enjoy a sunset walk on the beach? We need to check that off our must-do-on-vacation list."

"Add in pick up seashells and we've had a successful first day." I thought about meeting Max Winter at dinner. Maybe it was a coincidence, but it just felt off. Especially with Marvin and Tina out of town. I hoped we wouldn't "run into" them as well this week.

Greg studied me. "Are you okay?"

"Just thinking. And I'm going to stop that right now. Let's talk about when we're doing this wedding thing. I want to have a firmish date when we go home so we can start looking at venues." I leaned on his arm as we walked. "I can't wait to be Mrs. King."

"Sure, we can talk about this 'wedding thing.' Just be careful what you wish for." He kissed me on the top of my head. "I hear I can be a handful."

When we were almost back to the bed-and-breakfast we ran into Bill and Mary Sullivan. I hadn't talked to Bill after the meeting on Tuesday, but I wasn't surprised to see that Mary had gotten him out of town before he throttled the mayor.

Greg reached out his hand. "Bill, so nice to see you. I didn't realize our secret-hideaway town was so popular with the South Cove crew."

"You'd be surprised who you'd run into here." Bill shook Greg's hand, then kissed me on the cheek.

"We've been coming to Apple Valley for years. It's close enough we can sneak away for a night without feeling like we're putting the business in danger." Mary gave me a hug. "Your aunt didn't mention you were getting away this week."

"We weren't sure we could swing it. You know Greg's schedule." I squeezed Mary back. She was my aunt Jackie's best friend and a lovely woman, despite that flaw. I met Bill's gaze. "Are you okay? The last time I saw you, things were a little tense."

"Mayor Baylor only thinks about money. There are more things to consider when you're courting a new business. Like the yarn shop. The woman who runs that is a perfect new South Cove resident. She's here for the enjoyment." Bill looked down at his wife for confirmation.

"That's true. And it reminds me. You need to come to Crissy's shop next Wednesday. We're doing a community crochet project, making blankets for the NICU unit at the hospital. The yarns she bought were all so soft for the newborns' tender skin. You'll love working with it." Mary pulled a flyer out of her bag. "Here's the information. Be sure to bring Amy and your new barista."

Greg chuckled and I jabbed an elbow to his ribs. "I'm sure Evie would love to come. She needs to be more involved in community activities anyway."

"Well, we won't keep you two. I'm sure you have lots to chat about." Mary squeezed my arm. Aunt Jackie must have told her we were starting to plan the wedding details. "Come to the yarn shop next week. Crissy called it A Pirate's Yarn. Isn't that cute?"

After they'd disappeared into the night Greg took my arm and we continued our walk. "You really shouldn't force a blanket you made on an innocent baby."

"You don't know I can't crochet. It's not knitting." I wondered if my statement was true. I hadn't done either for a long time. "Maybe I can be a water boy for the group or something that doesn't involve me being creative."

"That's my girl. Accept your limitations." He kissed the back of my neck as we opened the door to the lobby. A fire glowed in the living room. And a plate of cookies sat on the coffee table, along with a carafe that was labeled with the words "hot chocolate." The owners had mentioned that we and a single female were their only guests until the weekend. "Do you want to sit and talk here? Or go upstairs?"

"Can you run and get my sweater and my planner? Then we can talk down here about some dates and venues." There was no way I was turning down hot chocolate and cookies.

He kissed me. "Don't eat all the cookies."

After he left I heard someone talking in what the owner had called the breakfast room. Thinking it was her, I grabbed a cookie and headed to the doorway. Instead of the pleasant, gray-haired woman who'd checked us in that morning, a redhead in a too-tight dress stood in the room, her back to me. She was talking on the phone. I stepped back but paused out of sight as I listened. I knew it wasn't my business, but you can tell a lot about a person by listening in on a conversation they don't think anyone else can hear. I did it a lot at my shop, mostly out of boredom, but sometimes it gave me an insider's look into what the customer might be interested in buying. No need to push books on a busy businessperson who only wants coffee. At least that was my excuse. Tonight it was just for fun.

"Look, it's not my fault you let her leave with it. You had to know that Dad trusted her more than either one of us. I can't believe he'd side with a wife rather than his own son. Of course you did put him through the wringer. You're lucky he left you anything in the will." The woman laughed. "Besides, I have a plan B if I need it."

I didn't like her tone, and because I didn't need to know anything more about her, I went back to the fire and poured two cups of cocoa, which turned out to be very delicious.

Greg came back and I forgot about the woman and her plan B. We looked at our online calendar and started planning out the wedding. May was too busy with festivals, and besides, Aunt Jackie and Harrold were already booked to go on an Alaskan cruise. If we wanted to do it outside, July would be too hot. So, it looked like I was going to be a stereotypical June bride. We were writing down venue options when the woman stormed out of the breakfast nook.

She took one look at us and hurried to the stairs, not saying a word.

Greg met my gaze. "I take it she's the other guest?"

"Afraid so. And she's having inheritance issues. I guess her father must have passed recently."

He raised an eyebrow, then shook his head. "I don't want to know."

Chapter 3

Friday morning I was beginning to think we could really pull off a full vacation. Four more days. Greg hadn't had any work calls. I'd had a few, mostly from my aunt, checking on our status of changing around her role and hours. We'd put Evie on nights, with a day shift on Saturday to fill out her hours to full time. So far she was doing amazing, but my aunt kept dropping in and checking on her. Then she'd call me with a list of things she thought Evie was doing wrong. Which really meant Evie wasn't doing it Jackie's way. I promised to work with Evie when I got back, then gently reminded my aunt I was on vacation. Once, she'd called and quickly hung up. I'd called back, worried something was wrong. Harrold answered and apologized for disturbing our vacation. I guess he'd caught her calling me. I loved my new uncle.

We were sitting at the pool, discussing today's nonagenda, when I got a call from City Hall. I picked up and met Greg's gaze as I answered. "Hi, Amy. What's up?"

"It's not Amy. It's Esmeralda. I just wanted to warn you that Greg shouldn't answer his phone today. Marvin's on the warpath. I guess his developer is getting threatening phone calls, and Marvin wants Greg to take care of it. I told him that since this Max guy doesn't live or work in South Cove Greg has no jurisdiction. But I guess he thinks Bakerstown PD is giving the guy the runaround."

"What does he want Greg to do about it?" Now I had Greg's attention and he pointed, indicating I should put it on speaker. "Hold that answer, I'm putting this on speaker so Greg can hear."

"Hey, Greg," Esmeralda said after I'd set the phone down. "Sorry to bother you on vacation, but I wanted you to be aware of this."

"No worries; what's going on again?"

Esmeralda told him what she'd just told me and then added, "Anyway, he's promised this guy that you can find out who's calling him and put a stop to it. Well, I overheard him say 'arrest the guy,' but you know Marvin and his dramatic solutions."

"I can't even step in. Especially if Bakerstown has been made aware of the issue. I take it Winter lives there?" Greg leaned back and closed his eyes.

"Yep. A nice little oceanside estate just a few miles out of town. I looked it up. It's worth a fortune. And all in Bakerstown's jurisdiction. Construction development must be a cash cow for this guy."

From the amount of money he'd wanted to give me for an option on my house and land, I didn't doubt it. I was a little worried that Greg would tell her we were on our way, but instead he sat up and winked at me.

"Just tell Marvin that you've tried to call with no luck. And no one knows where Jill and I went. Can you tell Toby and call Jill's aunt? Warn Bill and Mary too since we ran into them here. I wouldn't put it past Marvin to drive up here to find me. We might not be able to shut down the rumor mill, but maybe we can slow it down for a few more days. I'll be back in town on Monday."

"Sounds good. And have a great vacation. Tell Jill she'll be a beautiful June bride." And with that, Esmeralda disconnected.

"Huh. Sometimes she worries me with what she says. How did she know we'd decided on June?" I sipped my mimosa, but Greg set his aside and poured himself a cup of coffee. And with that, the vacation mood was broken. Even if we could keep Mayor Baylor from finding us, Greg was going to be on guard until we left.

"She has her ways." He made wiggles with his fingers. "And don't look so upset about the coffee. I don't know if we'll be called back or not, but if it's going to happen, it will be in the next few hours. I know Marvin. He doesn't do anything on weekends he doesn't have to."

"Okay, but it makes me mad that he can mess with our vacation this way." I drained my mimosa and took his.

"He's not. If we haven't heard anything else by five, we're good for the rest of the weekend." He leaned over and kissed me. "Orange juice tastes nice on your lips."

"Oh, you sweet talker. You know just the right thing to say." I leaned back and relaxed in the sun.

No other call came before five, so before we left for dinner, Greg tucked his phone in the top dresser drawer at the bed-and-breakfast. I stared at him. "Are you sure? Do you want to put it in my purse?"

He reached for my purse and put that in the drawer as well. "You don't have a lot of cash in there, do you?"

"I gave you what cash I had at the beach." I watched as he put my purse with his phone. "You're kidding. We're going to be out of touch for an hour?"

He nodded. "Maybe two or three, depending on how long I can keep you awake."

"Why Greg King, you've got a reckless side." I put my arm through his as we left the room. He stopped to hang up the Do Not Disturb sign and made sure the door was locked.

He put his arm around me as we walked down the stairs. "I don't get to show it much, but we *are* on vacation."

It was midnight when the phone in the drawer started ringing. Then, when we ignored that phone, my phone started ringing, but it was even more muffled because it was in my purse. Then Greg's started again. He sat up from bed and shrugged his shoulder. "Sorry. I need to get that before they wake our hosts."

I mumbled something and put a pillow over my head when he turned on a light. I heard him chuckle before answering the phone.

"Greg King," he growled. "This had better be important."

I listened but didn't hear anything from the other side of the call. My pillow must have been blocking it. I pulled it off my head and sat up in bed, watching him. His sleepy, relaxed face had turned to stone in just a few seconds.

Finally, he spoke. Toby knew exactly where we were because he was in charge of Emma. Just in case. "Come get me. I'll be outside on the porch, waiting."

When he hung up he came over and sat on the bed. He rubbed my arm. I sighed. "The mayor decided to work this weekend?"

He shook his head. "No. Something else happened. A man showed up at City Hall tonight with a knife in his stomach. He fell into the station when Toby opened the door. He died on the way to the hospital."

"Oh no. Did he say what happened to him?" Now I was awake.

Greg shook his head. "Not a word. Look, Toby's coming to get me. You stay here until Monday and relax. I'm sure you have a few more books in your bag you were planning on reading before we went back."

"Are you sure? I can go home tonight too." I started to get up, but he sat next to me.

"Jill, we don't get out of town often and I'd like to know you at least got use of our room. If you want to make this a girls' weekend, call Amy and see if she doesn't mind bunking with you." He pulled me into a hug. "Just because I have to go back doesn't mean you should cut your time away."

I leaned into him. "You're pretty amazing, Mr. King."

"I know. That's why you're marrying me." He kissed me and then stood. "I need to pack. Do you need anything from me before I leave?"

I shook my head. I had an emergency credit card stashed if I needed anything big. And we'd brought my Jeep, so I'd be fine driving home. "Emma will be glad to see you, if you go home tonight."

"The way it works, I'll probably see her in the morning when I go home to shower and change. I'll give her your love." He pulled out his travel bag and started packing.

I lay back down, watching him and feeling guilty about staying. I sat back up. "Maybe I should…"

"Stop right there. You don't have to leave just because I do. Enjoy yourself. Go to that spa you were talking about. Go in that antique store you've been window-shopping since we got here. Take care of my Jill. Then come home Monday all rested." He glanced out the window. "That was fast. He must have been on his way when he called. There's Toby, I've got to go."

I stood and hugged him. "How did I get so lucky to find you?"

"You were in the middle of a murder investigation. Where else?" He kissed me and nodded to the bed. "Go get some sleep. I'll call you tomorrow when I have a break."

He turned off the light after I'd crawled into bed, then I heard the door open and shut. I lay there for what seemed like hours, wondering if he was right about me staying. Then I fell asleep.

When I woke up I texted Amy. I didn't call to wake her up, but I guess the effect was the same; she called a few minutes later, grumpy from being woken up. "What's wrong?"

"Nothing's wrong. Why would you ask that?" I curled up under the covers. It was chilly this morning. The fog must still be surrounding the village.

"Because you texted me at seven on a Saturday." Amy yawned as she waited for my answer.

"Okay, so I wanted to invite you to come share the rest of my vacation with me." Maybe this was a bad idea. At least this early in the morning.

"Won't Greg be a little irritated at the third wheel? Or did you two have a fight?"

I could hear the sounds of coffee being made. I'd go down to the breakfast room once I got Amy off the phone. "We didn't have a fight. He just had to go back to South Cove, so I thought we could do a girls' weekend here in Apple Valley. I'll buy the spa day."

"It's tempting. Hold on a second." She covered the phone, and I heard mumbles as she talked to Justin, her newlywed husband. Finally, she came back. "I'll be there within the hour. Justin is grading papers this weekend, so I'd be looking for something to do anyway. And cleaning isn't on top of my to-do list."

"Great." I gave her the address of the bed-and-breakfast. "I'll be downstairs in the breakfast room. I'll make sure there isn't an upcharge for having you, but I'm sure it will be fine. As long as I can stand your snoring."

"I don't snore." Amy sniffed.

"She does too," Justin called out to me from wherever he was in the kitchen.

"I'll see you soon." Laughing, I hung up and went to get showered and ready for the day. I'd take a book down and read during breakfast while I waited for Amy. Maybe I should wait to eat with her too. I pondered exactly how hungry I was as I got ready.

I was on my way down when my phone beeped with a text. Hoping it wasn't Amy telling me she'd changed her mind, I scrolled down to the new text. Greg had checked to see if I was awake.

I called him as I walked down the stairs. I set my stuff on a table, then went into the living room to take the call. "Hey you. I just got up. How's the investigation going?"

"I'm not that tired that I would slip and tell you. Stay out of my business, Missy." He chuckled. "I'm home with Emma and she wanted to say good morning."

"Put the phone down and I'll give her puppy love." I used my best baby talk voice to try to cheer up my puppy and ended with, "Mommy will be home on Monday and we'll go for a run."

"Sounds like a plan. Her tail started flopping on the floor when you said 'run.'" Greg paused and I heard the fridge open. "Do we have bacon somewhere? I'm missing my full breakfast from the lodging."

"There's some in the freezer. If I leave it in the fridge, it goes bad. Maybe we should start eating breakfast before I go in to work." I hoped he wouldn't say yes; I hated cooking in the morning.

"I'll think about it. I'm sure it would be my task. You barely make it to work on time as it is."

"That's not true." Now I wished I'd at least poured a cup of coffee before I went to the living room. I peeked into the breakfast room; it was empty.

So I hurried over to pour coffee before anyone came in. "Amy's on her way. I had to bribe her with a spa day on me."

"I'm sure you didn't have to bribe her too much, but whatever, it's your money." He paused. "Now that we have the wedding date kind of settled, we need to talk about a budget for the wedding and what we're going to do with our finances after the marriage. I'm going to push for joint accounting for the everyday stuff, but I'm willing to have some exceptions."

"I've been thinking about that too. I do have some exceptions. Mainly the Miss Emily fund and the house. I don't want your new wife to want to sell as soon as you remarry."

"You're planning on me remarrying? I think you're crazy. You're the last woman I'm going to change my life for."

"Wait, what does that mean? How are you changing your life?" I set down my cup wondering what I'd done wrong now.

"And look, I've got another call coming in. Have fun with Amy and I'll see you on Monday."

"Greg King, don't you hang up on me." But I was talking to dead air. I knew he was kidding me. It was his standard smooth-over technique when things got too serious. I put away the phone and said quietly, "I love you too."

"Don't tell me you chased away that darling hunk of man I've seen you with this last week." The woman from the other night stood in the doorway watching me. "Sorry, but I was eavesdropping. It's one of my favorite pastimes, especially when I'm out of town. You'd be surprised to learn what people will say when they're out in public. Me, I'm a little more reserved."

Except for when you're talking on the phone. I didn't say what I was thinking. "Hi, I'm Jill Gardner, and yes, I'm afraid my fiancé had to return home due to work commitments. What are you doing in Apple Valley? Vacation or business?"

"Vacation before I go visit family. It's complicated and I needed a week to unwind before I went into the lion's den. You know family." She smiled and held out a hand. "Rebecca Craft. So nice to meet you."

"Yeah, I have an aunt, so I get it." I nodded to the breakfast nook. "Do you want to join me for breakfast?"

"Actually, I'm heading out. I've got an appointment with an antiques appraiser in a little bit. I'm just down for some coffee and a yogurt to take back to my room. I'm not much of a breakfast girl."

"I love breakfast. Especially sweets. Greg, he loves the more savory dishes." I was about to tell her about his bacon hunt when I realized she wasn't even listening anymore. When I'd reached down to pick up my coffee cup, she'd gone into the breakfast nook. I whispered to the empty room, "I guess girl bonding time is over."

I settled on having a cinnamon roll while I waited for Amy and opened my book. It was a time travel/alternate universe novel I'd been waiting to start until I knew I had a chunk of reading time.

Amy showed up just as I was halfway finished. She laughed as she walked up to greet me. "I know that look. You're loving the book and I'm interrupting. Well, you shouldn't have called if you wanted to be alone."

I stood and gave her a hug. "I don't want to be alone. I called because I wanted to spend some time with my best friend. But the book—wow, it's good. Let me find our hostess and get you checked in. Then we'll drop off your bag and come down for breakfast."

"Great because I'm starving. I love Justin, but he's always so busy with work. Sometimes I feel alone even when he's in the room with me." She shook her head. "And I'm griping. Sorry. I know we're just getting to know each other. At least the part where we're together twenty-four seven. I guess you and Greg already have that part worked out."

"I think you're always adjusting to your significant other." I was starting to get worried about my friend. I knew getting used to marriage would take a while, but she was taking too long. At least in my opinion. "Justin's a good man. You two just need time to figure everything out. And you don't have to worry about it this weekend. We're going to have fun."

Rebecca came into the room and poured another cup of coffee. "In my experience, if you don't immediately settle into marriage, there's a good chance it will not work out. My brother just got divorced and he was never happy with his wife. She always thought she was too good for him."

With that proclamation, Rebecca left the breakfast nook with her coffee, yogurt, and a banana.

Amy's eyes were saucers when she turned toward me. "Okay, who is that and do you think she's right?"

I shook my head. Rebecca was becoming a bit of a pain in the behind. "That's just an angry woman. She's had a loss recently. Don't listen to her. Justin loves you and you love Justin. Every couple has issues at first." I took her arm and led her to the living room/reception desk, where our hostess was working and trying not to listen in to our conversations. If Rebecca's brother was anything like her, there was a good reason his marriage didn't work. And it was him. "Let's get this weekend started."

Chapter 4

We were at the spa, our faces slathered with goop, our eyes covered with cucumbers, and our feet soaking in water while we got our fingernails polished and painted, when Amy brought up the reason for Greg's absence. "I take it Marvin got ahold of Greg? Sorry, I'd hoped we'd got the word out that you two weren't to be disturbed."

She hadn't said much since we'd left the bed-and-breakfast, so her words shocked me a little. I knew she needed time to process, so I'd been thinking about the venues and wondering if my first choice, a remodeled mission just down the coast, would be available. I'd sent an email to the event planner, but it had been late on Friday. "What? Oh, no, Mayor Baylor didn't find Greg. I guess you didn't hear. There was an accident in town."

"What?"

I heard Amy's feet splash in the water as her technician responded to the action. "Please, Miss, stay still. You're going to mess up your polish."

"Sorry." Amy took a deep breath. "What happened?"

I didn't want to say "murder" in front of the spa employees, but my technician filled in the missing parts. "If you're talking about what happened in South Cove, I heard it was a murder. My boyfriend works for Bakerstown PD. He said that guy had a knife in his gut when the night shift guy opened the door to the station. I always worry about Devin. He works nights too."

"That's so sad." Amy's nail girl spoke up. "Didn't that man from last week say he was working on a big deal in South Cove? You know, you had his wife, the big tipper? Honestly, I didn't think there was any land up for sale for the type of project he was talking about. I'm looking for a house, so I'm always looking through the local listings."

"Well, his wife told me he was dreaming. That the mayor guy was blowing smoke and he just needed to retire, like they'd talked about after the last development. They are so rich. I paid a month's rent on the tips she gave me last week."

"I wish I'd had her instead of him. He barely kept still for his nail work and then he just tipped me twenty dollars." She paused a minute, glancing up at Amy. "Of course we're more than happy with any tips we get. All we want is to provide you all great customer service."

Great catch, I thought as we moved from the manicure to the pedicure. I decided to change the subject. I really didn't want more reasons to not like Max Winter. Like the fact he was a poor tipper. "Amy, I think we have a wedding venue picked out."

She took my lead, and for the next hour our conversation was about the wedding and scheduling until we were left alone with a couple of glasses of champagne to wait for the last treatment.

When we were alone I looked at Amy. "So yeah, the guy was murdered. My nail technician had all the details right. He showed up at the police station, bleeding. I bet Toby was having a heart attack."

"Oh my word. Who do you think it was?" Amy sipped her wine.

I shrugged. "No clue. Greg didn't say anything when he called this morning. I wish it had been Max Winter. Wait, that sounded bad, didn't it? At least if it was, I'd have an alibi since I was here with Greg at the time."

"Yeah, but you could have hired me to do your dirty work." Amy laughed as she sipped her wine. "Seriously, Jill, you need to control yourself around developers and real estate people. I think the house is cursed: 'Don't try to buy the old Miss Emily house or you'll be sorry. Sorry and dead.'"

"It's not my fault mean people wind up dead. Max Winter treated everyone like a stepping-stone to the next deal. But if it had been him, Greg would have told me. I think." I snuggled into my fluffy robe. "Even during a spa day, I get sucked into these murder investigations. You really have to tell Greg it's not my fault this time."

"What do you mean? What clue did you hear that I didn't?" Now Amy was watching me, curiously.

"If it's Max, the wife was trying to get him to retire. She didn't want him doing this last deal. Maybe she got tired of waiting for him." I refilled my glass from the bottle they'd left us. I guess the wait for the massages was going to be longer than I'd expected.

Amy held out her glass as well. "Well, as a new participant to this whole marriage thing, I can testify that living with someone can drive you crazy.

I'm not sure about going to the point of murder, but Justin and I have had more than our share of fights the last few months."

I filled her glass to the top. "It will all work out. You and Justin are the perfect couple. You just have to find your rhythm. Marriage takes work. It's not all fifty-fifty. Most of the times it's one hundred percent one person, then it switches to the other person."

Amy looked at me through her wineglass. "How did you become so smart about relationships? I know you had one dissolve before. What makes now easier?"

"Maybe it's because I've been married and divorced. I know what to expect and it doesn't surprise me when I'm feeling left out or when Greg doesn't do or say what I think he should. Sometimes I think—no, let me change that—I know *most* of our fights are because one of us is assuming the other is thinking something they aren't. Or that they'll react one way rather than just telling them and letting them react." I took another sip from my glass. "I was a divorce lawyer, remember that. I saw so many people throw away their marriages without really working at the problems."

"Okay, now I feel like a whiner." Amy plopped back on the sofa. "All Justin said was he needed to grade papers and I went off about how he's always working. Maybe I need to understand his job more. I walk away from my job at five p.m. and don't look back unless Tina or the mayor calls me for some stupid thing. He's a professor who's working on tenure. I think he has a little more responsibility than I do."

I let her talk for a while. I found the best part of being a friend was letting the other person talk out the problem and find their own solution. Then, as I saw the door opening, I jumped in. "Sounds like you've got at least the start of an answer. I had to do the same thing with Greg. He can be called away at a moment's notice. I just had to learn to enjoy my time alone. Like today, with you. I think it's time for our massage."

We were led into separate rooms, and I stopped thinking about who had been murdered, about Amy's issues with Justin, or about my upcoming wedding. All I thought about was the feel of my muscles as they were massaged into a relaxed state.

After spa day ended, we took a walk down to the little shops that populated Main Street. When we came to a fiber and weave shop, Amy paused. "Did Mary invite you to the crochet class for the baby blankets? Isn't that the best thing? I love the way South Cove always bands together to help out others."

"She did." I wondered if Amy thought I shouldn't be invited due to my total inability to do anything crafty. But then I pushed the idea away. I was doing what I'd told Amy not to do. I was assuming what ideas were in her brain that may or may not be there. "I'm looking forward to trying something new. Mary said the yarn is really soft."

"Which makes it harder to work with." Amy studied a woven wall piece that seemed to mimic the ocean, with its waves blue, black, and a touch of white. "Don't worry, you'll be fine. But we might want you to use a standard weight yarn until you get comfortable with the stitches. I'll talk to Crissy if I see her before Wednesday and we'll get you set up."

Amy knew my weaknesses and loved me anyway. But somehow, finding the one craft project I would be successful at had become her personal mission in life. Me, I was happy I had reading to keep me busy. I could count on her for help with the wedding bits and bops I didn't even know I needed right now. I needed to order a book on wedding planning. Then I'd have a checklist. I pulled out my phone and made a note to check on Tuesday when I went into the bookstore.

"Let's go in and see what they want for this wall hanging. I think it would be perfect for Justin's office at the university." Amy grinned as she opened the door. "And maybe it would remind him about how much fun surfing is and we'd go more often since we're right here on the coast."

"Always an ulterior motive. I like it." I followed her into the shop and looked around to see if there was anything that called to me. I still needed a few things for the upstairs library I'd started setting up a few months ago, much to Greg's dismay. He'd been campaigning for a workout room, but I thought that would be better in the shed in the back once Toby moved out. It was bigger, and we could get more than just one machine and some free weights in there.

We window-shopped for the rest of the afternoon, then returned to the bed-and-breakfast. Our hostess was setting up the afternoon tea and cookies in the breakfast room. I stayed downstairs while Amy ran upstairs to drop off the bags.

"How was your day?" Our hostess—Tiffany, if I remembered correctly—asked. Greg had set up the reservation and handled most of our interactions, so I hadn't really talked to her before.

"We spent most of it at the spa. Now we're going to eat and chat more. I think it's been kind of perfect for a trip that turned into a girls' weekend." I picked up a macaroon and popped it into my mouth. It was sugar heaven.

"I was sorry to hear your fiancé had to leave, but it probably was for the better. Our other guest was a little too fixated on him for my tastes." Tiffany nervously adjusted the plates on the table. "I really shouldn't talk about her, but what she said was a little shocking."

"Don't worry about it. I'm used to people seeing Greg as man candy. Especially women who like the strong, alpha types. I'm just glad he's not a shopper. He and I are good." I picked up a second cookie. I knew I didn't have anything to worry about, but it made me mad when I heard things like this.

"Well, I'm glad for that. I would have felt horrible if something had happened." She adjusted the plate one more time. "Honestly, I've never said this about a guest before, but I'm very glad she's checking out today. She's always yelling at someone on her phone. Good riddance to bad rubbish, my mom used to say."

After Amy had rejoined me, we headed out to the main street and found a restaurant, Thai Blessings, for dinner. "I'm glad we chose this place. I'd been hoping to get to try it. Greg doesn't like a lot of Asian places. He said he'd gotten enough rice when he was growing up. I guess it was his mom's favorite side dish."

"Well, you know I'm always up to try someplace new. And it will give me something to do when Justin is working. Maybe this being different isn't such a bad thing after all." Amy opened the menu. "I'm starving. I can't believe spending the day at the spa would build up such an appetite."

We decided to get two different dishes and share them along with tea and a promise to check out the dessert menu. We were starting on an appetizer, when a couple of women passed by our table with the hostess. I watched as they were seated and started looking at their menu. "Well, isn't that interesting."

"What? Did you see a different dish we need to try?" Amy glanced around the room, finally settling on the two women. "Who are they?"

"I don't know the one woman, but the one in the red suit? That's Max Winter's wife." I pulled out my phone and said, louder than necessary, "Amy, look this way. I want a picture of you eating Thai food to send to Mom."

Amy frowned but turned toward me as I took several pictures of the women in the booth. I might have been a little far away, but I knew the woman was the one Max had indicated was his wife when he came to our table a few days ago. What had he called her? Connie? I texted the pictures to Greg with a note.

"What did you tell Mom?" Amy knew who I'd texted.

I put down the phone and lowered my voice. "I told him she was sitting here having dinner by us at the Thai restaurant I wanted to visit."

Greg's answer came back quickly.

Amy nodded, telling me to read it aloud.

"'Have a good evening.'" I set down the phone and watched the women talk. They didn't seem to be upset or sad. The person who had been murdered in South Cove must not be Max. I guess I was just projecting my wishes on the situation. My phone buzzed again. Amy looked at me expectantly.

"'Stop investigating and enjoy your weekend. Tell Amy hi.'" I tucked my phone into my purse and picked up my teacup. "What do you think of the venue choice for the wedding? I really hope they have the date open for us. Anything I should be worried about?"

* * * *

The next morning Amy was still asleep when I woke, so I decided to get dressed and head downstairs with my laptop. I could check email to see if the event coordinator had responded…as well as maybe do a little Google snooping to see if the news had anything on the man found in South Cove. The breakfast room was open and there was a table near the window where I could watch the sun break through the fog. I poured coffee, swirled a little chocolate syrup into the cup, and then topped it with whipped cream. Then I grabbed a couple of cookies to tide me over until Amy came down. I'd eat breakfast with her.

Opening my email, I scanned and deleted all the spam mail as I searched for important emails. It was just like flipping through snail mail. I got so much junk mail, it wasn't even funny. Both in hard copy and digital. I wondered if some marketing student at some university had studied the increase in unrequested advertising the average person had to deal with after the advent of email. The things I thought about.

After approving a last-minute time-off request from Deek on next week's schedule—he had a writing seminar he wanted to attend on Saturday—I closed out the program. None of the rest was pressing and could be handled on Monday when I was back home. Then I opened the book I'd started yesterday and got lost in the story.

By the time Amy came down for breakfast I'd almost finished.

"So, what did you find out?" Amy sat down with a cinnamon roll and coffee.

"About the wedding? The event planner hasn't gotten back to me." I sipped my coffee. I needed more.

"Don't play coy. I know you were researching the murder."

I stood and held up my coffee cup. "Let me get a refill before I disappoint you."

When I set back down I focused on her. "I forgot to look. I cleared out my email, answered one from Deek, and closed down the laptop. Anyway, what are our plans for today?"

Amy closed her eyes, but when she opened them and met my gaze, she was back in control of whatever demons were haunting her. "Let's spend the day at the beach. It's going to be perfect weather, and I need to refresh my tan. I've been inside way too much this fall."

"Sounds perfect." I wondered if she and Justin had fought again this morning after I left the room. I had a book to finish reading anyway. Spending the day lounging on the beach would help with my own confused thoughts. Sometimes you just had to veg.

Chapter 5

When I got home on Monday Emma was trying to break down the front door at the house to greet me. Greg wasn't home. It was close to noon, so the first thing I did after bringing in my luggage was change into running clothes and grab the leash. Emma went crazy. I leaned down and gave her a hug. "I know, I was gone too long and we didn't get in our runs. So we're going to remedy that right now."

I needed the run as much as Emma. Especially after the daily breakfast of cinnamon rolls. We made it down to the beach without seeing anyone. The beach was just as empty. Fall Mondays were glorious because we had less traffic and fewer tourists. Something a small business owner should never say or feel. But today I was just Jill who lived close enough to the beach to enjoy days like this.

When we were walking back Esmeralda crossed the street to meet us. "Welcome back, Jill. Sorry Greg's locked up with this new murder case."

"It's fine. I knew what I was getting into when I started dating a cop." I glanced at my sport watch. "Are you home for lunch?"

"Yes. I just needed to get out of there. So much anger and pain surround this investigation. I needed to clear my energy. I have a client coming in this evening and I'll be worthless to call in the spirits if I don't do a cleanse." She rolled her shoulders. "I'm glad you got to run today. Emma missed you while you were gone. She needed today."

Something about Esmeralda's tone made me look up at her. What wasn't she telling me? "Everything okay?"

"Yes, Jill, I'm fine." She shook her head, like I was a child who wasn't understanding the lesson. "I've got to go back. It's going to be a busy afternoon."

I nodded and watched her hurry back to her house. She actually drove her MINI Cooper up to the station every day. She said it was because she needed to keep it running, but I think she just didn't like the hike.

Emma whined and I started walking up to the house. "I know, Emma. Esmeralda's being weird. I felt it too."

When I'd gotten dinner planned and the steaks out of the freezer, I started to make a shopping list. I should go today, but I still had a few chapters left in that book I'd been loving all weekend. Besides, I was done driving for today. I'd go tomorrow after work. The good thing about having the early shift was I had lots of time to get things done afterward.

I curled up with the book and my phone rang. I considered ignoring it, but it might be Greg making sure I was home. Or, because Esmeralda had already told him I was home, he'd probably think something was wrong and send someone to check on me. I picked up the phone and checked the display. It wasn't Greg, it was Aunt Jackie. This one I couldn't ignore.

"Hi, Aunt Jackie. I was just about to call you. I'm home." I looked longingly at the book sitting next to me on the couch. I had a bad feeling reading wasn't going to be on my agenda today.

"I can't believe you stayed behind when Greg got called back." My aunt went right to what had been bothering her. I assumed she would have tried to call me this weekend, but Harrold probably stopped her.

"He said I should stay. Besides, I wasn't due back at the shop until tomorrow. Why would I come home early?" I knew I was going to get the marriage lecture, but I was going to stand my ground on this one. It wasn't the 1950s and I wasn't some housewife.

"Jill, you know men need structure in their lives. I'm sure we talked about this before." She clicked her tongue to show her disappointment in my answer.

"Let's just agree to disagree here. What's been going on at the shop? Anything I should know?"

"I told Deek to talk to you about his Saturday off. Which I'm sure you approved, but you may need to work that day, since Evie just told me she has unexpected family in town to visit and she'd like the evening shift off Friday and Saturday. I don't know. Maybe we should hire another person. It's getting hard to get all the hours covered. Especially if Greg pulls Toby this weekend."

"We can talk about it next week at the staff meeting. I want to make sure everyone has the hours they need before we hire someone else. I know we talked about hiring someone else once you went to managing full-time, but we made it work all summer. And we're going into a slower season."

I laid my hand on the book. I really didn't want to be talking shop right now, but my aunt thought I should spend more time on the business than I did. "Anything else?"

"I heard you called Amy and had her come up to meet you. Is she all right? She seemed a little off the last time I saw her."

Aunt Jackie loved Amy almost as much as she did me. "I think so. Maybe she just needed a weekend away. Learning how to be married can be overwhelming."

"You girls overthink everything. Back in my day, women were ecstatic to get married. The two of you seem like you're entering a long-term rental agreement. Or taking on a job you don't want. Being a wife is more of a gift than a job. I wish you could see that."

"I do. Most of the time. Amy does too; she's just getting in her own way, I think." I realized I was actually agreeing with my aunt. That didn't happen a lot. "Anyway, we had a fun spa day, then went out to eat and drank a few adult beverages. Then we chilled on the beach the rest of the time."

"Sounds like a relaxing time. I'm glad you got away."

Her tone had changed. "Tell Harrold hi, and I'll talk to you later."

"How did you know Harrold just walked in?"

Laughing, I hung up and picked up my book. I curled up on the couch with Emma beside me and got lost until Greg came home.

He crossed the living room and gave me a kiss, sinking down into the couch with me. "I would have figured you would have finished that one by now. Didn't you bring it along on the trip?"

"I would have, but Amy actually wanted to talk. Usually she's out surfing, but she didn't bring her board. And she doesn't rent. You would have thought I suggested she should wear rental bowling shoes. I guess it's just not done." I put in a bookmark and set the book aside. "How long are you home? Do we need to rush dinner, just in case?"

"Probably wouldn't be the worst idea. Even if I don't get called back, I'll be working in the study tonight. So far no one knows who our dead guy is. He's not a criminal, or at least not one that has been caught before. His prints came back clean."

"Not to change the subject when you're actually talking about an investigation. But did you find out anything about Max's wife? The woman in Apple Valley?"

He nodded.

"Really? I thought maybe there was something weird there." Sometimes talking to Greg was like pulling teeth.

He stood and pulled me to my feet. "Nothing you need to know. Let's go start dinner. I'm starving, and no one brought me any cookies today to get on my good side to ply me for information."

"It wasn't my fault. I was in Apple Valley." I thought about what Aunt Jackie had said to me about extending my vacation. "Hey, you aren't upset that I stayed at the bed-and-breakfast this weekend with Amy, right?"

He stopped walking and turned to me. "No. I told you to stay. Why would I be upset? Who said I was upset?"

"No one. Aunt Jackie called and basically told me I was being selfish." I leaned on his arm. "You'll tell me if you think I'm being selfish, right?"

"In a heartbeat." Greg started walking again toward the kitchen.

I followed him and watched as he checked the microwave for thawing meat. "What is that supposed to mean?"

He got out the steaks, then went to the refrigerator. "Do you want salad or some kind of potato with these?"

"I have a frozen mac and cheese I made last month I was going to pop in the oven." I pointed to the fridge. "It's on the second shelf."

"Sounds perfect." He took it out and put the pan into the oven. "Three fifty?"

"Yes. Are you going to answer my question?" I let Emma in from outside and she went to attack—I mean, greet—Greg because he'd been gone forever in her eyes.

He leaned down and gave Emma the love she was expecting and met my gaze. "Your aunt comes from a different time. I don't expect you to wait on me hand and foot. You're not required to be here at the house waiting for my return home. I thought you knew better than that."

My shoulders dropped. "I do. She just got me thinking. I love her, but she knows how to mess with my brain more ways than anyone should. Thanks for confirming, though."

"So how did the weekend go? I saw Justin Saturday eating at Lille's when I was picking up food for the station, so I knew she took you up on your offer. He says she's been a little tense since the wedding." He took a soda out of the fridge and offered it to me.

I took it and sat at the table. "She is freaking. I guess because they didn't live together, the adjustment is huge. She thinks he should be the fun Justin he was when they were dating. He's just trying to settle into a normal life."

"And there's the marriage thing. It gets in people's head. They have certain expectations of the other spouse, but they never tell them. So, like your aunt, they are disappointed when something happens that doesn't match their idea of what should be." He sipped his soda. "I like our normal life.

I know your aunt didn't approve of us living together before the wedding, but we're good together. And we'll be better together after we're married. You just have to swallow your fear and talk to me about our financial life."

"I'm not afraid of it." But maybe I was. I never told anyone how much money Miss Emily had left me. Greg knew part of it because of the gold coins we'd found, but not all of it. I used the fund as my own personal gift stash. I gave away money at Christmas to local charities. What if he wanted to use it for our lives? "Okay, maybe I am afraid that talking about it might change us."

"You can be rich or poor. I still love you. We just need to be totally honest with each other. No secrets about money, other people, or shopping." He smiled. "I may be reacting from my last failed marriage issues with some of these specific requirements. But I'll be honest with you."

"Except about investigations and things your job makes you keep secret." I held up a hand. "Don't take it the wrong way. I'm just saying, in your position there are exceptions. I'm not part of a spy ring, so I don't have exceptions that I'm calling. Let's sit down for dinner next Saturday if you're free and bring all our finance stuff to the table. Accounts, debts, credit accounts. Everything. We'll order pizza from the Winery."

"I don't know about Saturday, but the first night I'm not stuck in this investigation, it's a date." He stood and kissed me. "Now, I'm going to go take a shower and change. I'm praying for a quiet night."

I realized I hadn't told him about what the nail technician had said, but I figured that could wait until he was back downstairs. I went to the cupboard and grabbed a can of veggies to go with dinner. Then I seasoned the steaks and turned a timer on for the mac and cheese. I couldn't believe I'd let Aunt Jackie worry me. Greg was different. And that was one reason I loved him.

When he got downstairs he nodded at the meat. "You want me to grill? How much longer on the mac and cheese?"

"Fifteen should do it. You can start the grill and by the time it's clean and hot, you should be good to go." I held up a finger. "Hold on a second."

"What now?" He paused at the door.

"Do you want me to tell you what Ginger at the spa said about Mrs. Winter?"

"Actually, I don't. Not really. I want a quiet night with the woman I love. I'm sure that's not too much to ask, is it?" He looked tired.

"Then I won't tell you." I moved to the door. "We can sit outside while the steaks are grilling."

He sighed. "It's fine, tell me. I probably need to know. I can't believe even on a day off you run into someone who knows Max Winter." He paused. "I guess I should tell you that the woman we saw in Apple Valley isn't Mrs. Winter. I met the actual Mrs. this morning, when Marvin pulled me into the death threat discussion."

"Wait, what? Even Ginger at the spa thought Connie was his wife. She called her that several times and the woman let her. Either this Connie is a great actress, or maybe they are married?" Now my head was spinning.

"All I know is Mrs. Winter came into the station this morning and she wasn't the woman we saw in the restaurant." He sat down by me on the swing. "She wanted to check on the promises Marvin made to Max about South Cove stepping into the Bakerstown investigation. It broke my heart to tell her there wasn't anything we could be doing. Her name's Beth, by the way."

"What if each of them thinks they are the one and only Mrs. Winter? It happens all the time in books. A guy dies and two women come up to claim his fortune."

Greg pressed two fingers between his brows. He looked like I was beating him up.

"Jill, that's fiction."

"I'm not sure it is right now."

He took a big breath. "Point of order, Max isn't dead."

We stared at each other. Finally, Greg broke. "Well, it would give me more to talk to the wives about, but I'm not sure what my opening would be. I'd love to know why they thought he'd hid an entire family. Is that all you needed to tell me? Besides, like I told Beth, I'm not involved in the death threat investigation. If Bakerstown doesn't open a file, that's on them. Anything else I need to hear before we table this subject?"

I told him about Connie not being happy about this South Cove deal and that she'd wanted him to retire. "Maybe he can't retire because then he couldn't go back and forth between the two families."

"Or maybe he's struggling to keep everything afloat financially and that's why he can't quit." Greg stood and went to clean the grill with the wire brush as he thought. "The thought of having two wives makes me feel sick. Anyway, if there's nothing else, we're done talking about Max Winter and his wives. Go get me the spray oil and the steaks and I'll get these started."

I wasn't sure if he believed my theory, or if he was working on one of his own, but I could see that Ginger's information had piqued his interest. Max Winter had two women in his life. Maybe two families when other men had none. Mostly because they were jerks and didn't deserve one. But that was my opinion.

And as a good business owner in a small town, I usually didn't share my opinions with others outside my small cone-of-silence friends. I gathered the stuff Greg needed for grilling, checked on the mac and cheese, and decided to put the question of who exactly Max Winter was on the back burner. I was going to spend some quality time with my fiancé.

* * * *

The next morning Greg was already gone by the time my alarm went off. So instead of having breakfast, Emma and I decided to take an early morning run. It was bracing, but I loved watching the waves on the beach. Emma enjoyed chasing the gulls off her sand. She can get a little protective of what she considered her special running place.

Back home, I got ready for work and poured coffee to take with me. It wasn't that long a walk, but even after the run I needed my caffeine. My tote was filled with books I'd read over vacation. I had several ideas for my staff-pick-of-the-month article. I probably wouldn't have to write another one until the first of the year if I got all these book reports to Deek.

I unlocked the front door and turned on the lights and realized I already had a customer following me inside. "Good morning. It will take me a few minutes to get the coffee going."

"No problem. I didn't know what time you opened, so I've been watching for you. I'm unpacking stock today, and if I don't have coffee, I'll get my colors mixed up." The woman grinned as she followed me to the front. "Unless you'd rather I come back. I can be a little pushy."

"No worries. I don't think we've met. I'm Jill Gardner, and this is my place. I typically only work the morning shift, though." I flipped on coffee makers and dropped my tote on the floor. "What can I make you?"

"Coffee, large and black." She pointed to the display case, which Aunt Jackie must have filled yesterday. "And two of those black and white cookies. I haven't seen those since I was in New York."

"Our newest barista asked our bakery supplier if she could make them. They've been a hot seller." I set a cup aside to wait for the coffee to finish brewing and then got the cookies. "Do you want these to go?"

"Please. Oh, and I'm Crissy Newby. I own the yarn shop. Mary tells me you're coming to Wednesday's session." Crissy climbed onto one of the stools. She was a tiny thing, with her gray hair cut in a pixie. "I've been wanting to do a community event like this, but without my own shop I never could pull it off."

I poured the coffee and handed over it and the bag of cookies. "Well, welcome to South Cove. We're all about community service events, so I'm sure you'll fit right in."

She opened her wallet. "What do I owe you?"

I waved it away. "First taste is free. I'm your local coffee dealer. I want repeat customers."

"Not sure you want that on a T-shirt, but thank you." Chrissy laughed and headed out the door.

I got ready for my commuters. By the time Sadie arrived with her first drop-off for the week from Pies on the Fly, I had a line of customers. "Go ahead and set it in the back. I'll double-check your figures and text you if there's a discrepancy. Just give me the invoice and I'll sign it now."

"You're trusting." A man in a way-too-expensive suit tucked two dollars into the tip jar as he took his coffee cup. "She could short you and you wouldn't have anything to fight on since you signed for it."

I shook my head. "Now that's the thing about South Cove. We trust one another and will do anything to make it right if something happens."

He laughed and, as he left, he took a parting shot. "Until it does."

Chapter 6

Deek arrived just before Toby's shift started. I watched as he came around the counter, tucking his tote under the cabinet. "Let me guess. Greg has Toby's week booked."

Deek slipped an apron over his head. "Yep. I called Evie to see if she could help and I guess she has family coming in this week. Does this mean I can't have Saturday off?"

"No. I gave you the day off. I'll work your shift. Don't worry about it." I thought about the day. "And Evie's off too, so I'll just work the full day. Greg's busy anyway."

"Maybe you need to hire a temp or two." He restocked the coffee cups and grabbed the water pitcher to refill it with ice and water. "Saturdays are pretty busy."

"You're probably right. I'll call the temp agency today. I'm going to ask for someone who might want to work part-time. Unless you have a friend or two who's looking for work." I liked hiring people my staff knew. "Evie's too new to the area to have many friends. And Toby's friends are all in the police force, which gives us the same problem as we have with his schedule."

He set the water pitcher back on the counter. "Actually, I do have someone who might be interested. I'll call her and see if she can come down to talk to you tomorrow. Maybe we won't need a temp."

"Those are the words I love to hear." It wasn't that I was against hiring a temp, but to work at the bookstore, you needed to love books. That wasn't a question the temp agency screened for. The last woman they'd sent us hadn't read anything since high school. "If she can come during my shift, I'd appreciate it."

"I just texted her and she said she'd be here in the morning." He tucked his phone back in his pocket.

"I can't type on the phone that fast." I glanced around the semifilled dining area. "Let me refill the dessert case before I leave."

"Sounds good." Deek stepped up to help a customer. "Welcome to Coffee, Books, and More. What can I get you?"

After I'd finished getting Deek set up I ran into Evie coming down from the apartment. "Hey, I thought you were with family this week?"

"I would be, but Becky doesn't like to be out before noon. I'm meeting her for lunch." She reached down and stroked Homer's ears. Homer was her tan Pomeranian and always by her side. "We're probably going to be out most of the day, so I'm spending as much time with Homer as possible. She's not an animal lover."

"How is that even possible since she's related?" I reached over and stroked Homer's ears. "Who wouldn't love this furball?"

"Actually, she's my ex-sister-in-law. I was shocked when she called me asking to meet up this week. We didn't leave on the best terms. She took John's side in the divorce. I guess I understand, but it was hurtful because I'd thought we were friends." She glanced around the busy store. "I guess family trumps friendship."

"I've never had a sister, so I'm not the best person to talk to. Besides, you've met my aunt. So, in my situation, friendships are important too." I gave Homer one last pet. "Anyway, I heard this one woman talking to someone in her family about an inheritance when we were on vacation. If I heard one of my kids talking about me like that? I'd disown them. Of course, the guy was dead, so there was that. But he had to know this woman was a little snot, right?"

Evie laughed as she moved toward the back door. "You'd be surprised. Becky was, or I guess, *is* a horrible person and her father adored her. She was always nice to him, even at the end. John Senior was a lovely man. I don't understand how he raised two of the worst people I know. I've got to get Homer outside, he's squirming. Thanks again for the time off. I appreciate it."

"Not a problem," I called after her. But it really was a bit of a problem. Mostly because of Toby's reassignment at the job he worked for Greg. I really hoped Deek's friend turned out to be normal so I could hire her and have one more person to move around the schedule here. Especially going into the next few months. It was even more important then, because everyone saved their vacation time for the slower months.

It took me longer than I'd thought to refill the dessert cases, mostly because Deek was selling stuff just as fast as I was setting it in the case. When he'd taken the last piece of cheesecake for the third time, I narrowed my eyes at him. "Seriously?"

"It's the after lunch crowd. They've eaten lunch, now they want something sweet. And a book to read while it's slow." He shrugged. "What can I say? I always sell a lot of desserts during lunchtime."

"You suggest it with every transaction," I reminded him.

He cocked his head, watching me. "Are you telling me you want to sell less stuff at your store? Your aunt says I'm the highest seller of both books and treats for the last three weeks. I can slow down if you want, but you have to explain it to your aunt."

"You're horrible." I grabbed the empty cheesecake platter to send back to Sadie when she came in next week and went back to slice another cheesecake and put one in the fridge for later. I was just finishing when I heard Evie's door shut. I watched as she went down the backstairs and headed in the direction of Diamond Lille's. She was in a dress and was wearing heels and makeup. She looked like she was heading to work at a corporate job, not lunch with a family member. I felt bad for her because Evie had seemed less than enthusiastic about the meeting.

I finished stocking and Deek's line had slowed, so I thought he'd be okay without me. By this time I was hungry but didn't want to go to Lille's. I had my mind on the leftovers from the night before, so long as Greg hadn't popped in at the house and eaten them. I was probably safe since when he was working a case he tended to stay at the office and order in food for him and his guys. I grabbed my tote and headed home.

As I walked past Lille's, I heard my name being called. I turned and saw Evie standing by Lille's front entrance. I went over to chat, hoping it wouldn't take long. I was starving and had turned down half of the broken cookie Deek had offered me before I left. "Hey, I figured you'd be eating by now."

"Apparently Becky wasn't really on the road when she'd called. She was just leaving her room. She set up in Bakerstown for this week. I don't know why she didn't just stay with me." Evie shook her head. "I don't know what I'm saying. She would have hated the apartment and, of course, Homer."

"Sorry you had to wait, but you look amazing."

She ran her hand over the dress. "It's too much, right? I never know what to expect with her. I'll look like this and she'll show up in denim shorts and a tank. But if I have on jeans, she'll be wearing something designer."

"You should introduce her to Harper. Maybe something good can come from the visit. Hey, are you going to the yarn shop tomorrow night?" I was hoping someone had invited her.

"I wouldn't miss it." She nodded to the Mercedes pulling into the parking lot. "I'm going to get crap because Lille's doesn't have a valet."

"Well, she can pick the restaurant for tomorrow, then." I really didn't want to wait for a formal introduction, but I didn't want to leave Evie standing alone. Waiting for the car to be parked and the sister-in-law to get out, that was the correct path. I looked over at Evie, who was watching the car. "I'll leave as soon as you make sure it's her. I don't want to intrude on your lunch."

"Believe me, you wouldn't be intruding. I'm expecting to hear story after story about John and how amazing he's doing without me." She nodded to the car. "But I'll be fine. I'm sure you want to get home and see Emma after being gone so long last week."

"I've got a few minutes. I just don't want you standing here alone in case that's not her." I stood with Evie, feeling the nerves coming off my newest barista. Which she wouldn't be next week if I hired Deek's friend. Oh, the things I think about when I'm waiting.

The car door opened and a woman's leg showed as the occupant climbed out of the car. She adjusted a cotton sundress. Evie had been right on that note. She was casually dressed and the opposite of Evie's upscale look. When she shut the door and turned to look at the restaurant I gasped.

"Jill, what's wrong?" Evie squeezed my arm.

I shook off her arm and turned to leave. "Sorry, I just remembered something I need to do at home. Have a great lunch."

"Thanks, but you look white as a sheet," Evie pressed as I hurried away.

"I'm fine, just low blood sugar." I held up a hand to wave without turning back and hurried down the street.

Evie's sister-in-law was the same woman who had stayed at the bed-and-breakfast in Apple Valley. The woman who said she was here to get something from a relative. I needed to talk to Greg to see if he remembered anything she'd said before I told Evie. Because if what I remembered her saying was right, she still wasn't Evie's friend, and she was going to break her heart even more with this visit.

When I got home I texted Greg, but he responded with a quick *I'll need to talk about this later.* So, as I heated up the leftover macaroni and cheese for lunch, I tried to remember what Rebecca had said on the phone and to me directly. As I waited, I realized maybe it was mostly a feeling I'd gotten about her, especially after talking to my hostess. She wasn't a nice person.

Evie had that right. I'd just let things ride and see if she said anything to me if Evie decided to introduce us. I'd warn her to be careful, but from what she'd said about the woman, I thought Evie was already on guard.

I was glad I didn't have any siblings to argue with. Besides, my aunt wouldn't be leaving me much of an inheritance, so no one needed to fight with me over anything.

I sat at the table and went through the packet of mail I'd gotten while we were gone. One of the letters was from Winter Construction. I sighed and opened it. If this was his latest offer, at least I knew I wouldn't be getting any more friendly salesmen dropping by the house. I unfolded the pages and read the final offer. Half a million now to option and another guaranteed million if I sold. Man, the minihotel industry must be more financially rewarding than I'd expected. A lot of people were doing bed-and-breakfasts in the area and making a killing. I'd even talked to Greg about renting the shed short-term when Toby finally moved out. But I really didn't want people around me all the time who I didn't know.

It was a crazy amount of money to turn down, but the good news was I didn't have to actually say no to someone's face. I could just toss this into the trash with all the other junk mail. I flipped through the last few items that weren't junk and paid the couple of bills in the pile. I tucked them into my tote because I typically sent out my mail with the store mail. That way I didn't have mail sitting out with checks in it, waiting for someone to come off the beach, find my electric bill, and try to cash the check. I worried about things like that.

I updated my budget and finished my lunch. Then I dug the book I hadn't found time to read out of the bag and went out to the back porch. I needed to finish this because my dreams were being taken over by the plot. I needed to see if my solving of the who-did-it mystery was even close.

Toby came home, waved, and disappeared into his apartment. Then, about twenty minutes later, he came back out, his hair wet from a shower. He waved again and jumped into his truck. I guess Greg had sent him home to change because he must have slept at the station house.

I texted Greg: *You're running your staff into the ground. Toby just left without even stopping to chat.*

He was probably worried you'd ask if he could work a shift at the store. I hear you're a little short this week. Anyway, as long as he's back here in thirty, I'm not telling him he has to talk to his landlord.

That was the problem with working and living in a small town. Information flowed freely. Both rumors and truths. Greg was as much of a slave driver as my aunt. After he reminded me of my staffing issue,

I sent Aunt Jackie an email, asking for a list of what I needed to hire this woman who was coming in on Saturday to interview for the job. I knew we had a hiring packet somewhere, but I didn't have it on my laptop.

Emma lay down at my feet and I realized I was done working. The bookkeeping had been transferred as part of Aunt Jackie's new role. Deek was handling the author visits, including the planning. I'd already texted Sadie about more stock for the bakery showcase. The letter from Max Winter sat on the table, taunting me.

"I'll just do an internet search and see what I can find out about our developer." I heard Emma's sigh from under the table. Even she didn't believe I wasn't going to start investigating what had happened to Max.

I took a notebook from my drawer in the kitchen desk and opened it to a blank page. Then I wrote down his name and went searching on my computer.

The dwindling light in the kitchen told me I'd been researching too long. I had five pages of notes about projects and developments: completed, in progress, and hinted at. Whatever Connie had thought, Max didn't appear to be getting ready to retire or close his business. The South Cove project, and my house, was only one of five different plans he'd talked to City Councils in the area about. If she'd found out he'd lied about retiring, what else had he lied to her about? Maybe she didn't know he was married?

All good questions for Greg if he could find out who this Connie woman was and what her relationship with Max was. The women at the spa could have just assumed they were married. I knew I was obsessing over Max, but because I didn't have any idea who the murder victim was, this gave me an outlet for my sleuthing skills.

I had seen several notices of filing for court cases. I'd go into Bakerstown this weekend—no, they'd be closed. I'd go in on Monday. I couldn't leave town this week. Not with Deek and me being the only ones working. I leaned back and closed my eyes. What had I done? All I needed was for Deek's friend to not be an ax murderer, or at least be able to hide it well, and we'd have one more warm body to ease the stress.

A knock sounded at the door. Emma ran into the living room and I followed. She sat on my left side, waiting for me to open the door. I was pretty sure she already knew who was on the other side because she hadn't barked once. I swung open the door and Esmeralda stood there with a Dutch oven in her hands. "Hi, what are you doing here?"

"I brought over some soup and a loaf of bread for you. I know work is keeping you busy, so I thought you and Greg might enjoy this tonight."

Esmeralda held out the pot and I took it. "Careful, that's heavy. It's a tomato-based seafood stew."

"Thank you. But I'm not sure Greg's coming home for dinner tonight." As I set the heavy pot on the foyer table with the bread, Greg's truck pulled into the driveway. "Well, I guess I was wrong."

"I'll let you two have some privacy. I know it's hard to find time during investigations. I'll bring over something for tomorrow and pick up my pot then." She turned and left, waving at Greg as she opened the gate and crossed the road.

I waited at the door for Greg to come inside. "Hi, honey, welcome home."

"What did Esmeralda want?" He kissed me, then greeted Emma, whose tail was beating out a happy puppy tune.

"She brought us dinner. I hadn't started anything because I didn't know if you would be home." I picked up the Dutch oven and took it to the kitchen to put it on the stove. Opening the lid, the smell made my stomach growl. "It smells amazing."

"She brings a creole seafood stew to work sometimes to share. This smells like it. It was nice of her to think of us." Greg paused at the office and locked up his gun. "I do have to eat and run, so I'm glad dinner's ready. If not, I would have had to grab takeout in Bakerstown. I've got a meeting in about an hour."

"Then it's your lucky day." I went to get the stew on the table as I wondered how my fortune-telling neighbor had known I hadn't started dinner. Knowing that Greg was heading to Bakerstown tonight was kind of her job as the police dispatcher and admin for the station. But how had she known I hadn't been cooking all afternoon?

Too many questions today, not enough answers.

Chapter 7

Crissy was my first customer again the next day. This time she came in just a few minutes after me, rather than following me inside. She climbed on a stool and set down her wallet. "Good morning. I'm looking forward to the crochet class tonight. You're still coming, right?"

"I'm coming, but if something happens here at the shop, I may have to leave early. We're a little shorthanded." I poured her a coffee. "What can I get you from the treat display?"

"I'll stay with the black and whites; two please. That way I can have one with my lunch." She glanced around the shop. "How many employees do you have? I just hired someone part-time to allow me to keep the store open six days a week, but we close pretty early."

"I have six including my aunt and me, but she's gone to management only so I'm hiring another part-timer. I've got someone coming in today who I'm hoping will work out." I put the cookies into a bag and rang up the purchase. "The problem is two of my staff are in school and one has another job. A real job, with my fiancé at the police station. So, when he gets called in for extra hours, I need to cover his shifts. And this week we have a family visit and a workshop that's taking my other two out of commission."

Crissy handed me a credit card. "So, you're telling me I might need to hire another person too."

"Probably wouldn't be a bad idea." I finished the purchase and handed her back the card. Then I pulled out a cup and poured myself some coffee too. "How are you liking South Cove?"

"It's been nice. Mary has been helpful since I moved in. I live upstairs over the shop. I thought I might look for a house, but prices here are crazy.

I love your house. Mary showed it to me when she took me to Bakerstown the other day." Crissy talked fast. I wasn't sure if it was her normal pattern or the coffee. "Of course I'd like South Cove better without the murder that happened. I can't believe the guy just walked into the station bleeding and everything."

"I know." I didn't want to push, but if Crissy had some information, I'd love to hear it.

She looked at me. "You live with the police chief, right? You'd tell me if this was a high-crime place. Mary keeps saying it's not, but we had a murder. Here. Just down from my shop."

I saw the worry in her eyes. "South Cove is as safe as anywhere else. I mean, yes, we've had a few murders here, but it's totally safe. I feel comfortable walking alone at night here."

Crissy lowered her voice. "What about the homeless guy who sits out in front of the bike rental shop every day. Is he dangerous?"

I bit my lip to keep from laughing. "The guy in the Hawaiian shirt? Dustin Austin isn't homeless. He's just an old hippie surfer. He owns the bike shop and that building."

Crissy's hands flew up to her face. "Oh no. My cheeks should be burning. I can't believe I said something like that aloud. I'll just keep my opinions to myself until I know all the residents. I guess he's a nice guy."

I thought about Austin's dislike for me; but then, he loved Amy. "Yes, he's a nice guy. Like I said, just a little unusual."

"Well, now that I've embarrassed myself for the day, I'll head back to my shop. I hope you come tonight. We're going to have a blast and help babies. I even ordered treats for the night." She grabbed her cookies and coffee and headed out the door.

I liked Crissy. She was a lot like me, at least in her love for desserts.

My commuters started to come in and I was busy for a few hours. Finally, traffic to the shop slowed, and I saw a woman I hadn't served sitting and reading at one of the tables. She'd poured herself a glass of water. Refilling my own cup, I grabbed a notebook and pen and walked over to talk to her. I had a hunch this was Deek's friend and, hopefully, my newest barista.

"Good morning. I'm Jill Gardner, owner of Coffee, Books, and More. Are you Deek's friend?" I set my coffee cup on the table but stayed standing, just in case.

"Guilty as charged." The woman's smile was as bright as her short purple hair. "Although how that happened with me being old enough to be his grandmother, I'll never know. But the boy has good instincts about people. Except that just sounded like I was bragging on myself. Sorry, my name is Judith Dame. I hear you might have a job opening."

I nodded to the chair. "Mind if I sit?"

"Not at all." She put a bookmark into her book and moved it away from her water. "I'm very interested in part-time. I don't think I can fit a full-time position into my schedule, but if that's what you need, I'll consider it."

"Right now we're only looking for part-time. It might be more hours one week than another due to staffing issues. And in the summer, most of us work full-time hours, especially on festival weeks. So I need someone flexible. But if you're only looking for part-time, I can deal with that."

I wrote down her name and "part-time" under it. "I'll need a few things later if we decide this is a fit, but for now, let's just talk for a while." I pointed to the book. "Tell me why you're reading that book?"

She frowned and held it up. "This? It's a time travel women's fiction that got great reviews when it first came out, but it didn't set the world on fire. I think it's because it was a woman's fiction novel. The mainstream media doesn't get a heroine's journey most of the time."

I'd read the book too. And loved it. It was interesting, listening to her take on bookselling and the publishing machine. "What was the last book you read before this?"

She blushed, making the purple in her hair stand out. "A cowboy romance. Junk food for the mind. I hope you don't think poorly of me for my taste in reading. I do read a wide variety of genres."

"You could have lied and said something literary. Best book this year?"

She paused, thinking about the question. I could see when she hit on her answer. Her eyes lit up as she remembered the book. "*The Book of Two Ways*. Kind of time travel or alternate universe, some romance, a lot of Egyptian archaeology and mythology."

"I read that too. Really enjoyed it." I was liking her answers. "Tell me about a time when you worked for someone you didn't like."

"I don't know if I can. A job means you work with all kinds of people. Some are easier to get along with than others. You have a different vibe from some people. But in the end, if I'm hired, I'm here to work, not make friends." She sipped her water.

I was liking her more and more. I glanced down at the questions and set the pen down. "Tell me about you."

For the next half hour we talked about life and where the path had taken her. I told her about my life and how I'd ended up in South Cove. When we were done I nodded and opened a folder. "If you still want to work here, this is the new employee hire packet. I can't offer a huge salary, but you get to read all the ARCs you want. A discount on books and anything from the dessert case. And if you want more hours, we can get you those. The benefit package is also listed. Let me know. I'd love to have you start as soon as possible."

"Well, I'm not doing anything today. And I know our friend Deek is gone on Saturday. Why don't I fill this out and we can get started?" Judith held out a hand. "And I go by Judith, not Judy, just to be clear."

"Perfect." I stood and nodded to the register, where a customer had just arrived. "I'll be over there when you're done. You're officially on the clock."

I transferred the training duties to Deek when he came in and worked another few hours. Deek would close, so Judith would be our middle person for the next week or so, until she got comfortable working alone. At least I'd be able to get a lunch break on Saturday, when I was working from open to close.

When I finished my shift Greg was at the door. I smiled as I walked up to give him a kiss. "You have amazing timing. Have you eaten lunch?"

"Not yet. And I have to admit, I called earlier and talked to Deek. He told me when you'd be off. Want to grab an early dinner/late lunch at Lille's?" He took my tote and swung it over his back. "This feels a little light. Are you only bringing one or two books home?"

"Two. I have a thing at the yarn shop tonight. Didn't I tell you?" I thought I'd mentioned it.

"You did. That's why I carved out time to have at least one meal with you today." He checked a text on his phone, keyed in a few words, then tucked it back in his pocket.

"Do you have to go back?" I could feel my fish and chips disappearing out of my grasp.

"Nope. I asked Esmeralda to check on something for me. She just got the answer." He put his arm around me as we walked. "I told her the stew last night was amazing."

"I hope you thanked her for me too. She's a really good neighbor."

He chuckled. "When she's not getting into your head, right?"

"Or trying to convince me that I've got the gift too." I waved at Austin as we crossed the road to Lille's, but either he was asleep or he was ignoring me. "Crissy thought he was homeless."

Greg glanced back at the bike shop. "I have to admit, she's not the first one. We're always getting calls from tourists about a guy sleeping outside the bike shop. When I ask them to describe him, they seem disappointed when I explain that he owns the shop."

"Sometimes perception isn't reality." I went into Lille's and paused at the hostess station.

Carrie waved us over. "Lille's gone for the day. She's trying to find the mayor so she can give him a piece of her mind. I told her that it wouldn't live in that desolate space he has between his ears."

"She heard he was trying to bring in an upscale restaurant." I slipped into our favorite booth and took the menu Carrie handed me. "I can't believe how mad she was at the meeting."

"Yep, she's hot. She's been on fire about it since the business-to-business meeting. You guys have been out of town and missing the fireworks." Carrie gave Greg a menu. "And since she's off trying to change the mayor's mind, I've been doing longer shifts. I guess it's fine because Doc is busy with this new murder you brought him."

Greg held up his hands. "I didn't kill the guy. I'm working crazy hours too."

"I know, I'm just venting. Besides, telling Doc how I feel is like kicking a puppy. And if I did, all he'd say is quit. I'm not ready to become a kept woman, you know." Carrie pointed a couple who'd just come in to another booth. "Iced tea?"

"Perfect." I watched as she went to greet the new arrivals. When she was out of earshot I turned to Greg. "You don't think Lille was mad enough to do this, do you?"

"Stab a guy?" Greg shook his head. "It's not that I can't see her doing it, but I know Marvin would have been first on her list. Though if we find out this guy is attached to the mini hotel project, I'd have to admit, she'd be on my list of possible suspects. Just not very likely."

"Who else is on your list?" I leaned forward. "Now I mean, since you don't know who the guy is."

"That's the problem. It's hard to have a suspect list when the victim is a John Doe." He leaned closer and dropped the volume in his voice. "And more that that? I'm not going to tell you."

"You're mean." I laughed as Carrie dropped off the tea.

"Should I just get you the usual or are you going to surprise me?" Carrie pulled out her pad and a pen.

Greg pushed the menu toward her. "Stuffed meat loaf, mashed potatoes, brown gravy, and a side salad with ranch."

"And fish and chips for you?" Carrie didn't even look up.

"Well, yeah, I guess." Now my meal felt like a chore. Like I was in some sort of rut.

When she left I turned to Greg. "Do you think I'm boring?"

"Where on earth did that come from? No way. I'd like a little more boring if you want to dial up the characteristic." He took my hands in his. "You're my rock. I always know I can come home to you and you'll be there for me. Maybe pressing me for information you don't need, but there. I love you."

"I love you too. But this new barista I hired has been to Tibet. She walked the Great Wall. And she spent a year hiking the Appalachian Trail, alone." I shook my head. "The only other country I've been to is Mexico, and we stayed at an all-inclusive resort. I'm not sure that even counts as traveling."

"A lot of places in Mexico aren't safe right now." Greg squeezed my hand. "I didn't know you wanted to travel more. Maybe we should go to Canada for a vacation next year. That would be a different country."

"Judith has just done so much with her life. And I'm running a bookstore." I shook my head. "Sorry, I'm whining. I've just been thinking about the differences in our lives all afternoon."

"You were a lawyer. That takes determination and a lot of time." He sipped his tea. "You stepped out because it wasn't your life. You're happy running your bookstore and you know it. Look for the small changes you can make that will enrich your life, not blow it all up just because you think someone else is living more."

"I'm not blowing anything up." I leaned back and sighed. "I don't know what's wrong with me today. I think it's knowing I'm going to fail at this crochet thing tonight."

"You don't know that."

Carrie dropped off the food. "Hey, if you're going to A Pirate's Yarn later, would you tell Crissy I have two blankets done and will stop by Friday for more yarn?"

"Sure." I picked up a French fry and snapped it in two.

"A hundred blankets is a lofty goal, but I'm sure we'll reach it. Especially with everyone chipping in." Carrie patted my arm. "Every blanket counts."

When she walked away Greg started laughing. When I glared at him, he held up his hands. "Don't look at me. I already told you how wonderful you are. I can't fix the fact that you're craft handicapped."

"Handicapped is such a negative word. Maybe just challenged." I bit into my fish. At least my lunch wasn't going to disappoint me today.

When we were finished eating Greg walked me back to the house. He greeted Emma, then headed back out the door. "If you're going to run, would you text me when you're back at the house? I get a little nervous when there's a killer running around South Cove."

"You think it's one of us?" I rubbed Emma's head. "Anyway, don't answer that. Yes, we're going running as soon as I call Aunt Jackie and tell her I hired Judith. Then I'll change and we'll run. I don't want to ruin a perfect runner's high by calling my aunt."

"Do you think she's not going to like your hire?" Greg paused at the door.

I thought about his question for a second. "No, I don't think she's going to like Judith at all. But I like her, and I hired her. Jackie would have come up with some stupid reason not to hire her. I think they're a lot alike. Which is why I probably like Judith."

"Besides the fact their names both start with a 'J'?" He kissed me. "I've got to go solve this case and save the world. I'll be late, so don't wait up."

"I'll probably be sitting on the couch crocheting a few blankets to catch up with Carrie." I knew that wasn't true, but it sounded good.

"Sure, that could happen. Especially after one lesson." He tapped my nose. "You're an overachiever and expect perfection the first time out. That's why you're not good at these things."

I took Judith's application out of my tote and opened it so I could review it before I called my aunt. She'd hired people without my permission or input, so turnabout was fair play. Or something like that. I noticed she mentioned she wrote paranormal fiction. I wondered why she hadn't talked about it in the interview. The fact made me smile. She was searching out her dreams, just like Deek.

I dialed my aunt's number and got her voice mail. I decided to prewarn her in a message. "Hey, I hired Deek's friend today. She's working this week to be trained, so if you want to work with her, let me know. I'd love to give up part of Saturday's all-day shift. Call me. But not for a bit. I'm going for a run. I guess I'll see you at the yarn shop later. We can talk then."

I left my phone on the table and ran upstairs to change. When I got back I checked, but no call had come back. Either she was busy with Harrold or mad. Or both. I couldn't change what I did or how she felt, so I just needed to own it. Besides, she wouldn't make a scene at the class tonight. My aunt was too much of a lady for that.

No, I'd get a visit tomorrow during my shift when she thought I'd be alone. But I'd hired Judith, so she'd have to come early. And Crissy was taking my early morning alone time before the commuters hit. If I was lucky, we wouldn't have this conversation until after she'd met and maybe learned to like Judith. At least a little.

I clicked on Emma's leash and headed to the door. "Come on, girl, let's go running before Aunt Jackie shows up to yell at me in person."

Chapter 8

The yarn shop was already buzzing with people. I saw Mary and Aunt Jackie talking to Crissy near the front. Amy was waving at me from the other side of the room, and I hurried over to her, hoping my aunt hadn't seen me come in. I wasn't exactly hiding from her, more like delaying the conversation.

Evie stood next to Amy. I gave them each a hug. "Everything going all right with the family reunion this week."

"We're supposed to meet later. Sometime after nine. I think she's mad at me. I swear, I haven't stayed up this late for years. Last night she dragged me to the city to have coffee. I told her we could have a better cup at your place, but she wanted the time to talk." Evie yawned and took a sip of what must have been coffee in the CBM cup she'd brought with her. "Then she dropped the bombshell. The true reason she even showed up. She wants the mantel clock her father gave me for our wedding. She says it's a family heirloom and should stay with the family."

"You have got to be kidding." I'd wondered what Becky had wanted and when she'd tell Evie, since I'd heard her scheming at the bed-and-breakfast. "That's horrible. Your ex-father-in-law, when did he pass?"

"I didn't realize I'd mentioned that. It was a few months ago. I wasn't told until after the funeral had happened. I guess John didn't want me to run into his new girlfriend, but I sent a card to both of them. Then I made a donation to the local animal shelter in John Senior's name. He loved dogs. Somehow that skipped a generation; John hates them. Which made the donation all that sweeter for me." She grinned and nodded to the front of the room. "Looks like we're getting started. This should be fun."

Amy and I held back as Evie went to find us seats. I watched Evie as I leaned closer to Amy. "Can you believe that? I need to tell her I saw Becky at the bed-and-breakfast. I knew she was looking for something, but a wedding gift? That's cold."

"Some families are like that. Justin's mom gave me a pair of earrings she'd worn on her wedding day. Then his sister cornered me after the wedding and said if I ever divorced him, she wanted the earrings." Amy pointed to the front. "Should we move closer so you can see the demonstration?"

"I know how to crochet." Which was kind of true. I'd taken a class when I was in high school for an extra credit. The teacher said she passed me with a B due to determination rather than skill. "What did you tell your new sister-in-law?"

"I told her that I loved her brother, but if we ever got divorced, the earrings were still mine. No take backs allowed." Amy touched her ears, where a pair of black-gold-studded crosses shone in the bright light. "I think they're kind of me, don't you?"

I laughed and stopped by the table where crochet hooks and yarn were set out. "These are beautiful."

Crissy smiled and gave me a hug. "Like you and coffee, first skein's on me, along with a hook. Well, actually, five skeins because that's what you need to make your first blanket. The next ones are on your dime. Pick a color."

"Well played." I thought Crissy would fit into South Cove well. I reached for the blue on the table. It was a cross between royal blue and turquoise and the most beautiful color I'd ever seen, outside of the actual sky over the water at around two in the afternoon. "Is blue too cliché?"

"Not at all. Besides, I loved that color. It would be beautiful with a boy or a girl." She tucked five skeins and a hook into a bag. Then she pointed to a clipboard. "If you want to estimate how many blankets you'll be making, that will help us know when we're close to goal."

Amy snickered as she picked out a pretty yellow mixed with orange and red. "Yes, Jill, how many blankets will you be creating?"

"Due to my work schedule, I'll have to just do the one, but if I have extra time, I'll let you know." I shot a glare at Amy.

"I'll sign up for five, no, six. I'll help fill in for Jill's lack of motivation." Amy picked up a pen and wrote her name, cell number, and the number six.

"Give me that pen." I took it from her and wrote my own name and information. Then I put down the number three. It was out of my comfort level, but what good goal isn't? And this was for the babies.

Amy and I sat next to Evie, who was already working on her blanket. It looked so easy, maybe I hadn't just painted myself into a corner I would have to beg my way out of.

"What on earth are you thinking?" Amy whispered as we took out a skein of yarn and the hook. "Can you actually make three in four weeks?"

"Four weeks? No one said anything about this being a timed test." I leaned back into my seat, the crochet hook hanging heavy in my hand. Like a pair of handcuffs. I might just have Greg arrest me for being stupid. But I didn't think he'd get me out of this hole I'd just dug myself. I was in deep trouble. "Maybe I can buy three blankets?"

Amy just laughed.

"Quiet down, we're going to get started. Thank you all for being here, and for Coffee, Books, and More for sponsoring this night's rations of fun and excitement. I'll walk you through each step one at a time until you're feeling comfortable with becoming an outstanding hooker." Crissy paused as the group around her laughed.

I met Aunt Jackie's gaze. She hadn't talked to me about sponsoring the treats. It didn't surprise me because Mary was behind the event and they were friends. But I felt a twinge. Maybe we both needed to learn to respect each other's decisions. I let my gaze drop and focused on Crissy's instructions. To my surprise, the motions were feeling normal. Like some sort of muscle memory from those classes so long ago was waking up and taking over. The stitch she taught us was one I remembered. Triple stitch. And the pattern was easy, the same stitch over and over. Then there was a different couple of stitches at the end of the row and then you started again.

I could do this. I looked over at Amy's project, and even though she was farther along than I was, our blankets looked surprisingly similar. I smiled and kept working.

"Jill, tell me how you started the bookstore. Was it a lifelong dream?" Evie's question made me pause and look up.

"What?" I tried to focus on her words, but my fingers wanted my attention too. "Oh, no. I wanted to be a lawyer when I grew up. That's all."

"That's all? Being a lawyer is hard. Seven years of college? Did you not make it?" Evie shook her head. "That came out wrong. Like I meant you weren't smart enough, which you clearly are."

"Keep digging, Evie. I like seeing you sweat like this." Amy laughed as she watched the two of us talking.

"It's fine. Actually, I did become a lawyer. I didn't want to work corporate or criminal, so I chose family law. Which meant I got the divorce cases, the child custody, the emotionally draining yet not high-paying work. My law firm loved me because I was a workhorse. I booked a ton of hours, yet I was never quite good enough to be considered for partner." I focused on the blankct as I talked, and the motion calmed me. I hadn't talked about this part of my history forever. "Finally, I was burned out. So I took a week off and visited South Cove. I met Miss Emily and realized I wasn't living, I was surviving. I quit my job, sold my stock options, and bought the bookstore."

"Wow, that was courageous. I thought ending a bad marriage was a big step. You threw away a whole life and career." Evie glanced over at Amy. "So, were you a hotshot chef or something in your other life?"

"City planner. I worked with million-dollar projects and hotshot architects. Who were mostly also hot." Amy smiled as she thought about the life left behind. "I think you'll find that a lot of the residents left high-power, high-stress jobs to live here, where we have to work two or three jobs to survive. But we're happy. I love having time to surf. And I met my husband, Justin, here."

"Life's not all about work." I held up my blanket. Five rows in and it was beginning to look like a blanket. "Sometimes you get to help others and learn a new hobby."

When I got home I poured a glass of wine, turned on the cooking channel, and pulled out my soon-to-be blanket. I was still in the same spot when Greg got home. He relocked the door, then paused when he saw me on the couch. "You should be asleep. It's late."

"I was working on something." I held up my blanket. It was the size of a kitchen towel. "The edges are rough, but I think I'm supposed to put a border around it when it gets to be the right size. What do you think?"

He sank down on the couch next to me and picked up an edge of the blue fluff. He rubbed it between his fingers. He looked up at me and smiled. "I think you might have found a craft you're good at."

I took the blanket away from him and tucked it and the yarn back into my tote. I stood and headed to the stairs.

"Wait, what did I say?" Greg stood, watching me.

I turned back and shook my head. "You might have jinxed it."

* * * *

The next morning I had the shop all set up and was working on my blanket when Crissy came in. "Good morning. What can I get for you to go with your coffee?"

She met me at the couch and took the blanket in her hand. "This is good work for a beginner. Your stitches are a little loose, but they'll tighten up in time. Just don't try to fix it or they'll be too tight. It's a fine line."

"As are most things in life." I tucked away the project and headed to the coffee bar. "We have some amazing brownies we got in this morning."

"I'll take two." Crissy sat at the bar, clearly wanting to chat. "I thought last night went well. Mary was right, I needed to get to know the South Cove group. I've been asked to come talk to three ladies' groups. One even said they had an empty slot, and if I felt good about it, I could join. I've been accepted so quickly by the community. I feel at home."

"Good. But you have to realize there are a few in South Cove who don't appear to be part of the community, yet really do fit in with at least one of our groups."

She sighed. "You're talking about that man I accidentally called homeless. I am so sorry. I jumped to conclusions without having real facts. Appearances can be misleading."

"Sounds like you learned a lesson, so maybe my warning didn't fall on deaf ears. I'm glad." I handed her the coffee and a bag with the brownies. She handed me her card and I rang up the purchase. "I'm glad last night went well. I'm looking forward to next week. Will we learn a new pattern?"

She nodded. "That was my plan. Of course this time people will be buying the yarn, so I'll actually be making a profit, even it only half the people who were there last night come back. Your friend Evie had a hard night."

"What do you mean?" I hadn't hung around after Crissy called time because Amy offered me a ride home. Greg didn't like me walking home at night alone, so I took her up on it. "Did something happen after I left?"

Crissy nodded. "I was closing up and I heard her talking to a woman just outside the door. The woman started screaming at her that she had no idea what being a family meant. Evie walked away from her, but she just kept yelling and following her. I saw her disappear behind your shop, but I guess the woman didn't see her turn, so she paced for a while, then left."

"Evie has an ex-relative visiting." I didn't want to go into my barista's business, but Crissy deserved an explanation.

Crissy slipped off her stool. "Now *that* I understand. I've had my share of ex-relationships. Tell Evie I'm here if she wants to talk."

"It sounds like the visit might be over anyway. I feel bad when nice people get attacked. Evie is the best. The relative wants an antique Evie has."

"Sorry, I couldn't help overhearing. I may be able to help your friend evaluate the item." Judith came up to the coffee bar and nodded to Crissy.

"Hi, I'm Judith Dame and I'm the new barista. Or at least learning how to be the new barista."

"Crissy Newby. I own A Pirate's Yarn." Crissy shook hands with Judith.

"Nice to meet you. Anyway, I spent five years on the road as a researcher for an antiques show that valued old pieces for people."

I stared at her. "I can't believe that."

"Seriously. I did. I can bring in my books and look the item up. Do you know what it is?" Judith poured herself a cup of coffee and joined us at the bar.

I glanced at the door to the back room. I hated talking about Evie behind her back, but she deserved to know what this clock was worth before she let Becky bully her into giving it up. "Evie said it was a mantel clock."

"Oh, good. I have a lot of experience with clocks, I'll start some research tonight, but I need more information. If you can get a picture, I can be more specific." Judith's eyes sparkled with excitement.

"I'll bring it up with Evie as soon as I see her." I'd made a decision: I was telling Evie everything I knew about her sister-in-law and offering Judith's help. We were a family here in South Cove and she needed to know that we had her back. No matter what.

A regular came in and I moved to the counter.

Crissy picked up her bag and coffee. "Well, I'll see you on Wednesday. Judith, you should come by the shop. We're doing a community service project for the hospital and we meet each week on Wednesdays at six to learn a new pattern. At least for three more weeks."

"I'll check it out. Thanks." Judith followed me to the counter and greeted the customer. "Good morning. While Jill's pouring your coffee, can I get you a treat out of the case? I haven't tried everything, but what I have was amazing. I'm kind of addicted to the pumpkin cheesecake squares. Easy to eat on the run, but the taste reminds me of Thanksgiving dinner with my family."

"You know how to sell, that's for sure." The man—Joel, if I remembered his name right—pulled out his wallet and put away the phone he'd been staring at since he'd walked in the shop. "I'll take one. And if it's as good as you say, I'll buy two tomorrow and take one home to my wife."

"Sounds good." I handed him his large, black coffee and rang up his purchase while Judith packaged the treat. When we were done I handed him back his card. "Thanks, Joel. We'll see you tomorrow."

"It's a date." He chuckled as he headed out the door.

"Well done. You're a natural at this." I turned to Judith. I didn't tell her that she was better than I was at the selling part. I had a soft sell method.

I was here if you needed me, but I didn't suggest like Judith did. I had a feeling her training was going to go fast.

We worked through the next couple of hours, then I taught her how to add books to the computer inventory and how to shelve. I poured a cup of coffee and sat at the couch. I took out my yarn and partially completed blanket. "I'll be here if you need me. I'll handle the customers until you're done with those boxes."

"Sounds fun." Judith turned and started working.

I watched her as I added rows to my project. She was methodical and hit all the steps I'd shown her. She was going to work out fine.

Evie came in from the back, poured a cup of coffee, then sat down across from me.

"Bad night, huh?" I didn't look up, but I could see she looked like she hadn't gotten a lot of sleep.

"Horrible. I suppose you've already heard about what a butt Becky was. Luckily, she didn't see the path I took between the two buildings, so eventually she stopped yelling and went back to her hotel. She's determined to get that clock. Which makes me determined not to give it to her, family heirloom or not." She leaned back in the chair and closed her eyes.

"Look, Evie, there's something I need to tell you about your sister-in-law..." I heard the door bang shut and looked up. Becky was in the shop and steamrolling toward us.

She yelled as she came closer. "You are not going to win in this matter. If I have to, I'll take you to court."

I stood, holding a hand down to indicate that Evie should stay out of it. "You can't act that way if you're going to be in my shop."

Becky turned, her eyes burning with anger. "You. What are you doing here? I should have made a move on your boyfriend. Maybe then you'd stay out of my way."

"Greg wouldn't have taken you up on your offer anyway." I knew that. "Look, I know you and Evie have things to talk about, but this is a bookstore and coffee shop. If you can't control your anger, you'll have to leave."

"Try to make me." Becky growled out the words and stepped toward me, her fists clenched.

"She doesn't have to make you. Like Jill said, this is her bookstore." Toby, dressed in his police uniform, stood behind us. He must have walked in right after Becky. "Do you want to leave now? Or should I lock you up for disturbing the peace?"

Becky turned, and a bit of the determination fell off her aggressive stance. "I can talk to whoever I want. It's a free country."

"It might be a free country, but I've asked you to leave my shop. Either you leave alone or with Toby. I don't care either way." I stepped between her and Evie, just to make sure Becky didn't try something physical just to be stupid.

She glared around me at Evie. "You can't keep the clock from me. I will have it."

We watched as she marched out of the shop, giving Toby a glare as she passed by. The woman was a tornado of emotion.

I fell back down on the couch and Toby and Judith rushed to the seating area. "That was intense."

Evie was crying. "I'm so sorry. I'll just give her the stupid clock. Then she'll go away."

Judith sat next to her. "Honey, don't just give in. Let me do some research to see if I can find out where the clock came from and what it's worth. If you want to give it back then, that's up to you. But don't let her bully you. The angrier she gets, I'm thinking there's more to the story. Let's find out what she knows before we let her win."

"You don't even know me. Why are you stepping in like this?" Now tears did flow down Evie's cheeks.

"I don't like bullies. And good people should always win. It's a simple formula to live your life by." She squeezed Evie. "By the way, I'm Judith. I'm the newest member of the CBM family."

Toby sat by me where he could watch the door, just in case Becky returned. "I'm Toby. I work afternoon shifts mostly."

"Sorry about the short notice on our newest employee." I closed my eyes. "Wow, that woman is freaking crazy."

"What did she mean by putting the moves on Greg? Do you know Becky?" Evie wiped the tears off with a tissue.

I told her about meeting Becky and overhearing her conversation that night at the bed-and-breakfast.

"That had to be John, my ex. It's just the two of them now that John Senior is gone." Evie rubbed her face. "Both of them are selfish and only in it for themselves. Except when they want to gang up on someone. I have a message from John on my phone I haven't listened to. I bet he's trying to pave the way for Becky getting back the clock. So glad they're my ex-family." Evie met my gaze. "And I'm so sorry I brought this on you and the store."

"You don't have anything to be sorry about. We're family and we take care of our own. You just need to tell us if you see Becky again. I don't think she's going to stop."

Judith held up her hand. "Would it be all right if I got a picture of the clock? That way I should be able to get us more information tonight."

"Sounds good. Mind if I borrow her a minute? Homer is probably ready for a walk anyway." Evie stood and Judith followed her to the back of the shop.

I stood and looked at Toby. "Are you here for coffee or just checking in with me?"

"Actually, both. But I'm glad I decided to take my break now. You were good with Evie." He followed me to the coffee bar.

"I'm so glad you came when you did." I poured him coffee and grabbed a bottle of water for me. I didn't need more caffeine.

"You know I'm going to have to tell Greg."

I hadn't wanted to add this to Greg's worry list, but I agreed with Toby. We needed to keep Evie safe.

Chapter 9

The call came as soon as I arrived home. "Hey, Greg, how's the case going?"

"Which one? Seriously? Evie's sister-in-law is the woman from the bed-and-breakfast? What're the chances we not only run into Max Winter and his mistress or wife but also the woman who seems to enjoy screaming at the top of her lungs on Main Street late at night? At least ten of my complaint calls have been solved with Toby's report." Greg sighed, and I heard folders moving on his desk. "Anyway, I wanted to call to let you know I've got the guys watching the bookstore. Evie just needs to stay away from that woman. Even if I bring her in for disturbing the peace, she'll be out in hours with a good attorney."

"Judith's seeing if she can get a solid valuation on the clock Becky wants so bad. I think Evie just needs some time to get all the facts before she makes a decision. If the clock really is a family heirloom, she's willing to consider giving it back. But if it's just money Becky wants, that's another story." I stood at the back door and watched Emma run down the fence line in her daily vigil to keep the yard rabbit free.

"And who's Judith again?"

I left the door open and took the phone upstairs with me. I needed to change so I could run. It had been a crazy day. "She's our new barista. She also has some antique appraising experience and contacts. She can help Evie."

"Sounds like a plan. Hey, can you do me a favor for a few days?"

My hand froze on the dresser drawer handle. I knew what he was going to say. "You're kidding, right?"

"No, I just think with this Becky in the wind as well as the murder that just happened, I'd feel better if you didn't run by yourself. Maybe we should update the treadmill at the house, or I know—kick Toby out of the shed and make a workout gym."

"So what happens when he can't find affordable housing? You'll have your home gym, but I'll lose a barista and you'll lose a deputy." I pointed out the flaw in his plan. "I'll grudgingly stay home for a few days, but you'd better find one or more of them by Monday or I'm going to Bakerstown and joining the gym. And you're paying the membership fee."

He chuckled. "Tell Emma I'm sorry. I'll be late, so eat without me."

"Fine. And I don't love you anymore."

"And I don't love you any less." He lowered his voice. "See you soon."

I changed into sweats and a tank and decided to pull out a yoga DVD I'd bought the last time Amy tried to get me to attend classes with her. I didn't get it, but she loved yoga, so I didn't want to look stupid when I went to class. I had still looked stupid and quit after six weeks. "I'm just a runner," I'd told her, but she'd never given up asking me to go to class with her.

I let Emma inside and she sniffed my sweats. "Sorry, girl, we're grounded."

She went over to her kitchen bed and, after making three circles, lay down with a huff. Who said dogs don't have personalities and don't understand our language?

I tried not to laugh as I filled a water bottle. Then I grabbed my mat from its spot in the office, rolled it out, and started the video. Thirty minutes later I knew one thing.

I still hated yoga.

With my workout over, I glanced around the house, wondering what was next. I could do house cleaning or laundry, but we hadn't been home, so the house didn't look that bad. I put away the yoga stuff and went to grab laundry from upstairs. When the first load was started I went to the fridge. I hadn't eaten lunch, so I heated up soup and made a fruit salad. While I ate, I scrolled through the local news. A column by Darla on the murder caught my attention.

"'Unidentified man found bleeding at South Cove City Hall.'" I read the headline aloud. Well, she'd gotten part of the story right. The dead guy had found City Hall more than Toby had found him, but no one was probably talking to the press. I ran through the information, such as it was. It appeared Darla didn't know any more about the murder than I did.

I tapped my spoon on the table, thinking. Finally, curiosity got the better of me. I dialed the number for the South Cove Winery and asked to talk to Darla. When I was told she was out for the afternoon, I decided not to leave a message. It had been a bad idea anyway. If Greg found out, he would have been upset.

A knock sounded at the door. When I went to answer Esmeralda was there with another casserole. She pushed it into my hands. "Hey, what's this for?"

"I made a double batch. I thought you might enjoy it tonight." She paused a minute, listening to something I couldn't hear. "You've got company coming. I'll leave you alone."

"Hold up, I have your pot from earlier this week. Come in." I held the door open and she followed me inside. "I have to say, I appreciate the tasty meals, but I'm not quite sure what's going on."

"Can't a neighbor just want to share food?" Esmeralda walked into the kitchen and picked up her pot and serving spoon, which were on the table. "You can be cynical at times."

"And you can be cryptic."

Esmeralda started laughing. "You're right there. Anyway, your visitor is almost here. I'll see you soon. Come over later if you want to talk."

"I'm really not expecting anyone." I followed her out to the front porch and watched as Darla pulled her minivan into the driveway. "I guess I was wrong."

"I'm just better at tuning into the opportunities that are flying around as we speak." Esmeralda patted my arm. "Don't feel bad. I heard her telling Greg that she was coming to chat with you because he's been a little less than forthright."

"I should have known." I stepped forward to wait for Darla on the edge of the porch. "Thanks for dinner, again."

"You're most welcome, Jill. I hope your life slows down soon."

I was about to tell her that my life was always busy and she didn't have to keep making us dinner. But she was already out of the gate and almost halfway across the street when I thought about the perfect retort.

"Why did Esmeralda leave so fast? I would have loved to pick her brain on this murder case. Do you mind me coming inside? I need to get out of this heat." Darla stepped toward me and the door.

I didn't think it was that hot outside, but I didn't want Darla to think me rude. "Come on in. I was just hanging around the house."

"I'm trying to get a new angle on this murder. And your boyfriend isn't helping." Darla climbed the stairs and entered through the open door. She reached down and greeted Emma and then nodded to the kitchen. "Can I get some water?"

"Of course." I followed her into the kitchen, shutting my laptop as I passed by to put the casserole in the fridge. I took out our water pitcher and poured her and me a glass. "How's the Winery going?"

"It's good. Not as busy as summer, but fall has its own peaks and valleys. I'm sure we'll get slammed tomorrow night. I hear you're doing Saturday's shift on your own. I don't think I've seen you do that since your aunt came to town." Darla sat and sipped her water, watching my face.

"I know. But I'm not going to be totally alone. We hired a new barista who's working out nicely. And Evie might be available if her visitor goes home early." Shoot, I hadn't meant to mention that.

But Darla didn't seem to pick up on that issue. Maybe she hadn't heard about Becky's yelling fit the other night. "Family; you uproot your lives to be with them so they can visit, then they just disappear again. My folks do that to me all the time. Pop in for what they say is going to be a week, then disappear a few days later. Maybe I drive them crazy."

I could tell she said it like a joke, but I wasn't sure if she believed it. "I'm sure you're a gracious hostess. Maybe they want to see if the Winery's doing well. And when they do they decide to go on with their lives?"

"Possibly. My mom is certain I'm totally messing up the business every time she talks to me. Anyway, I didn't come by to tell you my sad story. I'm looking to see if anyone knows anything about this guy who was murdered. I think I might know who it is, but Greg won't talk to me. I think it's someone that Max Winter knows. I've seen a guy in the Winery a couple of times. Once with Max and once with this other guy. I heard him call the other guy John. He said his name was Gentry. But he paid cash for his drinks. Max paid for a round, but then he left. I made a joke that the rich guy should have left him a tab."

"What did he say to that?" I didn't think Greg knew this. He was probably avoiding Darla's calls thinking she was looking for information.

Darla sighed. "I must have struck a nerve because he said Max never worries about anyone but himself."

"That's harsh." I was definitely sending this bit of info in a text to Greg as soon as Darla left.

"I thought so. I've been trying to reach Max, but his wife says he's out of town at a construction site. Honestly, I was a little surprised he was married. He was a bit of a flirt at the Winery. I tried researching to get some basic facts, but I keep running into conflicting information." She pulled out her notebook. "All I have is that he lives outside of Bakerstown with his wife, but her name isn't listed on the property records. I think her name's Beth."

"That's weird." I wondered if the conflicting information was because Connie was holding herself up as Max's wife. If I gave up Connie's name and what I knew about Max, Greg would totally know who Darla had been chatting with. "What if you just leave the information with Esmeralda? Greg will probably call you once he knows you have a lead."

"You know, that's a good idea. I should have thought of that. Of course Greg's avoiding me because of my press connection. You'd be an excellent journalist if you didn't own a bookstore." She wrote down Esmeralda's name and underlined it three times.

I felt bad for sending her to badger Esmeralda, but at least I didn't have to drop the mistress bomb. She was the professional in the discussion, not me. "I think Greg would pull back his marriage proposal if I decided to write about murders. He has a fit when I stick my toe in the water around here. I'm not even allowed to run this week until he figures out what's going on."

"Oh? Does he think the murder has something to do with Miss Emily's house and the failed development?" Darla's pen hovered over the paper.

And I'd stepped in it again. "I doubt it. I'd made it perfectly clear to Mr. Winter that I wasn't selling. Not now, not ever. He offered me money for an option, but I want the house to survive me. Like it did Miss Emily. Maybe I can put it in a trust or something."

"You should talk to the people who run the Castle. They have a trust set up for what happens to the land and buildings due to all the historical artifacts they have. I bet you could give the house to a nonprofit, maybe something book-related, like a writers' commune, and have the trust manage it." Darla had forgotten all about why I couldn't run now. She was on her second-favorite subject, protecting South Cove for future generations. "Think about it. I'll see if I can find an attorney who works in preservation estates."

"I actually know a few myself." I smiled, and Darla realized what she'd said.

"Of course you do. And you probably could write it up yourself. But if you want any guidance or to talk it over, I'd love to be part of this. Preserving South Cove is my passion, rather than supporting the mayor's plan of tearing down every building to make newer, bigger ones. It's a crime what he wants to do to our town." She finished her water and stood. "I'd better get back to the Winery. Matt has a new band coming in to play tonight that he wants me to hear."

Emma and I watched her leave, then I closed the door. "I think Esmeralda's going to be mad at me, but Greg should be happy. Sometimes you can't please everyone."

Emma wagged her tail and I picked up a book I'd read a few chapters of last night. I needed to finish it so I could write a review for Deek's newsletter, but I'd gotten sidetracked with the vacation and then the blanket. "Let's hang out on the porch for a while, and if Greg's not home in a few hours, we'll put the casserole in the oven for our dinner."

Emma thought that was an excellent idea. At least the hanging out on the porch part. I wasn't sure she cared what I was going to eat for dinner, unless it meant she got a few bites. And if the taco casserole was as spicy as the soup had been, Emma was out of luck regarding human food today.

Greg texted me around nine and told me he'd be late. I let him know the casserole was in the oven on warm and I would be crashing around ten. I knew he wouldn't be home before I fell asleep, so I got out the vanilla bean ice cream and curled up on the couch with Emma. We turned on the cooking channel and watched as chefs competed to be the best and the fastest with items not of their choosing. When I turned it off Emma hurried over to the back door, waiting to be let out.

Our lives may not be exciting, but they were comfortable. I loved routine.

* * * *

The next morning Greg was already gone. A note on the table told me he loved me and he'd see me tonight, "come hell or high water." It was the punch line to my favorite joke and he loved using it.

I thought about the joke as I got ready for work, avoiding Emma's pitiful look as she realized we weren't running this morning.

A kid and his mom were sitting on the roof after a flood. The kid saw a hat going downstream, then upstream, then downstream again. He pointed out the hat to his mom. "Mom, there must be a fish under the hat."

"Oh, that's just Grandpa," his mom replied. "He said he was going to mow the lawn today, come hell or high water."

I wondered what kind of flood Greg was dealing with in the investigation. If I wasn't so shorthanded at the shop, I'd take over some cookies and coffee for his team today. And maybe I'd get some gossip. Or not.

I gave Emma an extra treat, packed my finished book and unfinished blanket in my tote, and headed out the door to open the shop. Crissy was waiting at the café table outside the entrance when I arrived. She was working on a blanket in the same blue I was using, but hers looked like a different pattern. She smiled as I came up. "Sorry if I kept you waiting."

"Oh, no. I came early. I need to go shopping and buy a new coffee maker, but since I don't have one, it gives me an excuse to come visit you every morning." She tucked the blanket into her own tote. "Besides, I always have a project to work on, just in case I have a minute or two."

"Come on in. You know the drill. It's going to be a few minutes before I can get you coffee." I unlocked the door and turned on the lights. "So, how do you like South Cove? Is living in town working out?"

"You know, I'm almost afraid to say anything, since I thought the bike rental shop owner was a homeless guy, but I swear, there's been a man sitting outside your shop at night after you close. It's like he's watching for something."

"Funny, no one's said anything. Typically, Toby and Tim keep a close eye out on the shops after hours because they're on duty then. I think they get bored waiting for something to happen. When did you first see this guy?" I pulled out a sheet of paper and started making notes.

"Last weekend? No, it was earlier in the week. Then I didn't see him on the weekend. I've got that balcony on my building, and I go there after dinner to enjoy the evening and get some knitting in." She watched my face. "Should I have called the cops?"

"Maybe tonight if you see him, you could call me." I wrote down my number on a business card and handed it to her. I'll call Greg and have him send someone to check. It was probably one of the town residents waiting for someone to get off work or something. "Your usual?"

I was just getting ready to leave the shop when Deek pulled me aside. "What's going on?"

He glanced toward Judith, who was cleaning up a coffee she'd dropped on the floor. "Look, if you don't think you'll be okay, I'll come in tomorrow."

"You have an event. One you probably paid money to attend. Judith and I will be all right. You forget how many mistakes you made at the coffee bar when you were just starting out." I patted Deek's arm. "Besides, Evie is coming in to work tonight since her sister-in-law seems to have disappeared. She said she'll do the closing shift tomorrow too."

"I just worry that it's too much for Judith. Maybe I should have sent you someone else." He watched as Judith rinsed the towel and then went back down on her hands and knees to finish the job.

"Someone younger?" I asked him.

To his credit, he blushed, and his skin almost matched the pink in his hair. "I didn't mean that. Well, okay, I did, but I worry about Judith. She's a nice person and I don't want anything bad to happen. I have a bad feeling about this weekend that I can't shake off."

"I don't think if there is an issue it's going to be with Judith. Evie, maybe, but we can't put our lives on hold because of a feeling. I let you off, I hired Judith. We'll be fine. You go learn things about writing." I swung my tote over my shoulder. "I need more books to read."

He laughed, and I saw his shoulders relax a bit. "I don't think that's true since we get new books in every week. Thanks for the book review, by the way. It's stellar."

"I'll be sending you three or four more next week as I work through the books I read on vacation." I waved to Judith. "I'll see you at ten tomorrow?"

"I'll be here with bells on. And maybe not such clumsy fingers." She waved back, grinning like she'd been named employee of the month rather than having just spilled a large black coffee.

I walked out of the shop and headed toward home, but a sound stopped me. Greg was hurrying across the road. He kissed me when he caught up to me and I glanced at my watch. "What, do you actually have time for lunch?"

"No, sorry." He nodded to the café table in front of my shop. "Mind if we sit for a second?"

"Uh-oh. What's wrong?" I sat and put my tote on the table.

He shook his head. "Of course you'd think something was wrong. Actually, I have a favor to ask you."

Now I was suspicious. "What, did you forget your mom's coming to town today?"

He grimaced. "Gosh, no. I would have called her and told her to stay home. Too much going on for me to deal with family drama. Anyway, I want you to go talk to Mrs. Winter. Bakerstown PD has asked me to see what I can find out about the family. Try to find out if Max is having an affair with this Connie or if there's more to this other relationship than just sex."

I pinched my arm. Pain shot up to my shoulder, so no, I wasn't asleep. "Wait, you want me to investigate for you? Like ask someone questions?"

"Exactly. I can't get anything out of her, and when I ask, her attorney steps in. Can you take her some cookies or something and see if she'll tell you?" He took my hand. "Please?"

"I don't think a box of cookies is going to get someone to tell me that her husband was cheating on her." I decided to take him up on his offer. "But I'll do my best. I just want one free get out of jail card, so when I do an unauthorized investigation you can't get mad."

"You want a card saying I won't get mad at you?" He dropped my hands. "I knew this was a bad idea."

"And yet you came to me anyway. Look, you know I want to do this. You want me to do this. So let's stop playing cute. I'll do it for a free pass on a future time when I step on your toes." I waited him out. It's really hard not to talk if you're waiting for someone else to speak, but I thought about the ice cream in the freezer I'd planned to eat as my dessert. I'd eat soup and a sandwich again for lunch and top if off with some vanilla ice cream with chocolate syrup.

Greg stood and pulled a piece of paper from his pocket. "Here's her address. You have a deal. But if you run into any trouble, you call the cops." He paused. "I'll let Bakerstown PD know you're going in case you have issues. Thank you for doing this."

The world must be moving into an ice age. Greg had asked me to investigate. I hurried home to get my car before he changed his mind.

Chapter 10

When I pulled up at the gate, I was shocked. Max Winter's house was as big as a normal hotel. Or maybe bigger. I pushed a button.

"May I help you?" a male voice asked. He sounded British. Did the Winters have a British butler for the oversize house?

"Hi, I'm Jill Gardner. I own Coffee, Books, and More in South Cove. Mr. Winter is talking to me about buying my house? I brought some cookies and wanted to know if I could talk to Mrs. Winter." I held up the box of cookies to the speaker, just in case it had a camera to show them.

"Please wait there a second."

It was actually three minutes, thirty seconds from the timer on my watch before the voice came back. "Mrs. Winter will see you. Please pull your car to the left side of the driveway near the front entrance. Someone will meet you at the top of the stairs."

The gate entrance slowly swung open. I used the time I was waiting to text Greg. *Being let in the gate. Holy crap, this house is huge.*

I tucked the phone into my purse and drove onto the grounds. Large trees arched over the driveway, and there were several marked spots near the area where I'd been directed to park. I got out of the Jeep, glad I hadn't decided to let Emma ride along. I would hate to have to let her do her business on the perfectly manicured grass, and even though I always picked up after her, somethings just weren't cleanable.

I carried the box up the stairs and was met by a woman in a business suit. I held out my hand. "Mrs. Winter, I'm Jill Gardner. Thank you for seeing me."

"Sorry to disappoint you, but I'm Mrs. Winter's secretary. Beth is out in the garden. I'm to show you the way." The woman ignored my hand

and moved down the porch. "You can leave the cookies on that table. The chef will send someone out for them."

I set down the box and made sure it was closed. "Okay."

The woman didn't say another word until we went through another black, wrought-iron gate and she paused at the edge of the patio. "Beth's on her way. Please have a seat. Can I have some iced tea brought out?"

"That would be nice." I went up the stairs to the patio and found a large couch and chairs near a waterfall fountain. I sat and glanced around; the garden, as the secretary had called it, was stunning. Lots of topiary and cobblestoned paths snaking through the deep green grass.

A woman climbed the stairs from the opposite side of the patio and smiled at me. "It's lovely, isn't it? I have to say, this is my favorite place in the entire estate. There's a leviathan walking path deeper into the garden. I try to use it daily as it helps me think."

She pushed a button and spoke to the speaker. "Please bring out refreshments."

"Already on their way, ma'am," the British-sounding man said.

She sat in a chair and leaned back, watching me. "Thank you for visiting, but I didn't think you and my husband were friends."

"Actually, we're not. I didn't, and still don't, want to sell my property. Especially not for a minihotel development. I don't think South Cove is the right place for that kind of establishment." I decided being honest with my feelings and thoughts might help me with this woman, who had already called me on the reason for my visit. "I wanted to talk to you. I've got something that's bothering me. Greg, my fiancé, mentioned that Max is dealing with death threats."

"Well, you're very direct, aren't you?" Beth stared out into the garden, and then the gate opened again. A man carrying a tray came in and set it on a table nearby. "Jeffrey, have you met Ms. Gardner? She is the homeowner who stood up to Max and his money."

"Nice to meet you, Miss. Do you want sugar or lemon in your tea?" Jeffrey was the British-sounding man. Unless there was more than one.

"Unsweetened is fine. Thank you." I held out my hand for my glass and saw that my cookies had been placed on a plate in the middle of the tray. I took a napkin from Jeffrey, and then he offered me a cookie. I was glad I'd brought my favorite chocolate chippers. I took one and set down the glass on the table. "I appreciate you seeing me. I suspect it's been a rough week for you."

"Yes, I suppose it has." Beth took her tea and two cookies. I was liking her more and more. "Max and I don't see eye to eye on all things, but I do love him. With him gone this week, I'm lost in that huge house."

Jeffrey cleared his throat and she looked up, as if she'd forgotten he was even there. "If there's nothing else?"

"Go watch your movies. I'll be fine out here with Ms. Gardner for a while." She smiled as he left the patio. "Jeffrey's been with us since we moved here from Utah over twenty years ago. My husband bought me a house with a butler. Not this house, a smaller estate farther north from here. It's outside Apple Valley. We still own the place of course, but I never get out there anymore. Max never sells a piece of property once he buys it. He's like you in that manner; he likes keeping houses the way they were when he found them. Even though he tears down houses for a living."

My first thought was that Max had set Connie up in Beth's first house. Which made me not like him even more. Or maybe my mind was just looking for connections. "There's a lot of history in these old estates and houses. I've heard rumors that some of the Hollywood royalty liked to build out here in the 'country' to get away from Los Angeles when they weren't shooting."

"You must see my Hollywood theater room. I haven't been able to trace it to her yet—the property kept changing hands between trusts and businesses—but I swear I found a lot of papers that seem to say Vivien Leigh lived here, at least for a while." Beth's eyes lit up for the first time since I'd arrived.

"I'd love that." I set down my cookie and turned toward her. "But I have to admit, I was sent here on a mission. My fiancé, Greg King, is the police detective looking into a death in South Cove. He's also helping the Bakerstown Police with your husband's death threats. Is there any reason you can think of that would explain these threats?"

Beth took a bite of one of the cookies. Then she totally ignored my question. "He seems like a nice man. You're very lucky. Hold him close."

"We're good together." I reached for my cookie, then pulled my hand back. "Mrs. Winter, did you know the man who was killed? Could it have been someone who was affiliated with your husband?"

She frowned at the last question. "I suspect you weren't sent here to talk about Max's business rivals. I understand you and Mr. King were out of town the day this man was killed. I heard you ran into him in Apple Valley at a restaurant. He calls me daily when he's away. He said Mr. King was a perfect gentleman and you were a little touchy."

"I've had developers try to strong-arm me into selling before and I'll probably have to deal with it again. Developers like your husband are gnats. Annoying, but not worth the effort of getting upset about." I brushed the crumbs off my jeans. I figured it was about time to leave. She wasn't going to talk about their marriage.

"No matter what you're thinking, my husband loves me. And I love him." She took another bite of cookie. "Your friend is very talented in the kitchen. I have my chef order all our desserts from Pies on the Fly."

"Sadie's a food goddess." I stood, knowing I wasn't getting anything more. "Thank you for your time. I hope I didn't upset you with my directness."

"I love direct people." She stood as well. "But I don't think you asked the question you were really sent here to ask. Anyway, please let me show you my Hollywood room. I don't get to show it off as much as I'd like to. I thought about bringing one of the local papers in to do an article on it, but it never seems like the right time."

I didn't feel like I had a choice now. If I just left, I was being rude to a woman who had invited me into her home. Besides, I really wanted to see what she'd collected. "I'd love to see it."

She pushed a button on a speaker on the table. "Jeffrey, we're coming in to see the Hollywood room. Will you make sure the dogs are somewhere else?"

I waited for her and started walking to the house when she met me. "Dogs? What kind? I have a golden retriever I love who is totally spoiled."

"We have three Shelties. I wanted a collie, but with my health condition, Max thought a smaller dog would be better. So I made up for the size of the collie with the number of the Shelties. I love my girls." She paused, looking at the house.

"Shelties are beautiful." I held out my arm for her to use to steady herself. She wasn't that old, so the health condition had to be something chronic, like arthritis or maybe something worse. "Do you have family nearby?"

She chuckled. "In a way. But we aren't really close. I have my dogs and my staff. Like I said, Jeffrey's been here for years. He's more a member of my family than a staff member."

Speaking of the British butler seemed to bring him out of a side door, and he hurried over to her other side. He gently put an arm around her waist. "I could get your chair or your walker, if you wanted."

"Then I'd look weak in front of our guest. That wouldn't do." She leaned her head into his shoulder. "This is fine. Leave me on the purple couch just inside the room. I'll let Jill wander around and see the good stuff."

Somehow in the conversation I'd gone from being Ms. Gardner to being Jill. "You know, my aunt is a Hollywood glamour expert. Maybe I could bring her around and let the two of you visit sometime next week? If that wouldn't be an imposition?"

"You are a sweet girl." She smiled at me as we headed back up the stairs to the house. "I'd like that a lot, if your aunt would really like to visit. I haven't had many female friends. Max is a tornado. Taking care of him takes up most of my time. It's been nice talking to another woman today."

Jeffrey snorted, and I got the feeling he didn't approve of Tornado Max taking all of Mrs. Winter's time.

"Then it's a date. I'll call and let you know when we can come." I held the door open and we stepped into the equivalent of a museum lobby. The air was chilly and the art on the wall was rare and expensive. I'd seen at least one of the paintings in my college humanities textbook. The marble flooring made me worry about Beth's stability, but I saw Jeffrey had already taken care of the situation. He moved a walker near a purple couch and helped Mrs. Winter onto the couch. Then he nodded and moved another speaker box close by just in case. The woman was well looked after.

I stepped into the room, following Jeffrey and Mrs. Winter, and gasped. Glass cases held gowns and movie posters. Each mannequin wore the jewelry that went with the dress, and the other items, like shoes and jackets, were exhibited nearby. It was beautifully displayed. "I can't believe you collected and staged all this. It's mind-blowing."

Mrs. Winter smiled, and even though I could see the weariness, I also could see she needed to show off her room. "I'm so glad you're enjoying it. Walk around. Ask me any questions you have. If I don't know, it's a piece of knowledge I need to find out. Vivien's been kind of my life's work. I think I'm about done and looking forward to making the next room all about another diva. I'm just not sure which one to pick."

I wandered through the room, amazed at how one person could have gathered all this memorabilia about a single person. There was a Playbill from her first stage appearance. And Mrs. Winter had surrounded each item with things and events that had happened the same year. It was painstakingly researched and developed.

My phone beeped with a text. It was Greg. *Everything okay?*

I quickly texted back, *Kind of amazing. I'll call you from the car.*

When I had circled the room I sat on the other end of the couch from Mrs. Winter and shook my head. "It's crazy good. You have a real knack for setting up displays. Every display has a theme and a lot of materials just to set the mood. You should do this professionally."

She blushed and rubbed one of her legs. "I would explore it as a career, but I go through spells when I can't walk. I have been feeling better this week. You would think with all that's going on, I'd be worn out. Instead, I've had time to breathe."

I glanced at my watch. It had been almost twenty minutes since I'd texted Greg. He'd be starting to worry again. I started to stand, but then saw a picture in a frame on the coffee table. There were several family shots, as well as ones at events where they were all dressed up. That was what this picture was, an event. The three of them stood and smiled for the camera, with Max in the middle of the two women.

I picked up the frame and showed it to Mrs. Winter. "Who is the woman with you and your husband?"

Her eyes dulled and she reached out her hand like she was unsure who I was talking about. Then she set it down face-first so the photo was no longer showing. "That's a friend of the family. Connie Middleton."

When I got into the car the first thing I did was set my phone up to the car speaker. Then I called Greg. When he answered I jumped into what I'd found out. "The other woman is a family friend according to the wife. Connie Middleton."

He listened as I told him everything that had happened up through the part when I was bringing my aunt for a meet up next week. "Hold the phone, you agreed to what?"

"She and Aunt Jackie will get along. Mrs. Winter needs some people to talk to who aren't paid to hang out with her. She's lonely. I could tell."

Greg didn't say anything for so long, I'd thought I'd lost him. Then his voice had changed to something soft. "Jill, you're such a good person. But maybe you should rethink visiting. Beth Winter may not be telling us everything she knows. I'd rather you and she didn't become fast friends just yet."

I decided to handle the conversation like I did most of our pre-arguments. I changed the subject. "Are you going to be home for dinner?"

"Probably not. The DA's coming over to talk over the suspect pool. I'll try to keep an open mind on your new friend." He chuckled. "I only have myself to blame. I sent you over there."

"She's a nice person. I don't think Max is very attentive. Yes, she has stuff, but I don't think he pays a lot of attention to her. They have a British butler."

"Jeffrey Hargrove? He's more than a butler. He runs the household, and he's also her attorney."

"You have got to be kidding. He brought us iced tea and cookies." I thought about the woman who'd greeted me. "And she has a secretary."

"Rich people have a lot of people around them. I guess Max likes attending charity events."

I heard voices on Greg's side of the conversation. "Sounds like you need to go."

"Yeah, Esmeralda says someone's here to talk to me. I'll call you later. Why don't you see if Amy can have dinner with you?"

And he hung up. No "goodbye." No "I love you." Someone must have just walked into his office and he had to get off the phone. I decided calling Amy was a good idea. I used my voice command to call her and caught her still at work. "Amy, what are you doing for dinner tonight?"

"Opening a can of soup. Justin's got his history group tonight, so he won't be home for dinner. Do you have a better idea?"

"Lille's at five thirty?" I checked my clock. I could make it home, let Emma out, and still have time to walk up to Lille's in time to meet Amy.

"Much better idea. Besides, I wanted to tell you about some gossip I heard at City Hall today." She'd dropped her voice, and I knew I couldn't push her because she didn't want to be overheard. Maybe it was about Max Winter. Mayor Baylor was still mad that I'd stopped the plans for the new development in South Cove.

Besides, Amy loved old Hollywood glamour actresses. She'd kill me if I didn't tell her about the Vivien Leigh shrine just up the road.

Chapter 11

Saturday morning there were already people lined up outside the shop when I arrived for work. I glanced around at the milling group of women and smiled. "Okay, is there a sample sale going on I don't know about?"

"How did you know?" The woman closest to me laughed. "Actually, Vintage Duds is doing a fall clearance of all the summer items. I love their sales. Pat's just a sweetheart. I bought most of my work wardrobe there last winter when I got a new job in the city. Everyone thinks I spent a fortune on clothes. And it makes me look good to the bosses when I dress up for the job."

"I need to watch my mail closer." I unlocked the door. "I would have opened earlier. I hate to have you all waiting."

"I think most of us have someone holding our place in line." She called out to the group. "Anyone not have a line holder? You can go first."

A couple of women blushed and raised their hands. One rushed to the coffee bar. "Coffee, black, please. I thought I was getting here early, but I guess I'm late. This is my first sale day."

"Well, let's get you on your way, then." I had a pot on timer that started before the doors opened. Mostly so I could have coffee first thing, but that wouldn't last through this crowd. As I poured, I started the lighter-blend pot and got coffee ready for the next pot too. "Four fifty."

The woman threw a ten at me and told me to keep the change. Then she ran out of the shop with her hot coffee.

"I hope I put that lid on tight enough," I mused, then greeted the next in line while ringing up the last order.

An hour later I'd served all the early birds and a few more who weren't in such a hurry to get to the shop. Or had line holders. I had started new pots of coffee and was refilling the dessert case when Greg came in. "Hey, what are you doing here?"

He glanced around the shop, which still looked like it had that morning. Usually I went around, cleaning and adjusting the tables back to where I liked them and set out some books for impulse buys. "You've been busy. Isn't Saturday morning usually slow?"

"Not when Vintage Duds has a clearance sale. Maybe I could ask Pat to give me a heads-up next time. I've been swamped since I arrived to open the shop." He started to respond, but I held up a finger. "Hold that thought."

I went back into the office storage area and pulled the two cheesecakes I'd taken out of the fridge a few minutes before. I'd replaced them with two from the freezer, but I thought maybe I might want to pull out another rack of cookies as well. I grabbed one from the fridge and took that and the cheesecakes out to the back counter behind the coffee bar. "I need to restock while we talk."

"Don't you have any help today? I know Deek's gone for the day and I pulled Toby, but I thought Evie was back to work." He glanced around the shop, which needed a good cleaning round, which I would do as soon as he left.

"She's closing, and typically, mornings are slow. Judith is coming in at ten. Like I said, today's morning crowd kind of blindsided me. I guess I should watch the community business board closer." I paused as I finished cutting the first cheesecake. "I didn't ask—are you here to talk as my fiancé or are you a customer?"

"Both. I feel bad we didn't get to talk last night when I got home. I can pour my own coffee." He moved to come around the coffee bar.

I held up a hand to stop him. "Sorry, no one behind the counter unless they're working here. Aunt Jackie's newest rule. And besides, you're too busy as it is. Let me pour you some coffee, and as soon as I get these cheesecakes and cookies in the treat case, I'll join you."

I filled a cup and then put a piece of the blueberry cheesecake on a plate and slid it toward him. "The cake sells better when one of the pieces are missing. Then it looks like it's popular."

"I like your reasoning." He grabbed a fork from over the counter because I'd forgotten to get him one. "How was dinner with Amy?"

"We had fun." I told him about the Hollywood glam room, as Amy and I had started calling it. I saw the look on his face when I was talking about Beth Winter. "Look, I know you think Beth might have secrets, but from my viewpoint—and that's why you sent me there—she's a nice person. Even though I don't think Max treats her very well. I think you need to look at this 'family friend,' as Beth called Connie. Also, I don't think Beth is healthy."

"You're right there. According to her lawyer, the stress of talking to the police has exasperated her health conditions. Therefore he's limiting any access, at least for a few days. Besides, I don't even have jurisdiction in that case and I'm busy with my own issues. As long as the mayor stays out of my to-do lists." He focused on the cake. "I love Sadie's cheesecake. Have you heard from her lately?"

"No, and it's killing me. I keep expecting to hear that Pastor Bill has popped the question, but I guess they're still on the slow path. They're doing pre-couples therapy to see if they are a good fit for marriage. I'm beginning to think this guy has a fear of commitment." I finished stocking and closed the display case. Then I poured myself some well-earned coffee. Saturdays ran different. I had no idea when my next customer would show, but I suspected I'd get some around lunchtime from the Vintage Duds event. Unless they went to Diamond Lille's for a meal that didn't consist of 100 percent sugar, fat, and caffeine. But what fun would that be on a girls' day? "I'm guessing this midmorning visit is to tell me you may not be home for dinner?"

"You're figuring out my schedule." He finished his cheesecake and set down the fork. "Well, I can't say Bill has commitment issues. He's been a pastor here with our church for close to twenty years. Maybe he's just taking it slow to make sure Sadie's ready to be a preacher's wife. I'm sure he's heard horror stories from his peers about jumping in too fast. He does a lot of premarital counseling for local couples too. He's got a class starting up in a couple of weeks. Do you want to go?"

I set down my coffee cup and stared at him. "What are you implying? Don't you think we're a good couple?"

"It's not that. I'm just seeing the issues Amy and Justin are dealing with now that they've become a married couple. I know you've been having problems talking about our financial future. Maybe having a structured time to walk through some possible scenarios would help us be more prepared for our new lives." He glanced up as the front door opened and a group of women came into the shop. "And that's the end of our time together. You think about it and go back to work. I'll sign us up as a "maybe" to hold our spot. If you don't want to do it, I'll do it by myself. I could use some sensitivity training when it comes to speaking to my upcoming new bride."

I giggled as he stood and kissed me. "Wow, I would look like the bad fiancée if I let you do it alone. Anyway, I'm not saying no. I'll think about it. But not today. Today I'm focused on running my shop and making sure Aunt Jackie doesn't have a chance to say 'I told you so' on anything. Especially my decision not to hire a temp or two."

He laughed as he held out his cup. "Can I get a refill to go?"

I took the cup as I made sure the other women were still wandering around the bookshop. I could see them watching us. I figured they were giving us a minute alone before descending on the coffee bar for refreshments. I put a cover on Greg's cup and handed it to him. "I guess I'll see you when I do. I'm not sure what I'll make for dinner."

"Oh yeah, I have a message from Esmeralda. She'll be bringing over a surprise and you're not supposed to cook tonight." He must have seen the question on my face because he shrugged. "Don't ask me. And no, I didn't ask why. I've learned it's better just to go with the flow when it comes to Esmeralda."

"Chicken. Anyway, I'll see you later." I called out the last part loud enough for the women to hear. I didn't want to run people away.

He held up his cup. "Definitely."

As soon as he left the shop, several women hurried to the coffee bar. "Can I get you anything? Something to drink? Maybe a treat?"

"If he has a brother, I'd love an introduction." One of the women pulled out a wallet and the others laughed. She leaned closer and slid me a business card. "I'm not kidding. Your husband is drop-dead gorgeous. I'm the only single one in the group, so if he does have a brother who's looking, here's my card."

I decided not to correct her on our relationship status because, well, it wasn't her business. I took the card and tucked it by the register. "I'll let him know. Now, what can I get for you?"

The next few hours were busy, but Judith arrived a half hour early and with her help, it wasn't a horrible Saturday. We were just walking through shift-change duties when Evie came down from the upstairs apartment. She put on an apron and started shelving books without saying "good morning" or anything else. I asked Judith to refresh the display case and went over to talk to her.

Evie focused on the fiction book she was trying to shelve in the travel section. She set it down and moved the cart over to the mystery section. "I'm having a bad day."

"What's going on?" I picked up the book and put it on the shelf in alphabetical order, not looking at Evie.

"John called last night. He said some horrible things, especially after I told him I was doing some research on the clock. He said I was always looking for free money and that's why I married him." She brushed a tear from her cheek. "Which is so not true."

"He was trying to get you to react and just give him the clock. You know his games." I rubbed her arm. "What has Judith found out about the value? Anything?"

Judith's voice carried from the coffee bar. "Not to eavesdrop, but I did hear my name. I have some estimates on your clock if you want them. A couple of my contacts still haven't gotten back to me, so these are just preliminary."

I turned to Evie. "Ready to find out why he's pushing you so hard?"

She frowned a bit at the question, then nodded.

There weren't any customers in the shop. We all met at a table near the coffee bar. Judith pulled out her phone. "I tracked down when your father-in-law bought the item."

"Ex—oh, never mind. John Senior bought it? Becky said it had been in the family forever." Evie scooted closer to Judith.

"Not unless 'forever' means fifteen years ago in her viewpoint. He bought it from an auction that March." Judith blew up the auction house listing. "See, it's right there. And he paid just about ten grand for it."

"We were married in June of that year. So Senior did buy it for me as a welcome-to-the-family gift." The listing had a picture of the clock, as well as the date of the sale and the name of the buyer. "John and Becky must have found the auction records and decided that money was part of their inheritance."

"Well, now, that's the thing. Your father-in-law got it for a steal. Apparently, this auction house was just starting out and didn't know how to reach out to the whale buyers. He bought several items from that lot and the next one. According to my friend, it gave the house enough money to hire a researcher and a marketer, and at the next sale they had more buyers there. So John Senior didn't get his deals anymore." Judith switched over to another email. "I have an offer from one of my contacts. Sight unseen, they'll give you twice what he paid for it. And I think that's a low offer. Sydney likes to get in fast with items. Sometimes he's burned, but a lot of times people think it's a great offer, so they take it. If he's offering twenty thousand, I bet it's worth at least thirty in an auction sale. Probably more."

"Thirty thousand? That's almost what I have left from the divorce settlement." Evie laughed at our shocked expressions. "I know, I should have gotten more, but John claimed all our assets were tied up with other debt projects. And I wanted out, so I told my attorney to take the offer. If that's true, I can sell it and buy a house. Well, not the whole house, but

I'll have enough to put down that I can afford to make the payments and still go to school. If I keep my job."

"What would you do with all your free time if you didn't work?" I teased her. Then I glanced over at Judith. "Thank you. You arrived right in the nick of time."

"I've been told I tend to do that." Judith beamed at us. "I just have a lot of contacts in different worlds. After all the estimates come in, we can sit down and I'll give you the names and contact information for the ones I totally trust."

"You're a lifesaver. Now I just have to call John back and tell him I'm not releasing the clock to him or Becky. Just to be safe, I moved it to a locker at the police station. Toby met with me yesterday and we transported it there. I didn't want anyone trying to break into my apartment to steal it." Evie leaned back into her chair. "I don't know what I would have done if Sasha hadn't recommended that I move here. I would have believed their lies about it being a family heirloom. I think John Senior must have known my marriage to his son wouldn't last. So he tried to provide for me without the kids knowing. If he'd put me in the will, they would have contested any gift to me."

"He sounds like he was a good man." The door opened and a few customers wandered in. I went to stand, but Judith beat me to it.

"You're off for the day. Evie and I can handle the rest of the shift." Judith squeezed Evie's shoulder as she walked by.

Evie wiped her eyes. "Judith is right. We've got it from here. Do you want me to do a deposit tonight?"

"Actually, I'll set one up now and take it. Then, unless we hit the magic number on the closing list, you can just put it in the safe. I had a really good morning." I followed Judith to the coffee bar and waited for her to finish her transaction. I opened the register and took out the cash over the amount my aunt had set for a "full" register. She'd set up very specific financial processes around the cash and the bank drops after we'd had some issues at the bank a few years back. But we rarely hit that level because a lot of our transactions now were mostly done on some type of a card.

I took the cash to the back, set up a deposit, and put it in one of the bank bags we stored in my desk. I noted the computer register we used for our accountant and then got ready to leave for the day.

Greg was sitting at a table in the front when I came out. After saying goodbye to Evie and Judith, I greeted him. "What brings you back here?"

"I was going to say coffee, but now I'm thinking maybe lunch?" He scanned the shop. "Looks like you're in a good spot to leave, at least for a bit."

"I could get some lunch." I pointed in the opposite direction from the diner. "But we have to walk to the bank first."

"No problem. I can use a walk and some out-of-office time." He reached for my tote and fake weighed it. "What? No books today?"

"I'll have you know I have three paperbacks in there. I just don't have any hardbacks to bring home." I tried to take back my tote, but he just put his arm around me. As we walked down the street, I glanced back at the shop. "You might have some issues with Evie's ex-family again. I think she's going to give them the bad news tonight."

"I spoke to her when I first came into the shop. She said she was calling her ex-husband tonight. I told her to let him know that his sister is already on my watch list due to her outbursts. I'll have Tim check in with her at the shop a few times tonight and again when she closes up."

"You don't think they'd try anything, do you?" Now I was worried about Evie. The good news was we'd put a good security system on the apartment when my aunt lived there, so if they did try anything when she was there, the police would know.

"I think they're just bullies. I told her to tell them that she'd given the clock to an auction house to have it appraised. That way they know it's not in the apartment. She should be fine. She's a smart woman." He shrugged. "And if they try anything stupid, we'll be watching."

"Thank you." I didn't feel totally comfortable with the plan, but I would once Evie sold the clock and used the money. "So, how's the investigation going?"

"You mean do I have a suspect? Or maybe I've identified the murder victim with Darla's new information?" He opened the door to the bank and waited for me to go inside. "Not any of your business."

"You're mean." I poked him in the side and then went to the business specialist teller, who was at a desk. "Hey, I'm doing an early deposit today."

"You sure are." Tara took my envelope. "Wait right here and I'll get you a receipt. I love that shirt on you."

"Thanks." I glanced down to check what I'd put on this morning because I didn't really remember. Clothes weren't my thing. I guess it was from being a lawyer, when I had to wear the same type of suit five days a week. Now, I bought clothes because they were comfortable. The white peasant blouse was an impulse buy when we'd been on one of our vacations. I'd paid way too much for it, but I loved the way it felt. And it had pretty embroidery on the sleeves.

When Tara came back she held out the receipt. "Are you two building your new house nearby?"

"I'm sorry, what new house?" I took the receipt and tucked it inside the tote Greg still carried.

"Oh, I assumed that since you sold the house on the edge of town you'd be building. Did you already buy another house? I know, it's none of my business, but I hate it when our favorite South Cove residents move away." She leaned against her desk.

"We didn't sell my house. Where did you hear that?" I glanced at Greg, who looked as confused as I felt.

Tara looked between the two of us. "Wow. I guess that's what I get for listening to gossip. Some guy came in to cash a check on an account out of the Bakerstown branch. It was sizable, so I had to call to get it cleared. While we were waiting, he mentioned that you'd just sold the house and would be coming into a lot of money soon."

"Do you remember who the man was?" Greg had stepped closer.

Tara shook her head. "I might be able to go through my notes. It was last week, and we keep a pretty good listing of who we have to go the extra mile for. Can I call you after I find it?"

Greg handed her his card. "Call me. I'd be interested in anything you can tell me about this man. I'm concerned about Jill's safety."

"Oh, I get it. I'm so sorry, it didn't feel like gossiping because he was feeding me all the information, but maybe that was the point." She tapped Greg's card on her desk. "I'll call as soon as I find something."

As we walked out of the bank and toward Lille's, I shivered.

"Are you cold?" Greg asked, pulling me closer.

I studied the now cloudy sky that had just a minute before been full of sun. I shook my head. "I'm just wondering why someone would assume I was selling the house. Again."

"I don't think that was the point. I think he wanted you to know that this wasn't over. That your telling Max no didn't change anything. And he just gave me another line of investigation. Who else is part of Coastal Investment Properties?"

Chapter 12

Greg didn't have to tell me to stay home after we finished lunch. He walked me to our door, gave Emma a hug, and kissed me. Lunch had been quiet, with both of us lost in our own thoughts. Greg pulled me into a hug.

"Look, it might just be someone who worked for Max and thought the project had been greenlighted. Who turns down an offer like you got? Probably not very many people." He put a finger under my chin and met my gaze. "It's going to be all right. Just let me do my job."

"Okay, Alpha Male Hero Character. Go save the world and my house. Emma and I will just stay here and play damsels in distress." I glanced toward the kitchen. "I'm pretty sure I have some ice cream to keep me company until you get home."

"I'll be home early. If I need to, I'll bring work home and camp out in my office. I don't feel comfortable leaving you alone out here."

"Actually, with Esmeralda popping in most afternoons to bring me food, I'm not feeling all that alone this week." I leaned on the doorway and glanced over at our neighbor's house. She must have still been at the station because her car wasn't in her driveway. "And Toby's around sleeping at times."

"Well, I'm going to be here more until we get this murder solved. I really didn't like the idea of some guy talking about the house selling to random people in town. If it had been an outsider, they might think you had money just sitting around. Maybe we should get more of a security system." He started to step inside to evaluate the house again, but I put a hand on his chest.

"Go to work. We'll be fine. You know Emma won't let anyone in the house I don't want here. And I know how to use a cell phone to call for help."

He kissed me again. "Just keep it charged this time."

I held up my phone so he could see the battery. "I'm good. See you tonight. Should I pull out something?"

"Yeah, surprise me." He waved and hurried down the stairs. I watched him pull out of the driveway, then closed and locked the door. Emma and I had just settled down on the couch with a cold soda and one of the books I'd brought home when a knock sounded at my door.

I went and let the door swing open, thinking it was Greg. "What did you forget?"

Esmeralda stood at the door with a bag in her hands. "I don't think I forgot anything. I brought you the fixings for chicken fajitas. I thought it might be fun to cook for a change."

I folded my arms. "What's going on? Why do you keep bringing us food?"

"I feel bad that the two of you aren't getting much time together. You've just gotten engaged and now Greg's off working a case at all hours." She swung the bag. "Take it. I'm not spelling you or anything like that."

"I didn't mean to imply that you were." Wow, the land mines in this conversation were huge. "I just wanted to know why you were taking care of us."

Now she did move the bag into my hand. "Oh, Jill. I'm not trying to take care of you. All I'm doing is trying to help you take care of yourself. I know how hard it is to be a cop's wife. Let me do this for you. It makes me feel better about you having to spend so much time alone."

"Well, that's stopping tonight. Greg has promised to be home at a reasonable hour and we'll make the fajitas together. Thank you. But please stop bringing us food. We're fine." I nodded to the kitchen. "Do you want to come in and talk?"

"No, I've got clients coming over tonight. Thank you for letting me do this today. I promise, I'll stop. I just didn't want you to feel alone. Like no one cared about you." Esmeralda turned and headed down the stairs.

"Thanks again for dinner. I'm sure it will be amazing." I relocked the door and took the bag into the kitchen. Esmeralda was acting weird. I thought about what she'd said. She didn't want me to feel alone. Maybe she was feeling alone. Her boyfriend lived halfway across the country. I knew she had friends, like Deek's mom, Rory, but maybe this was her way of saying she wanted to be friends with me too. I was going to take her cookies at work tomorrow and invite her to the almost weekly brunch I had with Amy.

With that mystery settled at least for now, I decided to spend my afternoon reading. My fingers were hurting from crocheting last night.

I guess I had to build up muscles for the craft. I was just getting into the story when my phone rang. I glanced at the display and saw it was the shop. "Hey, what's going on?"

"Sorry to bother you. I tried calling Toby, but…could you send one of the guys from the police station over here? I keep thinking I'm seeing John outside on the street." Evie's voice was strained, and I could tell she was upset.

"Sure, I'll call Greg right now. Are you and Judith safe?" I set down my book and grabbed my keys and tote. I wouldn't walk to the shop; this would be faster.

"We're fine, but I'd feel better if someone could go check on Homer. I just have a bad feeling." I heard her voice choke up. "I'd go myself, but I don't want to leave Judith alone."

"Don't go anywhere. I'm coming back and you can run upstairs with Toby or whoever Greg sends. Hold on a minute, I'm going to call Greg." I put the call on hold and dialed Greg's office number.

Tim answered. "Greg King's office, may I help you?"

"Is he there?"

"Jill? Is that you? You sound like you're running."

I was running. I'd locked Emma in the house and now I was heading to my car. "No time to chat. I need someone to go to the shop. Evie thinks she saw her ex-husband outside the bookstore."

"We're in a shift-change meeting, but I'll get someone over there now." He paused. "Jill, don't worry, it's going to be fine."

And then he was gone, and I was connected back to Evie. "Help is on the way. Do we have any customers to worry about?"

"No, it's just the two of us."

I started the car. "Go lock the back door. I'll be there in five minutes tops."

When I arrived at the shop Toby was already there. I relocked the front door after myself and turned the "Closed" sign over. We could deal with this, then reopen after I got Evie calmed down. I moved over to Judith, who was watching Toby and Evie talk. "What happened?"

Judith glanced at me and then at the other two. She took my arm and moved out of earshot. "I'm not really sure. We were going over the closing list when Evie looked out the window. I saw her face go white, but by the time I looked in the same direction, there wasn't anyone there. After she told me who she'd thought she'd seen I told her to call you and I went outside, but no one was out there. The area looked deserted."

I glanced at Evie. "I hate that they're messing with her this way."

Judith didn't say anything. Instead, she adjusted the napkin holders on the nearby tables. She didn't look at me.

"Wait, don't tell me that you think she imagined it." I stood in between us and Evie, just in case. I didn't want her to overhear our discussion.

Judith shook her head. "I don't know what to think. I know she's under a lot of stress. And stress can make you all kinds of crazy."

"Well, it's a good thing we have cameras outside, then." I left Judith in the dining room and moved toward the back. I stopped by Toby. "Have you checked the tape?"

He shook his head. "The cabinet is locked, remember? Your aunt put a lock on it a few years ago."

Which I had thought was stupid. I grabbed my tote and dug for my keys. It took a while, but we finally found the one that opened the cabinet. Toby ran the tape back and there, walking by the camera, was a man. He looked straight into the shop window, then waved at someone. Then he left. I glanced at Evie. "Is that your ex-husband?"

She nodded. "Now I feel stupid. John just walked by and waved, and I made a big deal out of it."

"Maybe he wanted you to overreact. If the police think you're crazy, he might think they'll start blowing you off and give him an opportunity to get to you and to the clock." I met Judith's gaze and she turned away first. I was going to have to explain how we supported each other to my newest barista. But I'd give her this one. We were all new to her. She probably didn't know who to trust yet. "Toby, can you take the tape back to Greg? I don't think John's going to do anything now, but I think he's announcing his presence. Evie, you need to be careful. Are you okay to keep working or do I need to finish your shift?"

"It will be a cold day in you-know-where before he messes with me like this again." Evie squared her shoulders, and a sense of pride flowed through me. She was going to be all right. "I can finish my shift. Don't worry."

"Tim and I will step up patrols past here tonight. Are you closing at nine?" He looked at me, but I pointed to Evie.

"Don't ask me. I'm off the clock."

I stayed around for a bit and then got out a box of cookies and wrote a marketing receipt for the register. It had been a while since I'd dropped off treats to Greg's crew. And they'd been quick to get here and make sure Evie was okay. I said my goodbyes and then crossed the street. The air was chilly but not horrible. I'd parked my car behind the store, so I'd go back and get it before I went home.

For now, it was time to see my boyfriend and see what we could do to get Evie's ex-husband off her back.

I opened the door to the police department lobby, but it was empty. Esmeralda didn't work as a dispatcher on the weekends. Which was why Tim had answered the phone. He was the low man at the station, so when the dispatcher was gone, he stepped in. On the weekends Esmeralda was South Cove's best fortune-teller. A job at which I knew she made at least three times, if not more, the money than she did as a dispatcher/receptionist. But she loved being around people. A lot more than I did.

A light was shining from Greg's office, and as I went inside, I realized he wasn't alone. Lille was there, and they were in what appeared to be a serious conversation. Greg looked up and frowned.

"Is everything okay at the shop?" He stood and walked over to greet me.

"Yes, fine. I mean, there was an issue, but he's gone now. Sorry, I didn't mean to interrupt." I shoved the box into his hands. "I'll talk to you later. Here's some cookies for your guys."

Lille smiled at me. Which took me by surprise. "I just brought Tiny's fried chicken for the station. It must be feed-the-ones-who-serve-and-protect day."

Greg kissed me on the cheek. "Thanks for the cookies. I'll call you later."

"Sounds good." I left the office wondering why Lille was still sitting there. Did she have information on the dead guy? Darla thought he'd been at the Winery. Maybe he also ate at the diner before someone stabbed him. There was no way Lille would tell me anything, but maybe Carrie would. Greg and I had already eaten lunch, and Esmerelda had brought over stuff for dinner, so I couldn't very well pop in and claim hunger.

I'd have to wait until Monday, when Carrie was back at work. My day off was filling up really fast. And I hadn't even asked Aunt Jackie if she wanted to go visit Beth's Hollywood room. Maybe I'd wait to take Aunt Jackie over there for a while. Things just seemed a bit unsettled around South Cove right now.

When I got home I curled up on the couch and worked on my blanket. Greg had texted that he'd be home around five, so I stayed on the couch with Emma by my side and the home improvement channel running on the television. They had just shown an outdoor backyard spa makeover complete with hot tub and outdoor shower when I heard the front door open. I waved him over to the couch. "You've got to see this."

"Unless it's a tape showing someone killing my victim in the City Hall parking lot, I'm not sure I can take any more input today. We put out a photo of the guy today to see if anyone had seen him in town. And guess what? Lille is certain she saw the guy having dinner several nights in her diner with your friend Max Winter."

"Yeah, Darla thinks she saw him too. She has a name for you. Did you ever call her back?" I pointed to the hot tub. "Maybe we should expand the deck so we could get one of those."

"It looks great, but what's this about Darla having a name for the guy? Why didn't she come see me?"

I muted the television. I didn't think we were going to get to chat about remodeling today. "She tried. She said you were avoiding her calls. I told her to leave a message with Esmeralda. Didn't you get it?"

"I've been a little busy." He took off his hat and ran a hand through his hair. "And I've been avoiding Darla because I thought she was wearing her reporter's hat, not trying to give me information. I guess I should go over and talk to her."

"At five on a Saturday? Are you crazy? The Winery is going to be crazy busy. Call her and tell her you'll meet her tomorrow. Maybe take her to coffee at Lille's? You probably need to apologize for ignoring her. And she said she thought his name was Gentry. Or John. Wait, that's Evie's ex-husband's name. I think I'm getting people confused now. It's been a long day." I kissed his cheek. "Go call her and lock up your gun. I'll get the stuff out for dinner and when you're done we'll make fajitas. Just in case you have to go back in. Unless you're full of Lille's chicken."

"I left that for the guys. I'm not going back in, and that's a good call on taking Darla to coffee." He stood and headed to the office. "How did I get so lucky to have such a smart girlfriend?"

"Fiancée," I corrected him as Emma and I headed to the kitchen. It was going to be a fun night.

I was taking out Esmeralda's fajita kit when I remembered I hadn't invited her to brunch. I dug my phone out of my tote and found her number in my contacts. I glanced out the living room window and didn't see a car in her driveway. Hopefully, I was calling in between her clients.

"Good evening, Jill. What's going on? Did I forget something in the dinner kit?" Esmeralda answered on the second ring.

"No, and shouldn't you know what I'm calling about?" I returned to the kitchen as we were talking and finished unpacking the bag. I set the cheese on the counter with the sour cream.

She laughed. "You know it doesn't work that way. What can I help you with? I saw Greg's truck in the drive, so I know he's finally home to spend some time with you."

"Yeah, we're just starting dinner. Anyway, I was wondering if you wanted to join Amy and me for brunch tomorrow. My treat. You've been feeding me all week." I tried to make the request sound casual, not like I just wanted to pay back a debt.

"Brunch? Let me check tomorrow's schedule. I know I have a few appointments, but I don't think they start until after noon."

As I waited for her to come back on the line, I paced back into the living room. I hoped she would be able to come. Not just because I owed her, but I realized I hadn't really spent much time with her just talking. This would give us a moment to find out more about each other.

"I'd love to come as long as I can be home before one. I'll need some time to get centered for my first reading."

"Great. If you want, we can walk up to Lille's together. I meet Amy there at nine most Sundays. This will be fun. And you're always welcome if you aren't working." I knew Esmeralda was one of the hardest workers in South Cove. But that didn't mean she couldn't carve out time for a little girl talk. And it might help Amy to talk to someone else besides me and Justin. Or me *about* Justin.

"I'll be waiting on the street in front of your house at eight forty-five." She paused a second, then added, "Thanks, Jill. This *will* be fun."

I said my goodbyes and then turned back around. Greg was watching me. Setting my phone on the coffee table, I said, "Esmeralda's going to join Amy and me for brunch tomorrow."

He followed me into the kitchen. "That was nice of you. I think she'd like having a few more friends around the area. I think that boyfriend of hers is trying to get her to move back to New Orleans."

I thought about what life in South Cove might look like without Esmeralda. And then a worse thought hit me. Maybe if she did leave, she'd take Max Winter up on his offer for her property. I'd be living across from a minihotel and all the traffic that would bring. I took the peppers over to wash them in the sink. "I hope that doesn't happen. For a lot of reasons."

Chapter 13

Sunday morning Amy slid next to me in our booth, leaving the other side for Esmeralda. "Where is she?"

"Bathroom. She saved a turtle from the middle of the road as we walked here and wanted to wash her hands." I set down my menu. I didn't know why I even looked at it anymore. Today was Sunday, so I'd have the South Cove special: a western omelet with hash browns inside along with a flaky biscuit. And then Tiny covered it with country gravy. It was carb heaven. "Why?"

"So why are we having brunch with her? What do you need to know? I can help tag team if I know what you're looking for." Amy opened her menu and studied the choices. I knew what she'd have by the time she was done too: a waffle with two eggs and a side of bacon. Sunday tradition.

"I'm not looking for any information. I just thought it would be nice to have brunch with her." I shook my head as I sipped the coffee our waitress had brought. I didn't know her name, but she was new. I had a rule: I never became attached to any of Lille's waitresses until they'd been there more than six months. So mainly I just knew Carrie. And Carrie didn't work weekends anymore, not since she and Doc got serious. "I'm not that insensitive. Besides, I don't know anything about the investigation this time, so it would be going in cold."

"I can't believe you're not investigating this. It seems right up your alley. A mysterious man who no one can identify walks into the station all bloody and dies before Toby can even get his name?" Amy shut her menu. "Classic South Cove."

"That's what's got Greg upset. It's so weird that no one knows this guy."
Esmeralda slipped into the other bench and smiled at Amy. "Thanks for
inviting me to your weekly brunch."

"Glad to have you." Amy waved at the new waitress, who held up a finger,
letting her know she'd been seen. "I'm starving. Have you two ordered?"

"Just drinks." I liked the new dynamic of the three of us at the Sunday
brunch table. Hopefully, the mix would work. Sometimes you just couldn't
mix friends. But Amy and Esmeralda both worked at City Hall so they
really had more time together than I did with my neighbor.

Esmeralda set her menu to the side. "I'm having the South Cove special.
It's the best."

"I know." I held up a hand to high five our new brunch mate, but she
didn't look up. I put down my hand, not meeting Amy's gaze. "Anyway,
I love it."

"You and Jill are a pair." Amy leaned back as the waitress came with
coffee and a cup. She nodded as the waitress held up the pot in a question.
"Please. And I think we're ready to order. I'd love a glass of orange juice
to go with the meal as well."

"Let me get that and then I'll be right back to take your order. If I don't
follow the steps Carrie taught me, I get lost." The woman scurried away.

"I give her two weeks," Amy said as she lifted her cup.

I watched the woman disappear into the kitchen. "Maybe a month.
Carrie's trying real hard to get her trained."

"If she's here next weekend, it will be a miracle," Esmeralda added.

After Amy had gotten her juice and our orders were into the kitchen,
we fell into an easy banter.

Amy looked between us. "You guys are serious about Greg not having
any leads. I can't believe it."

"He's had tough cases before." I came to his defense. "And both Lille
and Darla say they think the guy was hanging out here in South Cove a
few days before he died. I should ask Deek if he saw him at the bookstore."

"Yeah, because all the hardened killers hang out at bookstores before
they die." Amy laughed.

"He's the victim, not the killer. We don't know if he's even a criminal."
I was going to ask Carrie what she knew on Monday. But neither Amy
nor Esmeralda needed to know my plans for my day off. That way they
couldn't slip and tell Greg.

"You probably won't find anything here in town, Jill." Esmeralda talked
like she'd been reading my day planner. "Although taking a short trip out
of town might give you some information to build on."

As the food was being delivered, I ignored her fortune-telling. "Hey, Esmeralda, do you know Beth Winter? She's so interesting. I can't believe she built a shrine to Vivien Leigh in her house."

"Actually, Beth is a client. I can't go into a lot about what I know or how I know it. It wouldn't be fair to her." Esmerelda loaded up her fork with the omelet. "But I'll tell you this. That woman is a saint to still be married to Max. I would have killed him in his sleep. Or maybe at dinner. He's scum."

"Yeah, I got that feeling too. But Beth seems to love him, for all his faults." I hadn't realized that Esmeralda knew Beth. This brunch was getting interesting. "Her butler, Jeffrey, is crazy hot. I can't believe Max leaves them alone as much as he seems to."

"Max doesn't think Beth would stray. And besides, he's usually off chasing something else." She shook her head. "Seriously, I can't talk about Beth or Max. I know too much about the family. Even though I want to tell you so much about 'perfect' Max."

I'd never seen Esmeralda use air quotes before. I think Sunday brunches were going to be a lot more fun now that she was joining us. We changed the subject, and the time flew by as we talked and laughed.

Just before we were leaving, Greg came into the diner with Darla. He waved, said something to Darla, who turned toward a table, and then he came over to our booth.

He leaned over Amy and gave me a quick kiss. "I figured you three would be gone by now."

"The new waitress is trying to divide our bill. We might be here a while." Amy pushed away her milkshake, which we'd all ordered as a final splurge. "Justin and I are going shopping, then doing meal prep for next week. He swears it will save us tons on our food bill."

"So you're brown-bagging it next week?" I'd already finished my milkshake. I hoped my question wouldn't sound whiny. I could make something at home after work. I didn't have to take a lunch to my job. The waitress dropped off our credit cards and receipts with three pens, even though I'd told her I was buying Esmeralda's meal. She was going to lose pens the way she doled them out.

"Actually, just a few days. Justin's committing to brown bagging at least three of the five days, so I guess I need to do my part." Amy signed her receipt and then gently pushed past Greg before turning back to me. "The things we do for love, right? I'll see you Wednesday night?"

"I'm going to be almost ready to start a new blanket by then." I turned to Esmeralda. "We're crocheting blankets for the preemie babies at the hospital."

"I don't knit or crochet. It's not in my wheelhouse." Esmeralda stood and adjusted her tote.

I knew I had felt a no-craft kindred spirit with my neighbor. I started to raise my hand up for a high five.

Then she looked at me. "I'm quilting blankets for the project. Crissy said it would be all right. I've already got three done. I'm sure I'll meet my goal. I'm afraid I can't walk home with you; I'm running into Crissy's shop to help her box up the blankets the group has already dropped off. Thanks for the invite."

My hand dropped to my side as I watched both Amy and Esmeralda head to the door. Greg scooted in to sit by me for a second. "Man, you know how to clear a room. Go make nice with Darla. See what you can find out. I think Esmeralda knows more about Max and his wife than she's telling."

"Esmeralda isn't a big chatterer, especially around gossip." He leaned in and kissed me. Then he stood and tapped the table. "Sorry I ran off your friends. I'll see you at home."

I scooted out of the booth and headed to the door, waving at Darla as I left. The brunch had already been over before Greg showed up, so I didn't really blame him for Amy or Esmeralda leaving. My mind was on what Esmeralda had said about the Winters. I needed to talk to Beth again to see if she'd tell me more about Connie and her relationship with Max. And if she knew anyone named Gentry. I might need some dirt on Max if he came after my house again.

Tomorrow. Tomorrow I'd dig into all things Max Winter and see if I could find the name Gentry in any of the nooks and crannies where he stored his secrets. Maybe Max killed this guy, and if so, being in prison would keep him from going after my house.

Or he'd kill me and Greg would have to avenge my death. And not sell the house. We really needed to have that financial talk. I needed to know what I could do with the house. Darla's idea of giving it to a nonprofit was amazing, if I could find the right one.

I was almost home when a Land Rover pulled up next to me and the man inside rolled down his window.

"Are you Jill Gardner?" He leaned out of the window, watching me. The Rolex on his tanned arm gave me a good idea who it was that wanted to know.

"Why do you want to know?" I moved toward the inside edge of the sidewalk and tucked my tote next to my side with my arm. I had at least one hardback book inside if I needed to take a swing. What can I say? I always come prepared with at least one book.

"I think you know. I'm John Marshall, and my wife works for you, right?"

"Your ex-wife works for me. Why are you here stalking her? It's a little creepy, dude. Haven't you gotten on with your life yet? Get some closure going." I turned toward home but he kept talking.

"Look, all I want is what's mine. That was a wedding gift. I should have insisted that she put it into the asset distribution. It's only fair."

I tried not to spin around. But I failed. "From what I see, you got plenty of the assets in the divorce. I don't see Evie driving a Land Rover. Or dressing like she's on Martha's Vineyard. Just leave me alone. I'm not going to be your advocate in this discussion."

"I've had an upturn after the divorce. Anyway, tell Evie that I'm not giving up. She knows I don't lose. She should make it easy on herself." He started his car again and slipped on his shades. "I wouldn't want anything to happen to her or that mutt of hers."

"That sounded like a threat," I called after the Land Rover as it sped down the road, barely stopping at the highway to check for traffic. He turned right toward Bakerstown. I needed to tell Greg about this, but it could wait until he got home. I pulled my sweater closer as I hurried home. The sunny day had just turned cold.

Emma and I were outside on the back porch when Greg got home. He sat next to me on the bench. "The house smells wonderful. Is that a roast?"

"Yep. Roast beef, potatoes, carrots, and onions. I made an apple pie earlier, so it's sitting on the counter cooling. I thought it might be safer for the food for Emma and me to wait for you out here. She was very attentive when I was making the pie." I leaned my head on his shoulder. "Did Darla have some leads for you?"

"She did. But why are you upset? Don't tell me you're mad about the way the brunch ended." He rubbed my arm. "I didn't mean to scare your friends away."

"You didn't scare them away. We were finished anyway." I sat up and turned to face him. "Promise me you won't be mad."

He lifted my head off his shoulders and met my gaze. "Jill, what did you do?"

I shook my head. "I didn't do anything. I was just walking home. But here's what happened."

I spent the next fifteen minutes going over the run in with John Marshall. What the car looked like. What the man inside looked like. Finally, I held up my hands. "Stop asking me questions. We know it was John Marshall. He said so."

"Sometimes people lie."

I stared at him. "It was the guy on the security tape the other night. Evie identified him. Besides, no one else who works for me is or was married."

"What about this Judith? Maybe she's married."

I laughed. "One, this guy was at least ten years younger, maybe even more, than Judith. If he was her husband, I've got a lot more respect for her than I already did."

"That's sexist." Greg laughed as he shook his head. "I thought you were better than that."

I punched him in the arm. "I'm going in to check on dinner. Do you want to eat early?"

"Probably better. I've got to work in the office for a couple of hours tonight. Do you need my help with dinner?"

I stood and held open the door for Emma. "I've got everything done. I'll set the table and make some gravy and then let you know when it's ready."

"You're a good woman, Jill Gardner." He pulled me into his arms. "Soon-to-be Jill King. Or are you keeping your name?"

I blinked at the question. "I hadn't even thought about it."

He laughed as he followed me into the kitchen. "Great, now I've given you something else to stress over. Let me know when dinner's ready. I need to find Evie's ex so I can pay him a visit tomorrow. First, he scares Evie, then he tries to strong-arm you. I'm thinking I don't like this man."

"Well, I think that makes three of us. Four if you count Homer. Who would threaten a cute little dog like Homer?" I got plates out of the cabinet.

"A jerk." He kissed me on the forehead and headed to the office. "Don't let him get to you."

"I won't," I called after Greg, but honestly, I already had let John Marshall mess with my head. But he wouldn't for long. I set the table first, then focused on making gravy, thinking about how I could help Evie. I hated when my friends were being bullied. And I knew one thing about John Marshall. The man was a bully. And so was his sister.

* * * *

The next morning I set out my plan for the day while I drank my first cup of coffee. I had a lot of stops to make. And I needed to buy groceries too. Why was it when you had stuff to do, the routine chores always seemed to be urgent? I looked at the list and tried moving some things around. I wanted to talk to Carrie, but she would be in South Cove working. And I needed to go to the courthouse, see what I could find on Max Winter's other projects. Maybe there was a smoking gun there that might explain who this Gentry was, or at least give me some dirt to keep Max away from my house. I had an almost-empty notebook I tucked into my tote along with a book, just in case I had some time to kill somewhere. Then I made my shopping lists and put a load of laundry into the washer. I'd done two loads last night during commercials and then I'd folded clothes while I watched television. It was called multitasking, even when the other task was mind numbing relaxation. Sometimes I got my best ideas when I was watching a show.

I tucked my finished list into my tote and sipped my coffee. What was I forgetting?

Emma whined from her spot over by the door. She looked at me, then up at the hook where I kept her leash. I checked the clock.

"You're right. I have time to take you running." I glanced at my phone. Greg had asked me not to run and Esmeralda was at work. I peeked out the front door to check the weather. I was about to tell Emma it was okay to go when the black Land Rover from yesterday drove past my house. Really slow. We have a thirty mile per hour speed limit and I don't think he was even going ten.

"Sorry, girl, Greg doesn't want us out alone." I shut and locked the door and went upstairs to the treadmill. Slipping on my running shoes, I tried to clear my mind from the fear that seeing that car had caused. By the time I was done I was just mad. Mad that anyone was depriving my dog of a run she clearly deserved.

I decided to do grocery shopping tomorrow night after work. That way, Emma could come with me on my trip to Bakerstown. I wouldn't be able to take her inside Beth's house, but she had that great deck where it looked like no one ever sat. I'd stop by the bookstore and pick up more cookies and a book about Vivien Leigh I'd ordered last week. Maybe she hadn't read this one.

I jumped in the shower and got ready for my day.

I pulled the Jeep into my parking spot behind the shop. We had four with signs. One for the apartment resident. One for me. One for Aunt Jackie. And one that just said Coffee, Books, and More. Greg used it a lot when he stopped in for a visit. Today, a black Land Rover was parked in that spot.

And no one was inside.

Chapter 14

I had to give it to Greg. He was there before I'd expected him. He parked his truck behind the Land Rover and came over to the Jeep. He leaned in the window and rubbed Emma's head. "Stay here."

"I hope you're talking to her and not me," I tried to joke, but I didn't have the strength to fight. I was too worried about Evie.

The back door to the bookstore opened and Evie stepped out on the small deck. "Hi, guys. What are you doing here?"

I could see when she saw the Land Rover. Her face fell.

I tried to open the door, but Greg was still blocking my exit. "Greg, I need to be with her. She's terrified."

"Okay, change of plans. You and Emma go into the shop. Lock all the doors, including the one that goes up to the apartment. I've still got a key to the apartment, so as soon as you're locked in, I'll go check it out. Toby is out front. Don't let anyone inside unless it's me or Toby."

"I'm not an idiot." I climbed out of the Jeep and opened the back door. Snipping on the leash, I slapped my leg. "Come on, girl. Let's go see Evie."

Emma jumped out but waited for me to grab my tote from Greg. He nodded to the porch. "Go be with her. Find out what she knows, if anything. And lock your car."

I dug for my keys as we walked. By the time I was on the porch and moving Evie inside, I had the keys in my hand, and I remote-locked it. Then I shut us inside and locked the back door. "So, have you seen anything?"

"No. I've been working on a schedule for this summer. I'm going to take summer school so I can finish this degree faster. I'd just realized I was out of coffee, so I came down to get some from the storeroom. I was going to pay you back, I promise." She glanced to the stairs and moved that way.

"Sorry, no, you're staying down here with me until Greg can find your ex." I saw the worry on her face. "I take it Homer's still in the apartment?"

"Yes. I didn't want to bring him downstairs, mostly because he was still asleep on the couch when I left. And I know you don't love dogs in the shop."

I pulled out my phone and texted Greg. "I don't mind dogs in the shop. That's Aunt Jackie. Also, it's hard to keep an eye on them while you're working. Once, when she was a puppy, Emma followed some guy who'd stopped in to grab a coffee outside and I didn't see it. By the time the line cleared she was all the way across the road and at the police station. Greg had to bring her back. I've asked him to grab Homer for us if he can."

"Thank you." The raw emotion in Evie's voice told me all there was to know about her ex and his love for animals. Or nonlove in this situation.

I put my arm around her and led her out to the shop. "No problem. Now, let's make some coffee and chill while Greg investigates."

I started some coffee and Evie sat on one of the stools, watching out the window. She picked up a straw and started bending it.

"You know, you probably should be open on Sundays in the fall. There's quite a bit of traffic out there you're missing." Evie shrugged. "I was watching out the window a lot yesterday."

I leaned on the counter as the coffee brewed. "You're right. I've been holding off because it lets us all have a real weekend, but maybe we'll change it up and only close on Monday. I know traffic then is slow. People are either coming or going from the bed-and-breakfasts. Now that we have Judith, I could give half of you Sundays off and half Tuesdays, to go with your Monday."

"I'd work the Sunday shift to get Monday and Tuesday off. I could do homework or study groups or just stack all my classes on those days if possible." A sound upstairs made her look up, like she could see through the flooring.

I decided to change the subject. "Tell me about when you told John you weren't giving the clock back. I know he was angry, but what did he say?"

"He said I was selfish and always looking out for just me." Evie sighed. "Then he went through all the reasons he had known I was cheating on him, listing off people like my ex-boss at the library to the produce manager at the grocery store where I shopped. When he went into detail about what I'd been doing with these imaginary lovers, I told him he was an idiot and hung up on him."

I poured our coffees, then went to sit next to her. "You're saying he doesn't take rejection well."

She started laughing and nodded. "You can say that."

"Well, once Greg gets done with him, I don't think he'll be hanging around South Cove much longer. Greg has zero tolerance for bullies. Especially those who pick on women." I sipped my coffee. "I don't think I asked, what are you going to school for?"

This time when Evie started talking her face lit up with joy. "I've always wanted to be a counselor. I know, I'm old to be starting now, but some of my credits are still good. I won't have to retake all my bachelor classes. And I could be in graduate school in two years if I push, three if I don't."

The front door swung open and we both jumped.

Toby held up his hands showing the set of keys he held. "Hey, boss. Other boss told me to unlock the door. Sorry if I scared you."

Greg came inside and locked the door behind him. "Toby's always sucking up to you. I don't know why he doesn't treat me with some respect. I'm pretty sure I pay better than you do."

Toby nodded as he crossed the floor. "True, but the criminals don't tip me for taking them down to the station. Anyway, I didn't see anything. Well, except for a black Land Rover plowing over the parking sign in the back. Greg's lucky he didn't back up into his truck a few times just for fun."

"I would have been very upset had he done that. Right now I'm only mad." Greg came around Toby and handed Homer to Evie. "Here's your guard dog. I thought he was going to bite me when I came into the apartment. He did not like me in there without you."

"Homer's such a good boy." Evie crushed him to her chest, then let him lick her neck. "Thank you for bringing him down. I know it was silly, but I'm not sure what John would do if he got hold of him. I know he'd hold him for ransom, but I'm not sure how he'd be when I finally got Homer back."

"I found traces of him trying to break in the back door, but he saw the security camera. I'm going to take these over to his hotel to see if I can get him to sit down for a quick chat. If so, your worries will be over. I can be very convincing." Greg rubbed Emma's head. She'd come over and sat between Greg and Toby as soon as they'd settled into the shop. She loved both men in her life.

"He probably thought I'd be working today." Evie sipped her coffee. "I sure can pick them. If I ever talk about dating again, just hold up a picture of John. That should shock me out of it."

"I think I'll let it slip that the new owner is coming to the station tomorrow to pick up the item." Greg stepped over and poured himself a cup of coffee. "That should get him to leave. He'll have lost."

"You would think." Evie's voice was quiet and thoughtful.

I watched her, not knowing if she was being sarcastic or not. "What are you thinking, Evie?"

She shook herself out of what appeared to be a light trance. "Don't worry about it. I'm sure Greg's right. Letting him know that it's been sold should be enough."

I could tell she was lying, but I didn't know why. Or exactly what she was lying about.

I went to the dessert case and boxed up a dozen cookies.

Greg watched and held out his hand. "Thanks, hon."

"Sorry, not for you. I'm visiting Beth Winter again and I hate going empty-handed." I finished my coffee and turned off the pot, dumping the coffee grounds into a trash can. "Time to break up the party. I need to lock up."

Toby and Evie held up their keys.

"Okay, so I'm not the only one who can lock up; I get it." I called Emma to my side and picked up my tote and the box of cookies. "And Greg?"

"Yes?"

"Tell Mr. Marshall that he owes me fifteen hundred to replace the sign." I paused at the back door.

"Don't tell me you spent fifteen hundred on just one of those signs. They're cute and all, but that's a lot of money." Greg started following me outside.

"I didn't. Five hundred is for the sign, the rest is for pain and suffering. I'm going to have nightmares for weeks." I left the shop and unlocked my Jeep. After I got Emma settled, we took off for Bakerstown for our visit.

When I got to the Winter estate, I pushed the buzzer. A non-English-sounding woman answered. "I'm here to see Beth Winter. I'm Jill Gardner?"

"I know who you are, Miss Gardner, but I'm afraid Ms. Winter isn't taking visitors right now. Have a great day."

I started to explain how I'd only be a minute, but the button on the box had gone from green to red. No one was listening to me. I put the Jeep in reverse, then parked across the street, where I could see through the gate to the grounds beyond.

A man walked across the driveway near the house. I got out the binoculars I kept in the glove box for bird watching. Well, they were supposed to be for bird watching and that's what I'd told Greg when he'd found them one day. I just hadn't picked up the hobby yet. I focused in on the walker. It was Jeffrey. And he was heading toward someone already in the yard. Beth Winter sat on a park bench near a pond. He leaned down and kissed her. I set down my binoculars. "Whoa. I didn't expect that. Maybe that's what Max is worried about. Beth and Jeffrey."

Emma whined in the back seat.

"Well, you're no help." I hadn't wanted to see that kiss. Now I couldn't get it out of my head. I glanced at my watch. I needed to get to the courthouse today or I'd have to hurry off shift another day this week. Besides, as I thought about my plan, Emma didn't need to be locked in my car, even on a mild day, for very long. I picked up my phone and dialed a number.

"Caroline Dresser, how may I help you?"

I was still pulling out my notebook. "Hi, Caroline, I need some records of properties copied. Can you guys do that?"

"There's a dollar per page fee."

"That will work." I listed off all the properties I'd found online that Max had been involved with for the last five years. "And anything during that time for permits filed by a Coastal Investment Properties. When will that be ready?"

"You can pick them up in ten minutes at the cashier's office. I've had these pulled for a week. The man who ordered them never came by to get them. I was about to shred them. He didn't even leave a number and he swore he'd be in last Monday."

"Did he tell you his name?" I held my breath.

"Yes, I wrote it on the invoice. Gentry Floods. It sounds like a country western singer, right?"

"I'll be there in ten." Someone was watching out for me. I got the property information I was looking for as well as Greg's victim's full name. I should get paid for doing this kind of stuff. Of course Gentry Floods sounded like a made-up name. Before I started the car, I opened Facebook to see if there was anyone by that name. And hit pay dirt. He was real.

I started the car and pulled out onto the road. I glanced over at the gate. Beth and Jeffrey were still sitting there. I didn't know whether to be happy they'd found each other or sad for Beth's marriage. On the other hand, Max wasn't a pillar of virtue. It was all so confusing.

I called Greg on the way to the courthouse. I got his voice mail. "Hey, I think your dead guy might be Gentry Floods. Call me when you get this and I'll explain."

Emma barked at a tree as we drove by. Or probably at a squirrel in the tree. So I added before I hung up, "Emma says hi."

When I got to the cashier's office the woman was on the phone. I waited probably a little impatiently until she said, "Sorry, Dave, I've got a customer."

She smiled after she hung up. "That was my husband. He wanted to tell me all about the garden he's planning for next spring. I don't even like vegetables."

I smiled back, "Sorry to be in a rush, but my dog's in the car and I don't want her to get bored and think the seats are chew toys."

"Did you roll down the windows? It can get really hot in there even on nonsunny days." The woman stood a little in her chair, trying to see out the large front windows.

Another reason I needed to get out of here, I mused, but I let it go. "Of course. Anyway, I'm picking up some copies. Caroline said she'd have it here under my name, Jill Gardner. Or maybe Gentry Floods?"

"Oh, yeah. I had that pile on my desk for a week and just sent it back upstairs. Have you been out of town?" She peered at me over her glasses.

"Actually, yes. What do I owe you?" I didn't want to spend more time explaining. I pulled out my credit card and waited for her to process the charge.

When she gave me back my card and the documents I hurried out of the lobby. Before I got to the door, I heard her tell the next person in line, "She left her dog in the car. I hope he's okay."

I wanted to turn around and say *If you hadn't been talking to your husband on work time, I would have been in and out of here five minutes ago.* But I held my tongue and pushed the door open.

I knew I wasn't a bad dog owner. But I hurried to the Jeep, just in case. I rubbed Emma's head. "Are you thirsty? Do you want some water?"

She ignored my concern and barked at a car that had just pulled up next to the Jeep.

"Okay, then, next stop is home." I really hadn't gotten much done in Bakerstown today because I'd brought Emma with me. Well, that and the bookstore incident. Maybe if I texted Greg, he'd give me the go-ahead to take her running. I sure could use the exercise.

I pulled the car onto the highway and turned up the music. I was ready to go home.

When I got there, and because I hadn't eaten lunch yet and the fridge was pretty bare because I'd hadn't gone to the store, I left Emma in the house and walked back into town and to Lille's diner.

The hostess stand said "Seat yourself," so I hurried over to my favorite booth. I could watch the door, the kitchen, and most of the dining room from this spot. Not that I was nosy or anything. I just liked knowing what was going on. A new waitress with Lynda on her name tag stopped at my booth.

"What can I get you to drink?" She stared at the order pad, not making eye contact.

"Iced tea. No, make that a vanilla milkshake. It's been a crazy day." I smiled in case she looked up. "Are you new here, Lynda?"

"What?" She looked up from the order pad and tucked the pen into her pocket. "Yeah, I'm new, but my name's Cassidy, not Lynda. The owner told me to wear this until mine comes in. But she's not ordering it until after my first paycheck. She says most people don't stay around."

I had to agree with that, but Cassidy didn't need to know it. "Well, it's lovely to meet you, Cassidy. I'm glad you chose to work in South Cove."

"Actually I want to go south to LA to work. They get crazy tips, but it's so expensive. My boyfriend's working for a place in Bakerstown, so I looked there first. But no one was hiring." She glanced at her notepad. "Sorry, I'll go make you your milkshake."

I had a feeling Cassidy definitely wouldn't be here long enough to have her own name tag. I pulled a book out of my tote and got lost in the story. At least as lost as I could in a diner. When she finally brought me my fish and chips I inhaled them. I felt like I hadn't eaten in weeks.

"Jill, is that you?" Esmeralda hurried over to my booth.

I wiped tartar sauce off my chin and smiled. "What are you doing here?"

"Picking up chicken for the guys. They're eating dinner at the station because Greg just brought in a suspect. And we identified the victim. Greg said he had a little birdie that was helping him. I'm assuming that's you?"

I lowered my voice. "Was it Gentry Floods?"

She nodded. "How did you find that out?"

I looked around the almost empty dining room and leaned closer. "He was looking into Max Winter. So, is Max the suspect?"

Esmeralda mirrored my scan of the room. "You can't tell Greg I told you, but rumors fly fast here in South Cove. It's not Max Winter that Greg's looking at. It's Jeffrey Hargrove, his wife's lawyer. Can you believe it?"

I actually could because Jeffrey had been acting weird when I met him. Weird, and then kissing his employer. "So, Greg won't be home for dinner. How late is it?"

"It's four thirty." Esmeralda waved at Tiny, who had just brought two large bags out of the kitchen. "I thought you knew he wasn't coming home for dinner because you were here so late. He's been so busy today, maybe he forgot to let you know."

I wasn't worried that Greg hadn't texted me about dinner. Honestly, I'd been busy too. I sipped what was left of my milkshake. "Actually, I didn't even look at the clock. I hadn't had lunch, so I came here to eat. It's been a crazy day. But now that I have a little bit of time, maybe I'll run into Bakerstown for groceries tonight."

She frowned and looked back at the bags on the counter. "Look, I've got to get back to the station, but do you want me to stop by when I get off? I have a client coming at seven, but I could hang out for a bit."

I patted my book. "I'm fine. I've got a good book, and we really do need someone to go shopping. And Greg's busy with this case."

"If you're sure." Esmeralda didn't look like she believed I was fine.

I waved her away. "Go back to work and tell Greg I'm heading back into Bakerstown to get groceries. That way I won't have to go tomorrow after work. Can I get anything from the store for you?"

I finally got her to leave, taking the food and my message back to Greg. I did need to get groceries, and this was the perfect time to do it. When I got home from the store I'd grab a quart of ice cream and start reading through Max's construction plans. If they were as dry as I expected, Greg might find me asleep on the couch. Or maybe I'd find Gentry Flood's name on one of the property subcontractors' lists and I'd have the connection Greg needed to bring Max in for questioning rather than Jeffrey.

Chapter 15

Tuesday morning I woke up with a full refrigerator and cupboard, an empty ice cream carton, and a headache. Probably from the sugar high, but maybe from reading a stack of pages without seeing what I was looking for. Gentry Flood's name wasn't listed on any of the pages or in any of the contractors' listings. He might have owned or worked for one of the over two dozen subcontractors, but I would have to look up each company and hope Gentry had been enough of a bigwig to be on the website. If the company even had one.

I poured my coffee and sat at the table, hoping the magic liquid would do its work, and fast.

Greg came in from outside with Emma. "Whoa. You look like crap. Are you sure you want to go into work? Maybe you should call your aunt and have her sub for you."

I stared at him. "Why do you hate me?"

"I don't hate you, honey. What are you talking about?" He sat next to me and put his hand on my forehead, checking for a fever. "Well, you're not hot."

"You're not hot either. Are we done insulting each other?" I sipped my coffee after swiping his hand away from my head.

"You're in a mood. What's wrong and why don't you want to call your aunt?" He stood and took a bag of M&M's out of a box on top of the fridge. "Here. Eat some sugar. Maybe it will make you sweet."

"The saying is more accurate that it's the hair of the dog that bit me." But I shook a few into my hand and popped them into my mouth like they were pain pills. The chocolate burst into my mouth and did make me feel better. Somehow. "Anyway, I don't call my aunt to sub unless I'm dying and all the other baristas were in the car crash with me. She can be judgmental. And she'd guess I ate too much ice cream yesterday. You think Esmeralda can see secrets? My aunt has an uncanny way of seeing your deepest, darkest secrets. Especially when you're asking for a favor. Just don't ever do it."

He laughed and poured himself some coffee. "I think you're exaggerating, but I don't want to call your aunt either. You're sure you're okay? Maybe I should drive you in. At least that way you don't have to walk. I'm not sure you'd make it."

"Actually, I'm feeling better. Like I said, just too much ice cream last night. And a lot of reading boring, small-print contracts, looking for your victim's name." I pointed to the stack of papers on the counter. "And I got nada."

"That's the paperwork you got from the courthouse? From the person who knew Gentry?"

I didn't want to look at it, so I kept my gaze on the table. "That's the one. And I didn't say she knew Gentry. I said she had pulled the files and made copies for him, and he didn't come back with the fiftysome dollars. I think I got scammed."

"You're the one who took the chance. And it got me the name of my suspect. Doc compared dental records last night and it's him. So thank you for that. But why did you have to go back into Bakerstown for groceries last night? Why didn't you get them when you were in Bakerstown the first time?"

"Because believe it or not, grocery stores don't allow even good dogs like Emma inside. So I had to bring her home and go back. I didn't think I'd be gone so long the first time. But then the thing with Evie happened. Anything new on finding her ex?" I finished my coffee and stood to get a second cup. I still had time before I needed to leave. Especially if Greg was driving me.

"Actually, I had a good talk with him yesterday before your call and told him to leave Evie alone. He blustered, accused me of having an affair with her, and then agreed to leave her alone. But he insisted she would come crawling back to him. Sooner or later." Greg sipped his coffee. His gaze was a little distant, making me wonder what he'd actually said, but before I could ask, he spoke again. "He's just so convinced that Evie's his property, like a car or a house."

"Yeah, from what she said she didn't even question the way he treated her until he started being mean to Homer. Then her inner pet mommy jumped in and she realized how messed up their lives were." I smiled at the memory of our discussion. "Thank goodness for Homer."

"She would have gotten there. Evie's a strong woman." He glanced at the clock. "Are you letting me drive you to work?"

"Yeah, I'm just enjoying sitting here chatting with you. We've been too busy to do this since our trip out of town." I squeezed his hand. "Now that you have Gentry's name, are you going to be able to figure out why someone killed him?"

"I think it's going to be a lot easier. I have Jeffrey Hargrove at the station right now because Darla put the two of them together at her winery at least once. By the way, she says if you need her, all you have to do is call. She'll find someone to watch the Winery and she'll be right over. Why is she worried about you?"

"I'm not sure. But Esmeralda is having the same problem. You'd think I was a high school student alone at home with my parents off on a hunting trip. She's starting to freak me out a bit."

"Did you tell her that?" Greg got to the next step easily. I always hit every possible stop from A to Z, and then I'd start with the numbers.

"No, but I'm going to. I know she means well, but seriously."

"It's horrible having friends who care about you." He kissed me and then pointed to the clock. "We need to get going."

"Let me get my tote packed and I'll be ready. Can you make sure Emma's set up for the morning?"

He nodded. "I'll make sure my girl is fine for a half day alone. From the look she's giving me, you'd think we were taking off for a week."

"She likes having us home." I ran upstairs to grab a light jacket and the book I'd tried reading last night before I fell asleep. I was going to put this down as a DNR for myself and let someone else have a crack at it. It might have just been my mindset or it could be out of my wheelhouse for books, but I couldn't get into it, and I'd tried three different times. I grabbed my almost-finished blanket as well. I'd like to be done tomorrow so I could turn it in, but either way, I was going to start the new blanket with the new pattern Crissy was teaching us Wednesday. Crochet might not be my jam, but at least I wasn't horrible at it.

By the time Greg dropped me off at the shop, Crissy was already there, sitting at the table in front and working on her own blanket. "Sorry I'm late. I couldn't get going this morning."

Crissy nodded toward Greg's truck as he flipped a U-turn and went back to the police station. "If I had someone like that in my bed in the morning, I probably wouldn't leave the house either. You're a lucky woman."

I unlocked the door and flipped on the lights. I was a lucky woman and I knew it. My thoughts went to Evie and the way she'd looked yesterday. when she'd seen John's Land Rover. Why were some of us lucky and others had to fight to get out of bad relationships? "He's a good man and we're great together. I guess that's all you can ask for in a relationship, right? Do you want a pumpkin spice cookie? I heard Sadie dropped off a fresh batch yesterday with our regular order."

"Sounds perfect for a September morning. How's your blanket going? I've had several people wondering how you were fairing with the pattern." She sat on one of the stools, her credit card out of her wallet already to pay for her order.

"I'm kind of famous in town for not being able to craft. At all. So finishing this blanket is a pretty big goal for me." I started a second pot of coffee and poured a travel cup for Crissy and a large, ceramic cup for me. "I think I should be done this week. I was hoping for tomorrow, but I got sidetracked this weekend."

"I heard there was a guy trying to break into the coffee house yesterday." Crissy took the coffee from me and took a small sip. "I know it's hot, but I still haven't bought a coffee maker for the apartment. I should have insisted when I broke up with Phil that I got the espresso maker. That would have hurt him more than us breaking up, I think."

News traveled fast in South Cove. "Actually, it was more of a domestic disturbance. And Greg thinks he's got it handled, so you shouldn't worry."

Crissy blushed as I handed her the bag with the two cookies. "I'm pretty transparent, aren't I? It's just me over there in the apartment. If something happened, I wouldn't know what to do."

"Have you thought about getting a dog? Studies say that criminals avoid houses that have dogs. It doesn't have to be a big dog either. Just the sound of barking, I guess, makes them think twice about breaking in. There's a shelter in Bakerstown." I rang up her purchase and handed her back the credit card and receipt. "I know having Emma in the house makes me sleep better when the handsome cop is working late."

Crissy laughed. "I'll have to take that under advisement. I haven't owned a dog for years. My last one died at nineteen. Then I met Phil and he didn't like pets, so I didn't get a new dog. Maybe it's time to fix that error. And get a new espresso maker. Or maybe a handsome cop."

"But you'll still have to come to see me. I've enjoyed our morning visits." And as I thought about what I'd said, I realized it was true. When I first started Coffee, Books, and More, I didn't care if anyone came into the store. Then Aunt Jackie came into the business, and we started getting a lot of traffic. Now, I was making friends with my customers. And I knew most of their names. If they were repeaters.

"Of course I will. Where would I get my sugar fix? You know I'm not a baker." Crissy waved as she stepped away from the coffee bar. "See you tomorrow night. I've got some hot pink yarn set aside for you for the next project. And if you do three, we'll go with yellow."

I smiled as I got ready for my day. I turned on the stereo system, which I normally left off, and sang along with fun songs on the soft classic rock station. By the time my commuters started coming in, I was ready for them.

I'd made a plan to try to remember everyone's name; most of my baristas knew our customers better than I did. Well, at least their names. I could tell you everyone's order and, a lot of times, what they did for a living, but their name? Not so much. I'd made a point of calling everyone by their name when I gave them their coffee or, at worst, their credit card receipt back. And if they were cash customers, I'd bite the bullet and ask their name again, citing a faulty memory. Which was true.

Deek came in at eleven. I frowned and pointed to the clock. "You're early."

"Mom's been on my butt about cleaning my room. She doesn't get that I need to spend time writing this next book. If someone picks up the first one, I don't want to be one of those authors who can't deliver a book for years. I want to make some money with this career." He sank into a chair. "No offense meant to my current job."

"None taken." Honestly, if I didn't have the Miss Emily fund to smooth over the rough months at the bookstore, I might not be able to keep the shop going. Especially if something happened and I had to close for months. The thought had kept me up at nights before I had my slush fund. "So, you're here to write?"

"I'm going to be doing some character sketches. I learned this trick at the workshop last weekend and I'm anxious to try it out. I've kind of been doing it in my head, but now I have a structure." He stood and headed to the coffee bar. "Mind if I grab a coffee?"

"Not a problem." I held out a plate of the pumpkin spice cookies. "You probably need to taste test one of these to make sure you can sell them appropriately. By the way, Judith is amazing at selling. She's so natural at the art of the upsell. My aunt will be pleased. She's always trying to get me to learn how to do that. So, tell me your writer trick?"

"Thanks for the cookie." Deek leaned on the counter and set down his cup. As he talked, he waved the cookie around to emphasize his points. Finally, I got my own cookie. "You pick out someone in a crowded room, or a customer, and make up a story about their lives."

"So, someone you don't know?" I thought this game would be hard here at the bookstore because Deek seemed to know everyone.

"That's preferrable, but it could be someone you know. You just make up their story. Like there was this guy who came into the shop every day a few weeks ago. He'd buy a coffee, then write in this notebook. I stopped by and gave him a refill once, and his writing was dark and tight. You know, letters written really tight together? My description of him, in my head, was he was some sort of villain for the story. He kept watching the door, like he was waiting for someone. He came in every day at noon, then he'd leave about three. The next day, he'd repeat it. I wrote it from memory, including the brown leather jacket he wore every day and the shirt dress underneath without a tie. He always had two buttons undone. And he wore jeans. So maybe management, but not in some stuffy corporate job. Maybe he was in construction."

Deek kept talking and as I listened, I thought about the picture on Facebook for Gentry Floods. He'd worn a leather jacket with a dress shirt with an open neck.

It couldn't be. "What color was his hair?"

"The fictional character or the guy I based this on? He was blond in real life, but I felt that was too light for the dark character I was building. So in my story, he's dark hair, brown eyes. I'm not sure what color his eyes were in real life." He finished his coffee and sipped his coffee. "What, did you see the guy too?"

"Actually, kind of." I pulled out my phone and went to Facebook. I found his profile. "Do you think this is the guy?"

Deek squinted at the thumbnail. "It could be. Why?"

Instead of answering Deek, I dialed Greg's number. "I think Gentry spent some time here at the shop with Deek. Do you want to come over and interview him?"

I could hear the frustration in Greg's tone when he said he'd be right over. But it wasn't my fault my barista might have clues to the murder. I hung up and looked at the confused Deek. "Greg's coming by to talk to you. I'll stay later so you can get your hour of writing in, but first, I need you to talk to Greg about this guy. I think you saw the victim."

Chapter 16

Greg stayed late at work, but he sent me a text just before I went to bed. I frowned as I read the words, not sure what had led him to the action. I looked at Emma. "Greg said he signed us up for Pastor Bill's couples' finance class. I wonder what got him thinking about that. Are we doing two classes, then?"

Emma turned and hurried into the kitchen and checked her food level. I followed her and opened the door to let her out. "Don't worry about that. I won't let him change your food or put you on rations."

She didn't answer, just ran off the porch to do her business. Maybe she'd just been running to the door because it had been a while since I'd got up to let her out. I liked the idea of her worrying about her food, though, and I thought I'd use it with Greg in case we got in a fight about the class.

Sadie said she was attending the class that started up next month. It was on Wednesdays, so I was going to have to get my blankets done first. I had finished the first one and had it on the counter so I could take it to A Pirate's Yarn tomorrow night. Two more blankets. I put the yarn classes on the next two Wednesdays, then added our finance class for the next ten weeks.

Looking at the calendar made me smile. This was the first *us* activity since our engagement party, not counting our out-of-town trip. We were a real couple. Emma barked at the door, and we finished our nightly routine and headed upstairs.

The next morning Greg was gone again. I was beginning to think Esmeralda was right and he was ignoring me. More likely, with knowing the victim's name, the investigation had opened up. I knew Jeffrey was off the suspect list because he had accompanied Mrs. Winter to a fundraising event in Los Angeles that night and two days before and after. Not that he couldn't have left her there and driven back, but Greg had pictures of them at the event too close to the time Gentry was killed.

I had a little bit of time, so I pulled out my notebook and started writing down everything I knew about Mr. Floods. He had a horrible surname. I didn't write that down because that was only my opinion and I tried to keep the list objective. I wrote down the places he was seen. The Winery, Diamond Lille's, and my coffee shop. I tapped my pen on the paper and wrote, "So where was he staying? Or did he live close?" I wondered if Greg would tell me. If he was a contractor, that could be a tie to Max Winter.

So many questions with this investigation. Typically, I had a feeling for who the victim was by now. Gentry was as much of a ghost as he'd been when he stumbled into the police station, bleeding. I wrote down another question. "Where was he stabbed?" Toby hadn't heard a fight, or a scuffle outside the station. No one had reported one nearby. And as fast as Evie's encounter, well, shouting match with Becky had been reported, I found that hard to believe. Maybe he'd been dumped at the police station? Did they have cameras? They had to have some. Greg had put a camera on our house just a few months ago.

I put away the notebook and packed my tote. I gave Emma a quick hug after letting her out one last time. "Time to go make the doughnuts."

She looked at the stove, confused. Sometimes I thought my dog was a little too smart.

"It's a matter of speech," I tried to explain, but she'd already lost interest in our conversation and was heading back to her bed to sleep. I grabbed the two decorative pillows from the couch as I walked by and put them on the entry table. Emma could still get them if she was determined, but there was no need to make this bad habit easy on her. I locked the door and headed into town.

Crissy was sitting at the outside table when I arrived.

She stood, shoving her knitting into a bag. "Don't judge. I didn't have time to get into town to buy a coffee maker. And I hate buying online. It's always a little tight or too big. And then you have to figure out how to return it."

"I'm not complaining. I like seeing you in the morning." I unlocked the door and turned on the lights. "So, are you ready for tonight? I finished one blanket and I'm excited to get started on a second. I might not ever crochet again after doing these three, but it's been a blast."

"Now, don't give up so easily. My evil plan is to have you get hooked, and you'll need to buy all your yarn from me. Just like your evil, coffee lord domination plan." Crissy followed me into the coffee shop and pulled up a stool. "Actually, I feel blessed that Mary thought of this event. I've had more business the last week than I did the first full month I was open. I've gotten to know a lot of my neighbors. And we're helping out babies too. It's a total win-win."

"Well, I'm happy to be part of the fun." I started a second pot of coffee and then poured us each a cup. "Do you have time to chat a bit? I know you're probably swamped with the class tonight."

"I got most of it set up yesterday. Today's just about getting the yarn set out and bringing in chairs. Your aunt offered to donate the coffee and snacks again, but I told her I'd pay for the snacks and she could donate the coffee. You guys are really making me feel like I'm part of the community." She took the cup and then set it back down. "I need to tell you something."

"Okay, that sounds ominous." I sipped coffee, wondering what secret she was going to blurt out.

"No, it's just been bothering me. And since I called one of the business owners a homeless guy before, I'm trying to think before I judge."

I nodded. I'd been there. "You can only see things through the filter you have. You didn't know the history around Austin. Let's make a deal. If you're ever curious, come ask me. I'll tell you what I can and you can make the decision."

"Sounds perfect. Thank you, Jill." She sipped her coffee. "So, remember last week when I told you that woman was following Evie?"

I nodded but didn't say anything. I wanted her to feel comfortable and not cut her off by saying something she might take the wrong way.

"Anyway, I got the paper this morning, and I think I saw that same woman with the dead guy about a week ago. I was out on my balcony, working on the patterns for the baby blankets, and I heard voices over at your shop." She blushed. "Sometimes I can hear people chatting when they're sitting out at the tables. Usually, I tune it out, but the guy said something weird."

"What did he say?"

"He said the plan seemed simple enough and he didn't know why she wouldn't just let him do what he does best." She shook her head, trying to access the memory. "Or something like that. She responded that she wanted to try to trick her first. That it would be more fun her way. Does that even make sense? I didn't put the woman together with the one who was screaming at Evie until this morning, when I saw his picture. I think she was with this guy."

That didn't make any sense. Yet something about her description made me wonder what I had heard that night at the bed-and-breakfast. "You might want to go talk to Greg over at the police station if you really think he was talking to Becky."

"Do *you* really think so? I mean, it's dark. I know we have streetlamps, but I couldn't see him well. Don't you have cameras? Maybe you could check your footage?" Crissy looked up, hope shining on her face.

"Actually, that's too long ago. Our system dumps every two weeks to make room for the new data. If you'd come to me sooner, I could have checked the front camera." Whatever hope I'd seen in her face vanished with my words. "Really, if you think you saw him, you should tell Greg."

"I'll think about it." Crissy handed me her credit card, the subject now closed. "I'd better get going. Lots to do for tonight."

I rang up the coffee and charged her card. After she left a thought occurred to me. If she'd been up on her balcony like she said, how did Crissy overhear the couple talking? The conversation sounded like something Becky would say, but maybe Crissy was just trying to help Evie out? I grabbed my phone and texted a question to her.

Her answer came back immediately: *Yes, Becky talked about a new boyfriend. Why? Is someone else hanging around?*

Instead of answering her question, I called her. "Sorry to bother you, and no, no one else is hanging around. I was just wondering if you knew his name. Like we could be watching out for him, just in case."

"That's a pretty random just in case, but I'll trust your gut. However, I'm not going to be much help. She didn't tell me his name, just that he was in architecture and was working on a job near South Cove. His company sends him all over. She met him in New York. Which makes sense. Her last husband was in construction or development. Something like that. But she said they probably weren't going to last much longer. That he was getting clingy." She paused a minute. "Look, I hate to call Becky, but if you think this is important, I'd be glad to try to see if I could get his name."

"No, don't do that. I'm just trying to cover all the bases for you on this." I tried to lighten my voice, but inside I was scared. What if Becky had killed Gentry just to get him out of the way? "Are you okay to work tonight? Do we need to ask Toby to stop by during his shift?"

"I have his number on speed dial." Evie laughed. "Besides, Deek's been hanging out writing during my shift. He told me he wanted an excuse to have to sit his butt in a chair and if he goes home, he tends to play video games. So I'm good for the week. I'm sure John and Becky will give up when I sell this thing. Judith has three different houses ready to do an auction; I just need to say when and which one. I'm still doing some research to decide which auction house I prefer."

"Okay. Sounds like you've got a plan." The bell over the door rang and one of my commuters came inside. "Look, I've got to go. I guess you're not going to the yarn shop tonight?"

"No, I told Crissy I'd stop in early and pick up the new pattern and some more yarn. I'm going to hit my goal before the end of the month. It keeps me from eating when I'm home alone and nervous. Soon I'll have homework to do, but right now it's either crochet or eat a bag of chips." She sounded like she was moving around the apartment. "Sorry, you said you had to go. Chat later."

I hung up the phone and hurried to get Dr. Harris his coffee and sugar cookie. He always came in on Wednesdays and ordered the same thing: large black coffee and one sugar cookie. "I only have flower designs today, is that okay?"

"The design doesn't matter. It's gone before I get out of town." He took out his credit card. "How are things in the book world?"

We chatted for a few minutes before he left and my next regular arrived. The rest of the morning was filled with commuters, then a tour bus came into town. That kept me busy until Judith showed up at ten. She took over the coffee line and I went to the back and started refilling the dessert case. By the time I was done the crowd had left, and Judith and I leaned against the back counter, staring at the dining room, which looked like a small cyclone had touched down there.

"I don't think I said good morning when you came in." I leaned into the dessert case and took out two of the flower cookies. I held one out. "How are things going? Do you like the job?"

She took the cookie and laughed. "I love the job. Even when it's like this. I enjoy talking to people about books. I love working the coffee bar. And it's just enough physical activity that I don't feel guilty sitting and writing for hours when I'm not here."

"Well, that's great. Deek told me I need to work out more with weights. I've been meaning to add in a session a week, but it's been busy." I finished my cookie and grabbed a bin, a spray bottle of cleaner, and a rag. "I'll get this cleaned up for you and Deek."

Judith followed me with a second bin. "I'm here to help. I'll get the dishware and silver and you can get the paper stuff."

We worked together until the dining room was back to normal. I ran the small vacuum over the area and then went back to the coffee bar, where Judith was just finishing stacking the dishwasher. She turned it on and then studied the room. "Ready for the next tour bus. Can you believe a group of quilters from Omaha could be so messy?"

"I can, and after a few seasons you'll be more open-minded. Everyone can be messy." I rolled my shoulders. "I guess we should start on the shift closing list."

"You go sit and read. I'll do the list." Judith took the clipboard from underneath the counter. "Remember, I'm using this as my cardio for the day."

Holding up my hands in surrender, I laughed. "Don't worry about it. I won't steal your exercise time. Are you coming to the yarn shop tonight?"

"I wouldn't miss it. I'm looking forward to meeting more South Cove residents. So many people have asked me if I was attending. I feel like part of a big family." Judith grabbed the vacuum again. "I'll run this around the bookcases since you already did the dining room."

By the time Deek arrived Judith had finished both the closing shift list as well as the shift opening list and I had gotten deep into a women's fiction book that had just released. I'd been meaning to read it before release day, but I hadn't had the time. Having one more employee was going to open up a lot of time in my day, especially when Toby came back for his shifts.

I grabbed my tote and said goodbye just as a wave of customers came in. I paused, catching Deek's gaze, but he shook his head and waved his fingers, shooing me out of the shop. I guess I wasn't needed. My baristas were all grown up. I wondered if this was the empty nest feeling mothers got when their kids left home. Although if Deek was any example, kids didn't leave home anymore. They just moved into the basement.

Josh Thomas was sweeping the sidewalk outside his shop when I walked by. I smiled and nodded. "Good afternoon."

"Miss Gardner." He paused his sweeping. "I was going to call you about the woman who was yelling at your tenant the other day. But I saw Toby here, so I figured you were already alerted. And she hasn't come back since that incident, so I assume it was taken care of?"

"As far as I know, yes, but if you see her again, would you call Esmeralda or Greg? You don't have to call the emergency line, but it would be helpful to know if she's back in town again." I couldn't believe it. For once, my neighbor and antiques store owner Josh Thomas was going to be a help rather than just a pain in my side.

"I almost called a few weeks ago when the woman was sitting outside with that man every night. I mean, I know you can't just drag those tables and chairs inside, but it does bring out a certain type once the legitimate businesses close for the day. Maybe you could take in the chairs at least."

And once again we were back to it being my fault. "I'll consider that."

"That's all I want, some consideration for the issue." He started sweeping again.

I started to leave, then stopped. Josh's report was a lot like what Crissy had said. "Wait, you saw Becky earlier than last week with a man?"

"If that screeching woman's name is Becky, then yes, that's what I'm saying. They were outside your shop every night for at least five days. I can't verify every day because I had an engagement one night, but the other nights they were there. I told myself if they showed up one more night, I was going to call the station. But they weren't there, and I didn't see that horrible woman again until the night she yelled at your employee." He leaned on the broomstick a little. "Is there something going on I should know about?"

"No, I was just wondering." Now *I* needed to talk to Greg, but not until I went back to my own type of investigation, internet searches. "I've got to go let out my dog. See you at the next meeting."

"I'll send you my agenda items tomorrow so you can get them on the schedule," Josh called after me.

I kept walking, hoping I could say the wind was keeping me from hearing him. And maybe he wouldn't remember that there was no wind at all right then.

I let Emma out as soon as I got home and then opened my laptop. Becky didn't have a Facebook page. Probably because the mean girl didn't have any friends she could invite to like her.

Then I went back to Gentry's page. I scrolled through a bunch of off-color and totally inappropriate jokes. Most of which weren't even that funny. Finally, I hit pay dirt. He'd mentioned a girl he was dating. He posted that she was hot enough to burn and that she had an edge he loved. No wishy-washy girls for me, he claimed.

Well, if that didn't describe Becky, I didn't know what would. And when one of his friends challenged him about why she wasn't chiming in, he told the guy that she wasn't on the social media platform because, unlike him, she had more important things to do with her life.

From where I sat, that was less of a jab at the original questioner and more at Gentry himself. I wondered if there wasn't trouble in paradise after all.

I shot Greg the link to Gentry's Facebook page and then asked if he could talk.

My phone rang as soon as I finished the text.

"Where are you?"

Not the greeting I'd expected, but okay. "I'm home watching Emma chase rabbits. Why?"

"Just wondering. Especially when you sent me that link. So, what's so interesting about a Facebook page?"

"He had a mean girlfriend. And I've heard from two people today who said Becky had been hanging out at the tables by the shop late at night with some guy. Crissy thinks it was Gentry. Josh just thinks they both should be arrested. Or maybe that I should be arrested for not taking the tables and chairs in every night. But he verified Crissy's story."

"Maybe she was waiting for Evie. Didn't Evie say this sister-in-law was a night owl?"

I thought about that, then shook my head, even though Greg couldn't see me. "That doesn't work."

"Why?" I could hear the tiredness in that one word.

I threw my last card on the table and hoped it was enough. "They were seen before Becky reached out to Evie about visiting. Greg, I think she and Gentry were stalking Evie."

Chapter 17

Greg wasn't coming home for dinner. Of course after I threw another kink into his murder investigation, he might not ever come home again. I pushed the idea away and called Amy. It was a long shot, but maybe she'd be up for grabbing an early dinner at Lille's. I didn't feel like being alone right now. My mind was wandering in too many directions. And none of them were good.

"South Cove City Hall, may I help you?" Amy's chipper voice made me feel a little more connected. Greg had considered my information as me putting my nose in someplace it didn't belong. And even though his words weren't mean, his tone told me he wasn't happy that I was the one to bring him this news. It wasn't my fault I saw the connections when others didn't.

"Amy, hey, it's Jill. Do you have dinner plans with Justin?" I crossed my fingers just in case.

"Nope. The boy has a meeting with his history department chair. If I didn't know he adored me, I'd be suspicious of all these night appointments. At least most of them he does over Zoom at the house. This time the chair is taking him out to dinner at some fancy restaurant. Hopefully, it's about his tenure. I so want him to be happy here, and for us not to have to move to Nebraska." Amy chattered on about the cons of the newlyweds moving, which mostly centered on how far away from an ocean and surfing it was. "Sorry, I got off on a tangent. I take it you're on your own for dinner too. Want to meet at Lille's at five?"

"You got it. And thanks. I need a distraction."

"Really? What's going on? Typically, you're all happy couple. Is there trouble in paradise? Is it about the investigation? What did you do?"

"Why do you think I did something?" I glanced over and Emma whined. "Okay, yeah, it's typically me, but I just want some company tonight. Five will work great. I'll take Emma for a run and then get showered and meet you at Lille's."

"Okay, Trouble. But I expect a full report of your couple woes. Even if you have to make something up. It will make me feel better about dumping on you all the time." Amy greeted someone who'd come into the office. "Got to go. See you soon."

When she hung up I shot a look at Emma. "Traitor. You know you're my dog and not Greg's, so if we break up someday, you're with me."

Emma covered her eyes with her feet. I didn't think she liked that plan.

"Anyway, do you want to go running before I meet up with Aunt Amy for dinner?" Greg wouldn't be happy, but he wasn't happy with me right now anyway. Besides, he'd already talked to John.

She uncovered her eyes and ran to the door where her leash hung.

"I take it that's a yes." I rubbed her head. "Give me a minute to change and we'll get out of here."

A run would do me good. Exercise, food, and then the yarn shop group. What else could a girl want?

Emma and I didn't see another soul on the beach. Well, not unless you counted the seagulls she chased away from the water. I liked to think she was saving them from drowning, but really, I think she just liked to see them fly away. Emma considered the beach an extension of her yard. She shared the area well with humans, but when it came to birds, dogs, and other wildlife, she thought they should stay away.

As we ran, I thought about the connection between Becky and Gentry. Had she been his girlfriend? And if so, what had they been doing hanging out at the shop? Were they trying to catch Evie when she took Homer for a walk? Just a quick, unplanned meeting when Becky would happen to mention Dad's clock? I hadn't liked Becky from the first time I heard her, talking to what must have been John on the phone at the bed-and-breakfast. If she knew Gentry, could she have killed him? Or had they gotten into a fight that went bad? It could explain her irrational behavior around Evie. Sometimes murders were just accidents from heated arguments. No more and no less than that. Maybe she thought he'd be okay, so she left him at the police station. Then she drove back to Apple Valley to the bed-and-breakfast so she'd have an alibi, just in case.

Plausible, but cold if that was what happened. She'd been calm when I'd met her the next morning before she checked out. And where was she staying now? Why check out of Apple Valley when South Cove was just a short drive away?

"I'm seeing zebras now when I hear hoofbeats," I muttered as we finished our run and headed to the stairs to the parking lot.

Emma lifted her head and stared at me, a question in her eyes. I couldn't tell exactly what the question was, but I thought it was the same one Amy had almost asked. Was I crazy?

I scratched her back and we jogged up the stairs, although I had to admit she had a lot more energy that I did. "Let's go home and I'll feed you dinner. Then you'll need to entertain yourself until either I or Greg gets home later. Just don't eat the pillows."

We made our way up the hill to the house. I'd heard somewhere that people, and maybe dogs, never heard the "don't" part of a sentence. So, if you wanted someone to do something, you just told them to do it. If you didn't want them to do something, you just didn't tell them. Or phrased the sentence differently. Just in case, before I left to meet Amy I put the sofa cushions in the office and shut the door. I'd just bought new ones and the people at the home furnishings place were beginning to know my name.

When I got to the diner Evie was just leaving with a to-go bag in one hand and Homer's leash in the other. I leaned down and gave him a rub under the chin. "If it isn't my second-favorite dog and his owner. How are you, Evie?"

"Good. I'm meeting Judith before she leaves and we're having dinner. I wanted to thank her for her help, but she has a writers' meeting tonight with Deek and a few others, so takeout will have to do." She held up the bag. "Of course, when Tiny's cooking it doesn't matter where you eat, it's always amazing."

"Isn't that the truth." I nodded to the diner, where I could see Amy was already inside and talking to Carrie. "I decided since Greg's still at work I'd take advantage and meet up with Amy for dinner. It must be a theme today."

"I appreciate everything she's done for me. If I'd just given up the clock when Becky first asked, I'd be out a lot of money. Money that John Senior wanted me to have, not his greedy kids. I suspect even he knew that I wouldn't stay in the marriage forever." She glanced at her watch. "I'd better get going if I'm going to be done before I have to take over for Deek. I got him a hamburger too. Hopefully work's slow so he can eat while he's finishing up his shift."

"Tell everyone I said hi and to have a good evening. Like I said, if there's any trouble at the shop, call it in. I'll be at the yarn shop, so I'll stop in before I head home." Something was bothering me and I couldn't put my finger on it. Maybe it was all the talk about people hanging out at the outside tables.

"I'll be fine." She smiled and headed up the sidewalk to the main part of town and the bookstore.

I watched her for a couple of seconds, then headed inside to meet Amy. Carrie stood at the booth, talking to Amy. They both looked up as I walked in. "Hi, guys."

"Everything all right with Evie?" Amy nodded to the window. "I saw you talking with her."

"Just small talk. Although I'll be happy when she finishes selling that clock and she's not a target for her ex-husband or ex-sister-in-law." I scooted over in the booth and picked up the menu, which I knew by heart. "How are things, Carrie?"

"Good. But I think Evie's got some trouble heading her way. Lille said she told Greg about that guy who was killed and how he used to eat here. A lot."

"Yeah. She was at the station one day when I stopped in. What does that have to do with Evie?" I set down the menu.

"She was here with him a couple of times. I thought you already knew that." Carrie heard her name being called from the kitchen. "Tiny's got an order up for me. Iced tea for you?"

I nodded and watched her hurry away. Then I turned to Amy. "Evie didn't mention knowing the dead guy."

"Gentry. We should call him by his name, not 'the dead guy,'" Amy corrected me.

"Whatever. I can't believe she didn't say anything." I glanced at my watch.

"You won't have time before the class."

I looked up at her. "What?"

"I know what you're thinking. You want to stop by to ask Evie about Gentry. You won't have time before class, but as soon as it's over, I'll go over to the shop with you. Just in case Evie actually killed the guy. It's a long shot, but I'd rather not lose my best friend just to go home to an empty apartment and wait for my man to show up. Besides, if she is a murderer, I'll miss all the fun if I go home."

Carrie brought back my tea and took our orders. "I'd stay and chat, but as usual, I'm up to my eyeballs in alligators since Lille hasn't hired anyone. Or anyone who stayed, that is. I swear, I'm going to do my own hiring and she can just live with who I choose. Anything would be better than this."

After she walked away I sipped my tea. "I should have gotten a milkshake. It feels like that kind of night."

When we got to the yarn shop the place was packed. I bought my yarn and picked up my instructions for the next blanket. Then I dropped off my completed project on the table next to a pile of beautiful blankets. All prettier than the next, and all of them better crafted than mine. But it was done, and I'd made it. I tried to feel good about that. I checked off a box by my name on the flip chart and went to find Amy, who was supposed to be saving me a seat.

When I found her, she was sitting next to Darla, who was chatting with Judith. Amy popped up to go get her supplies and I sat down, putting my stuff on her chair. I turned to Judith. "Evie said you had a writer thing tonight with Deek."

Judith looked confused. "No, that's tomorrow night. She must have gotten confused. I just had dinner with her. She's such a sweetheart."

"Yeah, I know. I saw her at Lille's." I nodded to Darla. "How are things at the Winery?"

"Perfect. Matt's brought in a live band for the weekend and we're getting a ton of reservations for dinner on the outdoor patio. He's amazing at the marketing part of the job."

I thought from the glow on Darla's cheeks that Matt was amazing at a lot of things, especially those that kept my friend happy. "Sounds fun. If Greg ever catches the killer, maybe we can come down some night."

"So, things aren't going well?" Darla's eyes lit up. "Maybe if you walked me through what you know, we could brainstorm."

"Nope, I'm not playing investigation with you." I nodded to an empty chair. "Judith, grab that one and bring it over here so you can sit with us."

When she snared it just before another woman I grinned and gave her a thumbs-up. Leaning over, I said, "Nice snatch," when she returned.

"It's all in the swoop and grab." Judith sat down. "It helps that I'm old enough to be her grandmother. They tend to let me have my way. And I've got big news I just told Evie. The clock? It belonged to an old Hollywood star. That's going to make it worth even more at auction. There's already an interested party who wants to preempt the auction. Evie could get enough to pay cash for a house. Or darn close."

My hands were sweating. I didn't want to ask, especially because it could be a total coincidence and wasn't really happening, but I did anyway. "Who's the film star?"

"You won't believe it. Vivien Leigh! There's a local collector who has an open call out to all the auction houses for anything that's even rumored to be from Ms. Leigh. This clock is verified as part of her estate." Judith set up the yellow, green, and pink yarn on her lap for her project. "Everything's coming up roses for our Evie."

"If you don't count the years she spent in an unhappy marriage," Darla reminded Judith. "Or maybe you didn't know that."

"Sorry, you're right. I've heard rumors." Judith glanced over at me and then averted her gaze.

Crissy stood at the front of the class and clapped her hands together several times.

Saved by the bell. I was glad the conversation had been interrupted. It was getting a little uncomfortable for Judith. And I got uncomfortable when others were feeling that way. I thought about the clock and wondered if Beth was the "interested buyer." It would make sense. But then again, why was all of this so interconnected? Greg suspected Jeffrey had killed Gentry. Now, there was a connection between him and Becky, which made a connection to the clock and Evie, which brought us back to Beth.

Amy nudged my leg with her own and I realized that Crissy was demonstrating the new stitch and I was lost in my thoughts. I shook away the circular mess my thoughts had become and focused on Crissy and the new pattern. This time the hook felt more natural in my hand and my stitches were more even. Amy looked over and nodded. "This is really good. I can't believe we finally found a craft that works for you."

"I know. I told you I took a class in high school with all the homecrafts right? My teacher taught us knitting, crocheting, cross-stitching, and even quilting. But I really liked the crochet segment. We made hot pads for the kitchen. Aunt Jackie said they were passable."

Amy cracked up. "From your aunt that's high praise."

"I know." I looked around for where my aunt was hanging out. I hadn't seen her working on a blanket, but I knew she probably had already completed ten and had started another batch, just in case someone else, like me, didn't meet their quota. She was over with Mary, talking to Crissy. I waved at her and she nodded. Then her eyes widened and she pointed to the door.

I turned to see Toby Killian standing in the doorway, scanning the crowd. When he saw me, his shoulders dropped and he waved me over.

I set my stuff down, pulling the yarn loop larger as I tucked it in my tote bag. "Amy, save my seat, but if I'm not back in a few, I'm probably not coming back."

Amy looked up from a turn she was trying to navigate on the blanket. "Wait, what are you talking about? Why wouldn't you come back? Are you sick?"

I looked over at Darla, but she seemed focused on a conversation with Judith and wasn't looking my way. I dropped my voice and pointed at Toby. "He's here to see me and I don't think it's just to say hi."

I made my way through the crowd and a few people glanced over at the door as I approached. Maybe they'd just think it was a bookstore issue. A hand grabbed my arm and I looked down at a woman from one of the art galleries. She attended the business-to-business meetings a lot but, typical me, I didn't remember her name. Her face, her coffee, her business, but not her name.

"Everything all right?" she asked quietly.

"I think so. He's probably just checking in for next week's schedule. You know Toby moonlights with my coffee shop, right?" I smiled and hoped it looked easy and not fake.

The woman dropped her grip and nodded. I could see her relax with my words. "That's right, I'd forgotten about that. I should know that running a business is a twenty-four seven thing, right?"

I laughed and nodded. Then I hurried over to Toby and pointed to the door. "Let's talk outside. There are too many people listening."

"Smart idea." Toby took my arm and led me away from the yarn shop and across the street toward the bookstore.

"What's going on?" I asked when we were out of earshot. "Is everything okay?"

"There's a problem at the bookstore. Evie was attacked."

Chapter 18

"She was what?" I hurried across the street to the door to the shop. I tried to pull it open, but it was locked.

Toby caught up with me and pulled out his keys. "Hold on a minute, let me open the door. I locked it to keep people out while I was gone. Anyway, she's fine. Greg just wanted me to let you know what happened before someone saw something and worried you."

"Well, I am worried." I waited for Toby to open the door, then rushed inside to where Evie sat with Greg next to her. "Are you okay? What happened? Were we robbed?"

Greg stood up and put his arm around me. "Hold on, slugger, let us answer one question before the rest come flying out. Yes, Evie's all right. A little shaken up and we probably should close the bookstore for the night, but no one got hurt."

"What happened?" I met Evie's gaze, trying to slow my own breathing now that I knew she wasn't hurt. She looked scared, though, and I'd never seen her look so scared.

"Becky. She came into the bookstore and started yelling at me. Saying I knew the clock was worth money and I should give it to her and John. That I wasn't being fair." Evie shook her head. "I shouldn't have engaged. I knew Toby was coming over for some coffee because he'd called earlier and said he'd be in soon. But when she said I wasn't fair, something inside just broke, and I told her exactly what I thought of her and her brother. Well, she jumped at me and took me down to the floor. Toby must have come in then because the next thing I knew, he was pulling her off me."

"I'm so sorry this happened." I shrugged out of Greg's arms and pulled over a chair. "She's a horrible person."

"That's true." Evie rubbed her arms, then smiled, "At least I know where she's going to be tonight."

"And longer if I can charge her with assault and maybe some other things." Greg put his notebook in his pocket. "I've got to go back and do some paperwork on this. But I think I'll wait to question her until the morning. I'm sure I smelled alcohol on her when Tim took her to the station. It's in her best interests to sober up before talking to a police officer."

"That's going to make her spitting mad, staying in the jail all night." Evie stopped and then nodded. "Oh, that's your plan. You want her mad so she talks without thinking."

"That's the idea. I want to find out if she really did know Gentry. I want to spring that on her so she reacts to my knowing rather than just clamming up." Greg leaned over and kissed me. "Sorry, I might be late tonight."

"That's okay. I wasn't expecting you tonight anyway." I held up my tote. "And I have a new blanket pattern to play with."

"Jill, I'm sorry about this. I hate having my personal life affect work," Evie said after Greg and Toby left the shop.

I'd relocked the door and turned over the "Closed" sign, now we were just doing the closing tasks before I headed home. "You didn't bring this to work. She attacked you here. There's nothing for you to be sorry for. Are you sure you don't want to go upstairs? I'd be freaking out if something like that happened to me."

"That's one of the reasons I don't want to go upstairs. I am freaking out. I'm just glad she's locked up. She's such a dreadful person." Evie rubbed her arms like she was cold. "I'm going to be looking over my shoulder when I take Homer out tonight."

"I could wait around and go with you." I rinsed out the rag I'd been using to clean tables and hung it on the sink. "We're done here anyway."

"I'll be fine. If I let her get in my head, I'll regret it." Evie took a cookie out of the case and broke it in half. "You want part?"

I took the half. I had to. It was Sadie's chocolate chip surprise. Besides, I was saving Evie from having to eat the entire cookie. "I can see that. But if you want to talk, I'll be home alone tonight."

"I'm sorry about that too." Evie shook her head. "I've been saying sorry a lot lately."

"No need for that one; Greg was already working late." I thought about his irritation with me when I told him about the connection between Becky and Gentry. "And anyway, her showing up tonight saved him from having to go find her. I guess since she attacked you it's not a stretch to say she could have killed someone in a fit of rage."

"Yeah, but I don't think she'd go that far. Hurt someone. Make them pay. Maybe even torture someone with phone calls and pranks, but murder? That's another level. I'd hate to think that she has that in her. Not really." Evie turned off the lights and we walked to the office.

I was leaving through the back door, and then I'd sweep around to Main Street using the walkway through my building and Antiques by Thomas. I didn't want to walk the alleyway tonight, even if the light hadn't quite left the sky. I left her at the door, but before she shut it, I said, "That's what they always say when they find the serial killer next door. He was weird, but not that weird."

"You're twisted." Evie smiled and waved. "Thanks for saving me."

"I didn't save you, Toby did." I hurried out to the main street, then tucked my tote under my arm. The class was still in session over at the yarn shop and I could have gone back in, but I didn't want to answer questions. Especially not from Darla. That woman could smell a story.

My phone rang. "Hello?"

"Are you going home?" my aunt asked.

I glanced over at the yarn shop. She sat outside on a bench, watching me as we talked. "I think so. I closed the bookstore early, just letting you know."

"I saw that. I've been watching since you left with Toby. Everything okay?" Aunt Jackie sounded tired.

"Yeah. Kind of. Evie's sister-in-law—well, ex-sister-in-law—came in yelling and then, when Evie stood up for herself, she jumped her. Luckily, Toby was there, and he pulled her off Evie. She's over at the station now. Greg's letting her calm down." I hit the high points on what my aunt would want to know.

"Is Evie okay?"

Her question surprised me, but then I felt bad for assuming all she'd want to know was about the business. "She's shaken up. But physically she's fine."

"I bet you're worn out too. Go home and put your feet up. Maybe make some hot cocoa. Cuddle with that dog of yours. I suspect Greg won't be there for a while."

"No, he's tied up." I rolled my shoulders. "I'm going to walk home now."

"Why don't I stay on the phone with you until you get there? Just in case." My aunt nodded across the street at me. "We can talk about the treat situation."

I started walking. "The treat situation?"

"You realize our costs have gone up five percent this last year, and we haven't raised our prices at all."

My aunt went on to tell me all about the numbers for the last year. A feat I was impressed by because she was doing it from memory. When I got home Emma barked as I put the key in the lock.

"Sounds like you're home. I'm going back into the yarn shop. Lock the door."

"Yes, ma'am," I said to dead air. She'd hung up on me. I followed Emma outside and sat on the swing watching her. I felt bad for Evie. Someone she'd called family until last year had hurt her. Or tried to hurt her. No matter how crazy my aunt made me, I knew she'd never try to hurt me.

My phone rang again. Everyone was checking in with me tonight. "Hello?"

"Jill, it's Evie. I just wanted to thank you again for being so understanding about tonight's incident. I should have just ignored her or told her I was calling the police, but I let her get into my head." Evie sighed, and I heard a teapot going off. "I guess I'm not as okay with the divorce and dissolution of the family ties as I told my therapist last month when I canceled my future appointments."

"It's fine. You're not to blame here. You're just standing between them and what they want. To me, they sound like a bunch of spoiled children who want all the toys, even if they don't belong to them." The night was coming on and it was getting dark on the porch because I hadn't turned on the outside lights. I snapped my fingers and Emma came running to the door. "I hear your teapot going off. I'm going to make myself some hot cocoa. I keep whipped cream in the house just for nights like this."

Evie laughed, and the sound wasn't forced. Maybe she was calming down a bit. "I'm sticking to no-calorie tea. Working at the bookstore puts me way too close to cookies and cakes and all the other stuff I want but don't really need. Jill, you think I'm right about not giving in to John and Becky, don't you?"

"Yes. The gift was to you. Not to them. I think your ex-father-in-law wanted to make sure you were taken care of, especially because he couldn't count on his son to be fair in the divorce. Just get the clock sold and buy your house so we can get on with life here. I don't think Becky will be showing up in town anytime soon, but that means your ex might step up his intimidation plan." I made myself a single serving of cocoa and piled whipped cream on the top.

"I was just feeling a little comforted. Now you have me checking my locks again."

I sat at the table with my cocoa. "That was not my plan. But you can't let your guard down. I'm glad the clock is at the station with Greg."

"Me too. I'd hate to have it here with me. I'd never be able to leave the apartment without wondering if I'd be robbed."

After I hung up with Evie a thought occurred to me. I texted Greg, but instead of answering my question, he called me.

"Seriously? You think I'd leave an expensive clock out where one of my prisoners or their visitors could just walk in and grab it? Honey, do you really think I'm an idiot?" At least his tone was gentle.

"No, but I was thinking after I talked to Evie right now that maybe this was a plan to get someone inside the station to snatch the clock. I just didn't think the plan through." Now *I* felt like an idiot.

"Actually, I'd already thought about that scenario. I've told Toby no one comes in the station tonight. And I pulled Tim in too. If this was Miss Marshall's plan, she's going to be surprised at how seriously we take security around here. The clock is safe. Look, I've got to go. If I don't finish this paperwork, I'll never be home."

"Thanks for easing my mind."

He chuckled. "At least I know you're thinking through what could happen. This is a step up from when you started sticking your nose in my investigations."

"Hey, that's harsh," I complained.

"But maybe a little true?" He chuckled. "See you at home. I promise I'll be home soon."

I glanced at the clock. It was already nine. I would have just been getting home from the event at A Pirate's Yarn. I should try to head to bed, but I was too wound up after the incident. I went into the living room and turned on the television. Scrolling through the guide, I finally found a rom-com that had just started. Emma jumped on the couch and cuddled with me as we tried to get lost in the story.

* * * *

The next morning the smell of bacon frying woke me, and I hurried to get ready so I could have breakfast with Greg. The good thing about him getting lost in his investigations was eventually, when he was out of things to do, he would cook. Cooking for him was like my running. We needed the time to think things through. But with his cooking I got amazing food to eat. Which made me need to run more.

Emma was downstairs on her bed, watching Greg cook. I rubbed her head. "Hey, girl, I see you abandoned me for Greg again."

"I'm pretty sure it's not me she chose over you. I think it's the bacon." He kissed me and handed me a cup of coffee. "You were asleep by the time I got in, so I didn't wake you, but I had some news."

"You found Gentry's killer?" I took the coffee and curled up on one of the kitchen chairs. It was nice just having him in the house.

"I wish. No, I had a visitor at the station last night." He filled a couple of plates with eggs, bacon, and hash browns and set the food on the table. Then he refilled his coffee cup and sat down with me.

"And?" The food made my stomach growl and I picked up a slice of just-like-I-liked-it, crispy bacon. "O M G. He didn't show up, did he?"

"If you mean the brother, John Marshall, who shouldn't have even known his sister had been arrested since she didn't have time for a call yet? Give the girl a gold star." Greg ate a strip of bacon. "He was shocked I wouldn't let him inside. He said he was going to call his lawyer, but I didn't hear from Toby, so I guess his lawyer doesn't work nights."

"You seriously mean they planned this entire thing, thinking you'd have the clock out in the open for him to just walk away with?"

"Looks that way. Which means I might be able to charge John Marshall with a few things when I get his sister to talk this morning."

I filled my fork with potatoes and scrambled eggs. "How are you going to do that?"

"If she lawyers up, I'm going to tell her the charges, including this plan to rob the station and add up the years. That might make her want to throw her brother under the bus. She offered to provide physical comfort last night if I let her go. That's going into the charges too. Bribing a police officer with those kind of favors is a form of prostitution, right? I need to look some things up this morning before I call her into an interview room."

"I like the idea that maybe this will get them to leave Evie alone, but you need to ask about Gentry too."

Greg didn't answer, he just kept eating.

"Greg? Did you hear me?"

He looked up from his plate. "Did I hear you try to tell me how to do my job? Yes, dear, I heard you."

"I'm not..." I stopped, because actually, I *had* been telling him what to do and how to do it. "Sorry, I'm just worried about Evie."

"Evie told me that this auction if it's going to happen will be on Saturday, so we just have to get through a few more days. And I don't think either John or Becky Marshall is going to be hanging out in South Cove for at least the next few days. Hopefully, they'll just cross this town completely off their list. I don't like having visitors like them." He finished his eggs and glanced at the clock. "I'd better go relieve Toby. I bet he's beat. I'm sure she wasn't quiet last night, thinking about how she could clean up her life."

As he went upstairs to get ready for the day, I finished my breakfast, then opened my laptop. I had a few minutes before I needed to head into work. I still wondered if there was anything that would connect Becky to Gentry. Maybe she'd posted on his Facebook page. Or if I was lucky, there was a picture of the two of them together. That would give Greg a little more power to his questions.

I opened the page and scrolled down. There was a new post from a woman with a picture of her and Gentry. Not Becky, but the words caught my eye. When Greg came down I showed him the post. "Apparently Gentry had been dating this woman, and now she thinks he ghosted her for his ex-wife. She says she won't be around to pick up the pieces a second time when Becky blows him off for another guy."

"Well, it's not admissible evidence, but you're thinking Gentry was married to Becky? Did Evie know this?" He snapped a picture of the post with his phone. "I may need to chat with your barista today as well."

Well, this had taken a turn I hadn't expected. What had Evie known about Gentry? And why hadn't she told Greg about his connection to Becky sooner? I hated it when my snooping got people I liked in trouble.

Chapter 19

It wasn't a surprise to see Crissy waiting for me when I arrived to open the bookstore. She tucked her blanket into her tote and followed me inside.

"How did the class go? I'm sorry I had to leave early. I think I can follow the pattern, but if I have questions, can I stop by?" I asked as I turned on lights and made my way back to the coffee bar.

"Of course. That's what I'm here for. Was everything okay? I saw the police officer come and take you out of the class." Crissy climbed on the stool and waited for her coffee.

"That police officer is also one of my baristas. He needed to talk to me about the shop." I wondered how much to say, but I knew the rumor mill would be active today and she'd find out sooner or later. I poured a cup of coffee and handed it to Crissy. "Evie was working last night and had one of her former relatives come by and make a scene. Toby was checking on her and found them fighting. He needed me to make the call on closing early."

"Oh no. Is Evie all right? She didn't get arrested for the fight, did she?" Crissy asked, wide-eyed.

Leave it to Crissy to see the negative first. And no, Evie hadn't been arrested, but she might have more issues now that I pointed out something she'd been hiding to Greg this morning. But instead of letting my mouth run with my thoughts, I just shook my head. "Evie's fine. She was a little shaken up, so we closed up about an hour early. I didn't feel up to coming back to the class, so I went home and crashed."

"Well, I don't blame you. Emotional scenes like that drain me too. I had to listen to my parents fight all the time, so I don't like to hear even a minor quibble now." Crissy sipped her coffee. "Look, I appreciate your honesty in letting me know what's going on in town. I can tend to obsess about things and my mind always goes to the worst case scenario first. But today's another day, right? And since I had such a great sales day yesterday, I'm having three cookies today."

"You know how to party." I grabbed a sack and moved to the dessert case. "Which three?"

"Surprise me. And give me three different ones. I need to expand my horizons. At least in the food department." She dug in her purse for her wallet while I picked out the cookies. Then she handed me her credit card. "You know, I might not get a coffee maker. I'm enjoying this time with you immensely."

"I'm not open Sunday and Monday during the winter." I took her card and rang up the purchases.

"Okay, then, scratch that thought. I'd be a deranged person by the time you reopened. I'll go to Bakerstown on Sunday and get a coffee maker. I need to get new towels and a shower curtain for the apartment anyway."

After Crissy left I took a chance and tried to call Evie, but the call went to voice mail. A sign that she was probably already talking to Greg. If Gentry had been her brother-in-law, why didn't she say something? My commuters started arriving and I put the question away and got into my day.

When Deek arrived I realized I'd been busy all morning. I hadn't done any of the shift work and, worst, I hadn't had any quiet time to read. I had a book report due for Deek's newsletter and I hadn't finished it. I had plenty of books to choose from because I'd gotten several read over the miniholiday, but I needed to write three book reports a month. And I'd only been averaging two. Not the kind of example I wanted to set for my employees. I waved at him. "Hey, I'll get you that book review this week. Maybe the next couple of days will be quiet."

"You're kidding, right? You know we have a Fall Festival on Saturday. When I left the shop last night Evie said her traffic had increased all week and everyone said they were in for the festival." He tucked his tote under the cabinet and glanced around at the messy shop. "Wow, you've been busy."

"I didn't even get to sit down this morning." I grabbed one of the bins. "I'll get the tables cleaned before I leave. Is Judith coming today?"

"You really don't look at the shift schedule, do you?" He stocked the coffee takeout cups as he talked. "She's working a late shift half with me and half with Evie. I'll be around writing just in case something happens. I know Evie's been worried about her sister-in-law."

So, Deek didn't know. The rumor mill must not reach outside of Bakerstown, where he lived in his mother's basement. "Hey, I've got something to tell you."

He helped me clean tables as I went through what happened last night. After we were done he went back into the office and came out with two cheesecakes to refill the treat case. "I should have stayed through her shift. I had finished my words early, so I thought I'd go home and do some laundry. Mom has stopped making me meals and doing my laundry. I think it's a gentle hint that I need to find my own place. Man, I feel like a heel."

"You wouldn't have been able to stop it and Becky is now cooling off in the jail. It needed to happen, and Toby was here." I held out a plate for Deek to lay a slice of cheesecake, then put it in the display case. "Wait, was Toby here because you called him?"

He blushed before he answered. "I know Tim and Toby have been busy with this murder thing, so I told him I would write here at the coffee shop during Evie's shifts. Just to make sure nothing happened. When I left last night I texted him to let him know Evie was by herself. She only had two hours before close. I'm sorry I left."

My staff took care of one another. I loved that. "Don't be sorry. Becky might not have come inside the shop if she saw you there. It's been a weird couple of weeks. I'll be glad when Evie sells her clock and Greg finds out who killed Gentry."

"Speaking of Gentry, I'm pretty sure he was the guy hanging out here a few weeks ago. I called and left Greg a message today because I wasn't too sure about it when we talked. But after going through my notes, I'm pretty sure he was here. I asked Evie about him, and she said he wasn't there on her shift, but maybe she just didn't notice him. Especially because it's a new shift for her. Sometimes it's hard to keep all the faces in mind." He picked up the clipboard. "The floors look fine, so I'll grab them at the end of my shift. And I'm assuming you didn't get any books stocked from the size of the boxes in the office."

"Sorry, no, I didn't. I can stay later and do that while you deal with the walk-ins." My feet already hurt from standing most of the morning, but I was willing to do my part to keep the bookstore running.

"Don't worry about it. I'll show Judith how to do it when she gets here. She's really comfortable working with customers, so I want to take her out of her comfort zone for a bit. I think she's intimidated with the books because she so wants to be an author herself." He stepped forward and greeted a customer who'd walked in when my back was turned. "Are you here to browse the books or do you need some coffee? Or both?"

The man laughed and pointed to the bookshelves. "Right now, I need some reading material. I'm here for the festival and my wife is out shopping the sales. I want to be productive and get some reading in. I haven't had free time to read in months."

"Browse away. Although if you're a thriller fan, you'll love our selection over there under the speeding train sign." He pointed to the general area behind the couch.

"Perfect, thank you." The man hurried over and started glancing over the shelves.

"You're really good at this too," I commented when the guy was out of earshot.

Deek shrugged his shoulders. "I had a fifty-fifty shot. He looked like either a thriller guy or a true crime reader. I guess I had a feeling, as my mom would say."

Deek's mom was a fortune-teller like my neighbor, Esmeralda. She had her office farther up on the Pacific Coast Highway, so people tended to come from the city to see her. Esmeralda had her regulars, who came from the southern part of the state. I'd even seen a few Hollywood types going into her shop, wearing dark sunglasses and sometimes hoodies, but I knew who they were.

"Okay, if you don't need me, I'm heading home. I think a run with Emma is on the agenda, along with a long, hot bath afterward. I've got kinks in my kinks."

Deek held his hands over his ears. "I really don't want to know."

"I think it's knots on my knots, not kinks," Greg said as he came from behind me and put his arms around my waist. "And when did I say it was okay to start running again? How are you doing, Deek? Is your boss harassing you?"

"No more than usual. Jackie's the one who makes me question everything I do, not Jill." He nodded to the door. "I've got more customers. You weren't kidding when you said it was busy today."

Greg and I stepped away from the counter after I grabbed my tote bag. I'd already stuffed a couple of new books in there because I figured I wouldn't see Greg for a few days. "This is a nice surprise. Oh, are you here to talk to Evie?"

"No, I'm here to see if you have time for lunch. I know I shouldn't be hungry, but I'm starving. Maybe making breakfast is a bad idea."

I tucked my arm through his and shook my head. "Making time for meals is never a bad idea. Your body is probably just trying to catch up from all those days you didn't eat when you were investigating this case."

"That is why I love you. You don't want me to miss meals. It's almost like you care for me." He held the door open.

I walked through and gently punched him on the arm. "You're a dork. And stop teasing me about my addiction to food."

"I was being serious. You actually care if I've eaten during the day. It's a nice change of pace from the previous marriage." He put his arm around me as we strolled toward Diamond Lille's. "Next you're going to ask if I've seen my doctor lately, and not just to get a life insurance policy."

I shook my head. "You give me such low bars to be better than wife number one. I don't even have to stretch to step over them."

"You're right. I should up my expectations. Maybe we should talk about the amount of time you spend reading."

"Oh, now you're just being crazy." I leaned into his shoulder. This was comfortable. We were a perfect match. We both knew the other's buttons, but we chose not to push them. Unless we needed to. "Deek's feeling bad about leaving Evie alone last night."

"He didn't invite the crazy lady to attack Evie. He just wasn't there to stop it, but Toby was, so there's no problem, right?" He glanced over at me. "That's what I told him."

Greg studied me, then nodded. "And that explains why Toby was so fast on the scene. I wondered how he knew just when to be there. Deek called him when he left."

"Well, actually, texted him, but yes. That's what I found out this morning."

He smiled. "Your crew is the exact reason I love South Cove so much. They take care of one another. Even when the person they're protecting doesn't seem to realize the danger they're in."

"You talked to Evie." The road was empty, so we crossed over and into Lille's parking lot.

"This morning. She told me she knew Gentry was Becky's ex, but she didn't think she could have killed him, so she didn't tell anyone. I didn't have the heart to tell her she was protecting the wrong person. Becky is a slimeball, and now she's at least on my radar for Gentry's death. It would help if I could find a murder weapon." He pointed me to the diner door. "No more talk about the case or the investigation or Becky or clocks or Evie or cheating developers or even what you want for Christmas. We need a quiet hour."

"I would like to discuss my favorite jewelry types," I kidded as Carrie pointed us to our favorite booth as we walked into the diner. Lille was nowhere to be seen. Thursday lunch must not be her shift.

After we ordered I leaned back and watched him. "You look tired."

"Guilty as charged. I'm at the point of the investigation when I question everything and anything, especially the decisions I've made since the investigation started." He closed his eyes and then sat forward. "And I'm breaking my own rule. So, you want jewelry for Christmas?"

"Silver settings or chains. But not really. I was thinking we might want to look at our porch and upgrade some of the furniture out there. The table is so uneven, we don't use it. And I'd love to have one of those heaters so we could sit out there on chilly nights just relaxing and watching the stars." I sipped from the iced tea Carrie had just dropped off. "And a reading lounger would be awesome. Although today I might just fall asleep in it."

"You look tired too. Long shift?"

I nodded, setting my tea out of harm's way. "Busy shift. Deek reminded me that Fall Festival had started. I'd blocked it out of my mind. It's a good thing we're not doing much. We'll serve free apple cider on Saturday to customers, but we're not doing anything else. We need to get the shelves restocked, but Judith and Deek are finishing that this afternoon. Evie's all right to work tonight, correct?"

"Why would you ask that?" Greg leaned back and let Carrie set down a hot turkey sandwich with gravy that almost dripped off the plate. The smell made me wish I'd ordered the same. Although I liked Tiny's hot roast beef plate better. He looked up and smiled, "Carrie, tell Tiny I've died and gone to heaven."

"Which means he likes it," I translated Greg-speak to Carrie.

She beamed at him as she dropped off my lunch in front of me. "He'll be happy you said something. I guess some guy questioned his cooking skills a few weeks ago and it hurt his feelings. I wish that guy would come back so I could give him a piece of my mind. Nobody hurts my Tiny."

After she left Greg shook his head. "You are all itching for a fight to save the honor of your teammates."

"South Cove Strong." I dug into my shrimp po'boy sandwich and blessed the day Tiny came to work for Lille. "I can't believe anyone complained about Tiny's food. It sounds like something Evie's ex would do."

As soon as the words came out of my mouth, we locked gazes. Greg waved Carrie down. She nodded, letting us know she'd be right over. I set my sandwich down on the plate. "You don't think it was John, do you?"

"If so, I'm wondering if anyone saw who he was dining with. He doesn't seem like the type of guy to eat alone. And if it was the same night Evie saw him outside, we might be able to charge him with stalking. It wouldn't stick—not with a good lawyer—but it might make him think about bothering her again."

I waited for Carrie to come back to the table and thought that if it was Evie's ex, the fact that we cared about one another might be the piece of information that helped her stay safe from him.

Carrie let us know that she hadn't been working that night. But Tiny was in the kitchen, and the guy actually stormed back there to tell him how horrible his method of cooking steak was, not to mention the mashed potatoes. "You can go back and talk to Tiny if you want."

Greg excused himself and headed across the diner.

Carrie watched him. "When your man gets something in his head he acts. I would have finished my lunch first."

I laughed and picked up my fork. "Which is exactly what I'm going to do. Thanks, Carrie. He appreciates the info even if it's a wild-goose chase."

She nodded, but before she left the table, she said, "Sometimes those are the best kind. Let me know if he wants that reheated."

Chapter 20

When Greg came back from the kitchen he said he didn't want his meal reheated. "This is fine, Jill."

I watched as he started eating again. "Okay, so are you going to tell me what Tiny said? Or at least give me a clue?"

He looked up. "Silver jewelry, right?"

When I didn't laugh he set his fork down and took a drink of his iced tea. "I'll tell you this much. I've got a sketch artist coming down to talk to Tiny. I don't hold out much hope since it's been a while and he was more focused on the words than the guy's face. But he did say he was having dinner with another man. And with Lille's statement that she thought Gentry was here before he died, it's worth having the Bakerstown sketch artist spend a couple of hours. So, can we talk about anything else?"

I dipped a French fry into Tiny's special sauce. I'd figured out it was horseradish and ketchup years ago, but his still tasted better than mine. I guess it was in the ratio. "Well, we can't make any dinner or travel plans until you're done with this investigation. I'm almost done with redecorating the library upstairs. Toby still has no plans to move out of your home gym. So I guess we're out of topics."

"Okay, fine. I don't think even if it is John, now that we know Gentry was his ex-brother-in-law, I'm probably just tying up loose ends here. Evie told me that John thought his sister was stupid to divorce Gentry. And she didn't think it could be him because he was supposed to be working in Canada on some big project." He picked up his fork. "Can I eat now, and can we please talk about something else?"

"Sorry, I know I push sometimes. It's just this one is so close, with Evie being involved and all." I held up my hands. "Oh, I know, Emma has a vet appointment next Monday. Do you want to take her or should I?"

"Jill, you know I can't get away if this investigation is still going on. Besides, didn't you set it on a Monday so you would be off?"

I dumped another fry and grinned. "Of course I did. But it gave us something else to talk about, right?"

"You're pushing my buttons, girl." He pointed his fork at me.

I shrugged. "Probably should get used to it. Anyway, I'm going to check in with Aunt Jackie this afternoon about the event. I know she's going to ask about dinner with her and Harrold. Should I set a date in the future or push her off again?"

"Go ahead and set it. We need to live our lives someday." He glanced at his phone, which had just started beeping. "I'm sure this investigation should be tied up in a month or so. I've got to go. Can you get this?"

"Sure." I leaned in for a kiss and then he was gone. "The life of a police wife. He's here and then he's not."

Carrie stopped by and picked up his plate. "Everything all right, dear?"

"Work called." I pulled out a credit card for the bill. "Go ahead and run our bill. I'm going to head home."

"Do you want a milkshake for the road? My treat?" Carrie took the card and tucked it in her apron, then picked up my plate.

"That's sweet of you. Of course I do. Vanilla, please." I wouldn't want to run until later, but we had plenty of time. And I needed to call my aunt anyway. A call to Jackie was never short.

"Is there any other flavor for you?" Carrie laughed and disappeared.

I thought about what she'd said. Was I in a rut? Should I expand my horizons? Maybe I should run Emma on the trail rather than on the beach today? It was just a few more steps away, but I didn't even think of it. I had a routine. Which included trying to solve Greg's investigations. Which always got me in trouble. And he'd kind of said it was okay to run, at least he knew I was doing it. Rationalization 101, my favorite class.

After signing for lunch and getting back my credit card and my milkshake, I made a decision. I would try one new thing a day. Like tomorrow, if Carrie asked me about a milkshake, I would say, "Chocolate, please." Or maybe strawberry. They used fresh strawberries in a sugar sauce. I headed outside and wondered if this was why I had a routine. Because I never could make a decision.

No matter. I'd do one new thing. Starting today. I'd already decided running the trail would be my one new thing. I hadn't been on it since the coffee house had sponsored a fun run that hadn't turned out to be so much fun for one of the organizers. I pulled out my phone and dialed my aunt, hoping I could get two things done at the same time. Walking home and talking to my aunt.

I'd been foolish to try.

"Jill, why are you calling me from the street? Do you need me to come downstairs?" my aunt asked as soon as the connection was made.

"No, Aunt Jackie, I'm just passing by. I had lunch with Greg just now at Lille's, so I'm walking home now. I wanted to know if there was anything I needed for the festival on Saturday." I waved at the upstairs window of the building my new uncle had his model train shop in, The Train Station.

"I can't think of anything. I called Sadie and added more of those autumn flower cookies for our delivery on Saturday. I ordered the holiday cups, and it showed that they were delivered yesterday. Would you check with Deek or Evie to see if they are in the office?"

"Of course." And this was why I called my aunt. I might have remembered all this, but it might have been too late. "Anything else?"

"You did pick up the apple cider, cinnamon sticks, and the two Crock-Pots when you were at the store Monday, right?"

I thought of the shopping list in my tote. Where I'd put it right after our last staff meeting when we planned what CBM's fall "event" would be. And then I'd completely forgotten it. "Of course I didn't forget. I'm heading into Bakerstown as soon as I get home. I was a little busy on Monday, so I planned to go this afternoon."

"If you say so, dear." My aunt clearly didn't believe me. Which was typical. Especially because I'd just made up the excuse on the fly. "As long as the event goes as planned, I'm not worried about it."

We said our goodbyes and I thought about anything else I might want to do while I was in Bakerstown. I'd check my own shopping list, and maybe if I planned meals right next week, I wouldn't have to go back on Monday. By the time I got home I had a list in my head. I pulled out the shopping list from my tote, quickly added the other items I'd thought of, and then went through the kitchen, looking for things that were low or missing. I even wrote out suggested meals for the next week and a half on the calendar. Pleased with my proactive planning, I gave Emma a kiss and told her we'd run when I got back.

Then I turned on the tunes and drove into Bakerstown.

The grocery store wasn't as crowded as I'd expected. I guess Thursday afternoon wasn't a standard shopping time. And they had the Crock-Pots I'd thought I might have to make a trip to the big box store to get. I was standing in front of the ice cream freezers looking for a few quart containers to add to my stash at home when Beth Winter pushed her cart next to me.

"I'm a big fan of salted caramel. Especially if it has a bit of chocolate in it. I find most recipe blends could be enhanced with a touch of chocolate, don't you?" She reached for a quart and put it into her cart next to a fresh salmon and some French bread from the bakery.

"Beth, I didn't expect to run into you today." I took her suggestion on the ice cream and put two in my almost full cart. "I'm surprised you do your own shopping."

She laughed and glanced around. "I don't. I asked to come along with my chef today just to see what's out there. It's hard to plan meals if you don't get to see what's being sold in stores, don't you think?"

"I tend to plan my meals first, then make my list. But if I see something that grabs my attention, I might switch things up when I get home." I enjoyed talking to Beth. "I've been meaning to come by; in fact, I did one day, but you were busy."

To her credit, the woman blushed, even though she didn't know what I'd seen. "Oh yes, my secretary told me you called. I wasn't feeling well so I spent the day in my bedroom, sleeping. I tend to sleep a lot lately."

Liar, liar. But I wouldn't call her on it. From what I'd seen, her husband had his own little side dish, so why not her? "I'll stop back by when I have time. I'd love to talk to you about your Vivien collection. I'm wondering how you find the items."

She gave me a strange look, but then brushed off the question. "Actually, the antique brokers know what I like. Sometimes they come to me with an item, sometimes they tell me about an upcoming auction. I don't attend those much anymore. I send Jeffrey. I'm afraid he's my eyes and ears. Look, I know your fiancé thinks Jeffrey was involved in that awful murder. But he met with that man to inquire about a Vivien piece I was interested in. When Jeffrey found out the man didn't even have possession of the item, he started working with the dealer who's working with the true owner. He had no reason to kill someone who didn't even possess the item we were trying to buy."

"So, you know about the clock." I let the statement stand and watched Beth struggle with not letting her shock show.

"*You* know about the clock?" She paused, then nodded. "Of course you do. Mr. King probably mentioned it."

"Actually, no. I'm acquainted with the owner." I leaned on my cart.

"If she's interested in selling direct, have her give me a call." Beth pulled out a card. "I'd rather not risk losing it to some other collector. I can give her more than what she would get from an auction house."

"I'll let her know. But Beth, are you sure about Jeffrey?" I brought the question back. "The man was killed."

"Not by Jeffrey. He was with me in the city that night. I'd been wanting to attend an opening for a new painter. It had been on the calendar for months. I pretended to feel fine for a week before we went. Just so no one would tell me I couldn't go. It's hard to have so many people watching you. You don't have room to do anything foolish."

"They must care about you a lot." I hoped my words were correct.

"I hope that's true." She glanced up and saw a woman coming toward us. "And there is my babysitter. I guess my shopping spree is coming to an end. I'm glad I got to see you."

She left and met the woman, who had a full cart. The woman glanced over at me, checking, I guess, to see if I was some sort of hanger-on, or maybe a serial killer. But I must have looked normal, so she dropped her gaze almost as soon as she saw me.

The two of them moved slowly toward the checkout stands, but then I saw Beth's secretary join them. She took Beth's arm and they moved out of the store. The other woman, who must be the chef, put Beth's items in her cart, then grabbed a bag of chocolate chips and added it to the pile.

Maybe Beth hadn't been totally lying when she told me she'd been asleep the day I'd visited. She might not have been asleep at the exact moment, but the woman looked frailer than I remembered. Even when we chatted here at the store, she'd been holding on to the shopping cart like it was the only thing keeping her from sliding to the floor, exhausted.

I checked my list, then pulled out my phone and added a to-do item on next Monday's list. I was going to go visit Beth again. I think she needed a friend.

* * * *

I stopped at the bookstore and parked in the lot behind the buildings, bringing in the apple cider makings through the back. Then I found the fall-themed cups in a box near the door that went into the shop. From the number of empty boxes sitting around, Judith and Deek must have gotten most of the new stock checked in and up on the shelves for Saturday's event.

I was about to leave when Evie came into the office through the door that led to the stairs. "Oh, hi. I didn't expect to see you." She checked her watch. "I'm on shift at five, right?"

"Of course you are. I guess I didn't realize how late it was. I was just dropping off supplies for Saturday."

She glanced around the crowded office. "Jill, you're okay with me being here, right? I know with the whole Becky and John thing, it's been a little crazy. I know it's my fault."

"It's not your fault. The only thing you did was put your faith in the wrong man. I'm sure all of us have done something similar in our lives." I leaned against the door. I thought about Beth and her marriage to Max. "You were able to get out. This stuff is just residuals. It doesn't make up who you are now."

She wiped away tears. "I swear, you are the sweetest woman. I thought for sure I'd be fired after the whole incident with Becky and kicked out of the apartment. Everyone here has their lives together. Me? I'm a mess."

I walked over and gave her a quick hug. "Believe me, no one is as put together as we look. We're one crazy ex-sister-in-law from showing off our flaws. Besides, if we were perfect, what fun would that be?"

She laughed, and then Deek walked into the office.

"I thought I heard something back here." He glanced between Evie and me. "Everything okay?"

"Fine. I was just leaving again. Good job at getting the books stocked." I pointed to the empty boxes.

"We're not quite done, but we got a big chuck on the shelves. I wanted to save a few boxes for Evie, just in case she has a boring shift." He dodged a cup that Evie had picked up and thrown at him. "Hey, just trying to be helpful here."

"I hope I have a boring shift." She smoothed back her hair and tightened the scarf she had tied around her braids, which were swept up into a ponytail. "I could use it."

"I don't think it's going to happen. The midday shift was busy, as was Jill's. I think the Fall Festival frenzy has arrived." Deek frowned. "Maybe 'the Fall Festival frenzy has fallen' is better."

"Adding one more 'f' word doesn't change the fact that we're busy." I moved to the door. "I've got to get these groceries put away. Evie, if you need me, just call. I don't think I'll be busy tonight."

"Judith's here until seven, so I should be fine." Evie pulled on an apron.

Deek held up his hand. "I'm running to grab some food at Lille's, but I'll be back before Judith leaves. I need to finish this chapter. If Evie gets swamped, I'll clock in."

I watched as the two of them went into the coffee shop. Deek didn't fool me or Evie, but I could see the relief on her face when he listed off his schedule. Evie knew Becky wouldn't come back tonight, but her feelings told her she might.

And sometimes what you felt was more real than what you knew.

Chapter 21

Friday was busy, with more stocking and more customers. The store smelled like apple and cinnamon from the cider I'd set up behind the dessert case. Sadie stopped in early to drop off treats and promised another delivery early Saturday morning. I was wiped out when my shift ended. Deek refused my offer for help because Judith had come in with him. "But you're working a longer shift today. I could stay for a while."

"No need. We can handle this." He waved at the crowd wandering through the store. "You should have called me in early. Has it been this crazy all day?"

I nodded. I'd been busy with my commuters. Then the festival crowd had hit at eight and hadn't stopped. "I've filled the case twice and taken out all the cheesecakes, so they should be available to serve."

I hadn't seen Greg last night after I got home from shopping and I'd planned to talk to him this morning, but he'd already left before I got up. I went to fill a box with a dozen of the flower cookies. I hoped it wouldn't leave Evie short.

"Stopping to see Greg?" Deek nodded as I wrote down the box on the staff list. My aunt had put this list into place because she felt I ate too much of the sellable stock. I still did it, even if I might feel a little guilty when I wrote down the food. And bonus, it helped me track my sweet consumption. So now I limited myself to two treats a shift at the most.

"I haven't seen much of him this week. And with all these people in town, I might not see him until Monday night." I scanned the coffee shop and book area. Judith was talking to someone over by the women's fiction section. The woman already had three books in hand and Judith was suggesting another. "Judith has a natural sales ability."

"And it doesn't hurt that she reads a lot. I swear, she knows more books that I do. And it's in different genres. She's knowledgeable in women's fiction, historical, and international travel. I bought three books last week because she recommended them." Deek rang up a coffee and handed the customer her change and a receipt. As she left, he called out, "Have a great day. Anyway, we're good here. You go see the dude and go home."

"I'm taking you at your word. Call if you need me. Emma and I are running this afternoon, but that's all I have on my schedule besides watching a few movies and working on my second blanket." I put my tote over my shoulder and grabbed the cookie box. I greeted a few regulars who were enjoying the festival as I walked out.

The day was beautiful. Aunt Jackie would call it short-sleeve weather. Main Street was closed to vehicles for the festival and people were flowing into the streets, many with bags from the local arts and crafts businesses. I saw Crissy in front of her store, restocking yarn into a cute autumn colors display. I waved but didn't stop.

When I got to the station Tim was on the phones and Greg was standing in the lobby, talking to one of the locals.

I waited for him to finish assuring the woman that he'd look in to the theft of one of her garden gnomes early next week. The woman was leaving when he called after her, "Elizabeth, you know if it's just a prank, the gnome might already be back in its place by now."

"It's not a funny prank. I spent hours painting that statue," she mumbled as she made her way out of the station.

I stood from the chair I'd taken when I came inside and held out the box. "You deserve a treat for being so nice. Doesn't she get her gnomes stolen every year about this time?"

"Yes. And it's making me think it's on a fraternity's initiation list. One of these days I'm going to find the culprit and then I'll report the fraternity to the university. Justin tells me if I do, they'll be banned from bringing in new members for four years if we catch one."

"So now it's on your list to save the world from bad actors."

He pointed to the door. "She's really upset."

"I know. But it seems to be a fall tradition now." I opened the box and gave him and Tim a cookie. "Besides, I have something I need to tell you."

"Of course you do." He took the cookie and motioned to the conference room. "Put the cookies in there and then come into my office."

I dropped off the cookies and noticed there was already a taco bar set up for the officers. Greg brought in off-duty officers from Bakerstown when we had festivals. I didn't realize he fed them too. I went into Greg's office and sat on one of the chairs. "I should have brought more than a dozen cookies."

"That's fine. Sadie's dropping off an order around three. They'll have plenty of sugar to keep them going. What's up?" He signed a paper and moved it to his out-box. "I'm way behind on daily reports due to the investigation. Now we have to have a festival. I'm going to be running on sugar by the day's out."

"I ran into Beth at the grocery store yesterday," I started, but the look on his face made me stop. "What?"

"That's unlikely. Don't tell me you went to her house again." Greg leaned back in his chair.

"No, seriously, she was at the grocery store. Well, Beth, her chef, and her secretary. She had a few things in her cart. I guess she insists on going once in a while to see what's out there. She turned me on to a salted caramel ice cream that's amazing." I leaned forward in my chair.

"Interesting. Now can I get back to work? I promise I'll try the ice cream as soon as possible." He pulled out another file.

"Okay, but she told me that Jeffrey was talking to Gentry about Evie's clock. And when he found out that Gentry didn't have possession, he ended the conversation." I leaned back when Greg's attention focused on me. I hadn't meant to share the ice cream, but I'd brought it up. "Beth said she was Jeffrey's alibi for the day of the killing. I feel bad for her. She hides how she's really feeling because if she doesn't, they don't let her do things. Can you imagine?"

"I can't imagine anyone even listening to me when I suggest they don't do something." He raised an eyebrow, then tapped his pen on the desk and pulled a different file. He read a few pages, then nodded. "It matches what he told us when I pulled him in for questioning. In addition to the fact that he said Gentry was a slimeball. She just volunteered all this in the middle of the ice cream aisle?"

I picked a piece of lint off my pants. "Well, yes, after I asked her how she came across the items Vivien Leigh used to own. And, well, she knows we're engaged. So, she thought my information came from you and not Evie. I didn't mention her, except that I said I knew the real owner. She gave me a card and told her to have Evie call her."

He closed the file and rubbed his head. "Jeffrey was probably my best suspect in Gentry's killing, unless you look at Becky and her brother. At least this confirms that Gentry knew about the clock. Maybe he was pushing for a bigger share."

"Evie doesn't think either John or Becky are killers," I reminded him.

He tapped the file again. "Would you think the person you were married to or the person you ate Thanksgiving dinner with could be a murderer?"

Greg's phone rang and he answered it. He covered the mouthpiece. "Sorry, honey. I need to take this. I'll see you at home."

I'd been dismissed. On the way out of the station, I waved to Tim, who was on another call. Outside, the bright fall scene I'd left just a few minutes ago now looked menacing and suspicious. I made my way home and curled up on the couch with Emma, trying not to think of a world where family killed one another for money. Instead of taking Emma for a run, reading, or watching movies, I watched cooking shows.

I was still there when Greg came home at around eight.

He went into the kitchen and then came back out. "Have you eaten?"

I shook my head. "No. After you broke my faith in humanity I decided I'd just sit here watching good people make good food."

He turned off the television and pulled me up into his arms. "I'm going to change and put away my gun. Go get out something from the freezer and we'll make dinner. Maybe tacos?"

"Tacos are fun," I said. "I like tacos. Good people like tacos."

"You're a nut." He squeezed me and then gently pushed me toward the kitchen. "Go start dinner, woman. Your man needs to eat."

"Hold on a minute," I started, but then I saw the smile on his face. "You're trying to get me out of my funk."

"What? Me?" He disappeared into the office where he stored his gun.

I turned back and went into the kitchen, my black mood lifted at least a little. I still felt bad for Evie if one of her ex-family had really killed Gentry, but I didn't feel overwhelmed by the idea. I think I was more tired than I realized.

After he changed Greg came up behind me and gave me another hug. "Are you feeling better?"

"I don't know what got into me. All of a sudden the world was a gray place and I didn't want to even think about it. Poor Emma didn't even get her run." I put a tomato on the chopping block and started dicing it.

Greg took the knife from my hand. "You get the meat and beans ready. I'll use the sharp knives. You might have been depressed."

"Can it hit you just like that?" I checked the hamburger to see if it was thawed and set the microwave again. Then I took a can of black beans from the cabinet.

"You've been working yourself to the ground at the shop. Then you're running to Bakerstown. Between all that and worrying about Evie, I think you just needed to shut down for a bit. It happens to all of us." He put the chopped tomatoes into a small bowl and grabbed an onion from the basket on the counter. "You're the most positive person I know. You don't like seeing your friends in pain."

"Sadie's the most positive person we know. I'm gloomy Gloria compared to her." I put the beans in a pot and turned on the heat under them. "But I get your meaning. After my shift ends tomorrow I'm turning off my phones and taking a nap."

"I'll believe it when I see it. You and I are a little too much alike in the taking-on-too-much arena. I promise, as soon as this investigation is over, we're going on a real vacation. One where they can't call me back because we're too far away to come back." He dumped the chopped onion into another bowl, then reached for the hamburger from the microwave. "Hey, the Bakerstown Police chief called. They tracked down the death threat to Gentry's phone number. So, one mystery solved. Of course, since he's dead they don't know why, except the theory is Gentry felt slighted by Max cutting him out of upcoming developments."

I handed him a pan to cook the hamburger in. "And now you're going to ruin my evening by telling me that Max was in Apple Valley with Connie Middleton when Gentry was killed."

"Sorry, that's the alibi. I'm trying to find someone else who can verify it, but the bed-and-breakfast hostess claims he and Connie were there all night. That she would have heard if someone left the building. I'm not quite sure that's true, but he was definitely there the next morning." He looked up from the pan of hamburger he was crumbling as it fried. "I'm sorry, I know that would have been the easiest answer."

"Actually, it really doesn't matter because as long as I own the house, there are going to be developers trying to get me to sell. I've kind of come to terms with that. Darla gave me a good idea to leave the house in trust to a nonprofit. With specific instructions about what they can and can't do with the gift." I went back to the fridge to get the cheese and the soft tortilla shells. "I'm going to talk to a lawyer soon to see exactly what I can and can't do."

"I think that's an excellent idea. And if you go before I do, I'll move in with Jim. It will be the two brothers riding the trails again." He grabbed the colander and dumped the hamburger into the basket. He had already set up a pan underneath to catch the grease.

"Well, you could, or I could just leave you a life estate in the property. Either way, but if you want to move in with Jim, I won't bother."

He leaned over and kissed me. "Thank goodness. I really don't want to live with Jim. He's not all that much fun. I'll take your kind offer."

"You could just tell me that what's mine is yours and yours is mine in a few months." I handed him the taco seasoning and he started the mix back on the stove.

"I'd never say that. Well, except for Emma. She belongs to both of us, no matter when you got her. And I guess the kids. I'll take them if something happens to you."

I started laughing. I couldn't help it. Greg always made me feel better. No matter how bleak the situation or the subject matter of the conversation. "That's really thoughtful. Especially if they're still minors at the time."

He stirred the meat. "I'll figure out something. Kids know how to cook and stuff, right? Like when they're three?"

"Maybe we should stick with pets," I answered. "Are we ready to eat?"

* * * *

Saturday morning was twice as busy as Friday had been. I almost called in help, but then I got a short breather and thought I could actually get caught up. I was refilling the empty apple cider warmer when Crissy ran into my shop.

"Coffee, please, and three, no, four flower cookies. I didn't get a chance to eat this morning and I'm swamped over there." She glanced out the window. "I've got Mary watching the store while I come over here. I had to take a bathroom break first or I wouldn't have made it across the street. I know I need help."

"I'm thinking the same thing here." I poured her coffee and tucked the cookies into a bag. "Do you want some apple cider too? It's free."

She handed me her card. "Just ring me up and I'll get out of here. I was wondering if you would come to the NICU tomorrow with me. I told them I'd drop off some blankets early because they're totally out."

"Of course, what time?" I typically had brunch plans with Amy and now Esmeralda, but maybe this would be after that. Either way, I should help out with the event. Especially because I hadn't even finished my second blanket. My promise to Greg about me taking a relaxing after the Festival dissolved. Maybe Monday.

"I'd like to leave about two. If that works." Crissy took her receipt and card, putting both in her handbag along with the cookies. "Remind me how crazy I was today when the next festival occurs. Maybe I'll plan better."

"It's all in the luck of the day. Some festivals, like this one, are amazing. Some are less than that." I reached out for the book the next customer was holding. "See you tomorrow, Crissy. This is an amazing book. It's based on a true story."

The rest of the morning flew by. I hadn't heard from Evie, but she was working the late shift, so I hadn't expected to. I wondered if Greg had told her the full story about the night Becky was arrested. I almost groaned in pleasure when Deek and Sadie showed up at the same time. And about an hour before I'd expected either one.

"I'm so glad you're here. We're just about out of everything." I took the tray from Sadie and put it on the back counter. "And you too, Deek."

"I was beginning to feel overlooked." He washed his hands and put on an apron. "Can I help you get the rest?"

"Please. I have four more trays out there for you. I got a call from your aunt last night doubling today's order." Sadie held out the invoice for me. "I hope you can sell all of this today. It seemed like a lot."

"We probably needed it." I glanced over the list and then up at the clock. "But you're right, it's a lot more than I expected."

Deek came back inside with another tray. "Jackie tends to know things."

That was the truth. My aunt had owned a coffee shop for years before she'd sold out and retired to travel the world. Then she'd lost most of her retirement funds to a Ponzi scheme, and she'd come to South Cove to help with Coffee, Books, and More. I nodded to the back. "We'll trust her instincts here. I'll put this tray in the dessert case and we can put the others in the walk-in."

It took a few minutes to get the Pies on the Fly treats put away, and by then a line had formed at the counter, even though I'd been trying to do both. Deek stepped beside me. "Why don't you go finish up with Sadie and I'll work the line?"

"Sounds good." I handed off the coffee for the current order to the customer. "Have a great day."

"I'm getting a lot of my Christmas shopping done early. You wouldn't have any fantasy books for a younger reader you can recommend, would you?"

Deek held up a hand, stopping me from jumping in. "You go work with Sadie. I'm sure she has other stops."

"You're better at the young adult discussions anyway." I smiled at the woman who'd asked about the book. "I'm leaving you in good hands."

I went to the back, where Sadie was about halfway finished stocking the walk-in with the last tray. "Hey, let me help."

"I could have done it." Sadie nodded to the door leading out to the dining room. "I don't think I've seen the shop this busy since our read-in. I still have kids at church asking when the next one is."

"It's coming fast. Deek wants to do it annually, and I can't say no because we had a huge sale month because of the event. It paid for several new author events this summer." I put the last cheesecake in the fridge and closed the door. "So, what's going on with you and Pastor Bill?"

Sadie blushed and we took a few minutes catching up on each other's lives. Deek tucked his head in the door. "Sorry to bother you, but I'm slammed. Can you help?"

"Duty calls." I gave Sadie a hug. "Let's try to get together for an early dinner soon."

"Just call and give me a date. I'd love to spend more than five minutes with you." Sadie stacked the trays and I held open the door for her.

"I'll call Monday after I check my schedule." I washed my hands and turned to the next person in line. "What can I get started for you?"

Chapter 22

Sunday morning both Esmeralda and Amy bowed out of our weekly brunch. Amy and Justin were heading upstate to check out a winery. And Esmeralda had an emergency fortune-telling appointment. I didn't even raise my eyebrows when she told me why she couldn't come to brunch. I was getting better at accepting my neighbor for who and what she was. I hung up from the second call and refilled my coffee cup.

"So, are you free for the day?" Greg ate a piece of toast with a couple of over-easy eggs. I had turned down breakfast earlier because I'd thought I was going to brunch. "I'd offer to make you breakfast now, but I've got to get going soon. I've got an interview."

"That's okay. I'm just going to have some cereal." I went and fixed a bowl of the sweetened oat cereal I loved. I even ate it by the handfuls when I needed a snack. "I'm meeting Crissy at two to take a load of the blankets to the hospital today. I might go in and review last month's books since I've been putting it off. Aunt Jackie wanted it finished by Monday, and I don't want to spend tomorrow in numbers. I don't have to go grocery shopping, so I thought I'd spend tomorrow catching up on some reading."

"Really? I thought you might go see your new friend, Beth." Greg took his plate and rinsed it in the sink before setting it in the dishwasher.

"I would have if I'd needed to go to Bakerstown anyway. As it is, I just saw her, and we talked. I'll go see her next week. I don't want to wear out my welcome. She looked tired when I saw her at the grocery store. I bet she's resting today." I worried about Beth's health. She hadn't looked well the last two times I'd seen her.

"I'm impressed with your restraint." He leaned down and kissed me. "I'll be home early and we can fry chicken. Maybe we should invite your aunt and Harrold."

I loved my aunt, but I didn't want to see her today. "I'm tired. I appreciate the offer, but I'd rather just be with you tonight. I enjoyed our time on Friday."

He tousled my hair. "Okay, just the three of us. You, me, and Emma."

"Oh, I thought you were talking about the chicken." I closed my eyes. "I am so tired. I hope Crissy doesn't want me to drive us to the hospital."

"I'm sure she would have said something. She probably just wants the company. I've got to get going. See you tonight."

I watched as he hurried upstairs to change. Sometimes I wished Greg was a construction worker, or maybe a banker. That way he'd have regular hours. I already knew from Amy's husband that college professors didn't have nine-to-five hours. Justin worked as many hours as Greg, it seemed.

I puttered around the house for the rest of the morning, then decided to put my time to good use and head into the bookstore to finish up paperwork until I had to meet Crissy. If I stayed here, I was going to fall asleep on the couch. And who knew if I'd wake up in time to walk into town.

I gave Emma a treat and a hug, then grabbed my tote and headed into town. The walk seemed to wake me up a little, and by the time I reached the bookstore I felt better. Finally. Greg was right. I'd been burning the candle at both ends for a while. I took the pathway between the two buildings and went into the office through the back door. I'd learned my lesson about hanging out in the front area when we weren't open. People would bang on the door, wanting a book or coffee. I'd let them in and then someone else would come inside. I was open most of one Sunday a few months ago because I couldn't say no.

Now, I had a coffeepot in the back and, of course, treats in the walk-in, so I didn't have to go into the shop area unless I was looking for a book. And we kept the Advance Reader Copies in the office, so I usually had several books to choose from.

I started a half pot of coffee and grabbed some chocolate chippers from the fridge. Then I opened the computer and started working on the monthly accounting.

About one, I heard a door slam upstairs. Evie must be back from her weekly shopping. I'd heard her tell Deek she was going into Bakerstown today to get some groceries and dog food. I stood and stretched. Sometimes numbers made my eyes cross. Okay, so most of the times I reviewed the accounting my eyes wanted to cross. I went over to refill my coffee and grab a second cookie. I had an hour left and needed to review the staff wages to see if there was wiggle room for any raises. Especially for Deek.

As I moved back to the desk, with coffee and sugar to fortify me, I glanced out the window, expecting to see Evie's black SUV. There weren't any cars in the parking spots. I groaned at the still-overturned sign John had run over with his Land Rover. I hadn't heard from the insurance company. It probably wasn't enough to worry about, but I kind of wanted them to go after John for the costs. Petty, but there it was.

I heard noises again upstairs. Footsteps. Evie was running back and forth in the apartment. I wondered if Homer was giving her trouble. She'd asked me about what flea meds I used with Emma. Maybe she needed someone to hold him while she applied it.

I glanced at my watch. I could take a short break and then be back here to finish up the notes I wanted to take to Aunt Jackie next week.

I went up the inside stairs to the hallway. The door to Evie's apartment was open and I heard someone hit the table. Homer ran out of the apartment and jumped up on my legs, begging me to pick him up. I laughed and reached down for him. He jumped into my arms, then turned to the door, growling. "What's up, little man?"

I took a step toward the open apartment door but froze when John Marshall came out into the hallway.

"Well, you're not supposed to be here." He sucked on a finger where Homer must have bit him. "I guess I'll just have to take both of you. Who do you think Evie will worry about most? You or that rat dog of hers?"

"I'm not going anywhere with you and nether is Homer." Turning, I moved toward the stairs. Maybe I could get down and lock the door behind me before he followed.

"Can you run faster than a bullet? I'm a very good shot. I'll have you know, I train—a lot."

His words stopped me before I could get to the doorway. I looked over my shoulder. Maybe he was joking.

He held up a gun. "Trust but verify. I get it. Yes, I have a loaded gun. I was just going to shoot that dog and leave Evie a message, but I've learned hurting him just makes her mad. No, threatening to hurt him is more effective. And since I have you too, I guess she'll have to go get that clock and bring it here before my hand gets tired of holding the gun."

"You can't be serious." I rubbed Homer's back. He was shaking, but he still had a soft growl that came out every time he looked at John.

"Come on in the apartment. You can call Evie and explain the situation. I think she'll take it better from you. She doesn't seem to hear me when I talk to her anymore." He waved the gun and pushed the door open farther.

I could try to outrun his gun, but I knew how much Greg trained with his firearm. If John did even half that training, I'd be dead before I got to the bottom of the stairs. My only hope was that he would leave after Evie gave him the clock. Greg would know something was wrong if she went to get it. Even if she didn't tell him. Unfortunately, he'd think I was on my way to Bakerstown Hospital with Crissy.

"You're thinking too much. I can hear the gears working all the way over here. I don't see what other options you have right now. Not if you want to live. And if you don't want me to shoot the dog too." He waved his gun. "Please go into the apartment. I'd hate to have someone else walk in on our little discussion."

I tightened my grip on Homer and moved toward the open door. I didn't want the little dog to jump and cause John to shoot us. He might have the heart of a lion, but his body mass was no match for a grown man. "This isn't going to work. I'm supposed to be somewhere soon."

"Well, you're not going to make it, are you?" He nodded to the apartment. "Go inside. If you're good and Evie hurries, maybe you can still make your appointment. Although on a Sunday, I'm not sure where you think you're going."

I didn't want to show my hand any more than I already had. Besides, if Crissy came looking for me, he might hear her. Which would put her in danger too. I moved to the couch in the living room and sat down, Homer in my lap. I had to hold his collar because he had his teeth bared and was focused on John.

"He's such a little shit." John shut the door, then sat in the wing-backed chair. He tossed his phone to me. "Call her from this. We'll see if I still matter enough for her to answer my call."

I picked up the phone and opened the app.

"Don't get cute. Her number is on my recent calls. You don't have to pretend you know her number and dial the police station instead."

That had been my plan. I opened the recent page with one hand because I had to keep Homer in check. He was right; Evie's name was right at the top. The top of a whole list of calls she hadn't answered. She wasn't going to answer his call this time either. "This won't work."

His eyes narrowed. "What part of this won't work, in your expert opinion?"

I held up the phone so he could see the screen. "She hasn't picked up the last twenty calls. Why would she pick up this one?"

"Because you're going to be dead if she doesn't." He met my gaze and his eyes were black. Dead eyes.

"I want to talk to her, believe me. But if I call her from your phone, she isn't going to pick up. Let me use the landline. It will show the bookstore. She'll pick up a call from the bookstore."

He rubbed the back of his hand over his lips. Finally, he nodded. "You're right. I can't believe I'm saying this to a woman, but you have a point. Walk over to the landline on the wall. Don't try to escape. I'll have the gun on you the whole time."

I used his phone to make sure I was dialing Evie's number correctly. I didn't think I'd get many shots at it. John was on edge and he wasn't calming down. I tightened my grip on Homer as he squirmed to get out of my arms.

"Hey, Jill, what's going on?" Evie sounded like she was in a store. People were chatting around her. She must be in line. "Do you need me to work an extra shift?"

"When can you get home? There's an issue." I tried to keep my voice from shaking. "I'm in your apartment looking for the blankets to take to the hospital today. Homer's really upset."

"The blankets aren't due for another two weeks. And Homer loves you." Her voice turned wary.

"He's barking his head off and shaking. If I wasn't holding him, he'd be biting. Anyway, I need to meet Crissy at the police station at two to pick up the rest of the blankets that are stored there. Can you get here by then?"

"Jill, I don't know what you're talking about." She paused, and I could hear her talking to the clerk. "I'll be back in town in about thirty minutes. Can we talk then?"

"Good, so you're going to hurry back? I appreciate it. You know how Greg gets when I don't check in. He's a worrier." I willed all my angst into my words, hoping she'd get the clues I was sending. "I'll control Homer."

He took the phone away from me and pushed me down to the couch. "I hope you convinced her. Otherwise she's going to be less one dog and one boss."

He hung up the phone and then came to sit on the wing chair. "I guess it's you and me for a while. I'd ask you to make me something to eat, but I hear you're not the domestic type."

"I cook." I rubbed Homer's ears. "But not for you."

He picked up the gun and twisted it back and forth. "You'll be surprised at what I can make you do. But don't worry, I'm not hungry."

I leaned back on the couch to wait. Hopefully Crissy wouldn't come looking for me. And hopefully Greg would. "So, all this is for a clock?"

He snorted. "No. All this is for the money that rich broad in Bakerstown will pay for a stupid clock. I can't believe Dad gave it to Evie. He was always soft on her. You would have thought she was his kid, not me."

In for a penny. I decided to ask the million-dollar question. "So, you killed Gentry too? Your own brother-in-law?"

"Ex-brother-in-law. Once the divorce was over I thought I'd never have to see that loser again. Except Becky had this bright idea. We were back East. Gentry was here in California. He could get close to Evie and just take the clock. But I guess the guy wasn't as stupid as I thought. He decided to double-cross us and sell it to that Jeffrey guy. Of course, once the guy found out he didn't really have the clock, he stopped returning Gentry's calls. I guess he's got some morals, even if he's sleeping with his married boss." He set down the gun and picked up a crochet hook Evie had left on the table. "Not that I expect less of a woman. You're always looking for the next mark, aren't you?"

I didn't want to react to his oversimplification of Beth and Jeffrey's relationship. Instead, I turned it back to Max. "Well, I think in that relationship her husband is the one who went off the farm early. I think you should look at Max's actions before you throw stones at Beth."

"You women always stick together, don't you?" He turned the hook over and over in his hands. "It's never the woman's fault. And yet the damage is still done. Believe me, I know my sister screwed up that marriage. I'm just surprised Gentry figured it out. Like I said, the guy was an idiot."

"So, you met him to talk. Maybe renegotiate the deal he thought he had with Becky? Offer him more and you'd cut your sister out of part of her share?"

"Exactly." He glanced at his watch and set down the hook. Then he went to stand by the window, looking out on to the parking lot. "I finally find a woman who has a brain cell and she's unfortunately in the wrong place at the wrong time. Let's just be quiet for a bit while we wait for my ex-wife. I'd hate for her to get the wrong idea about the two of us."

I held Homer closer. He was still watching John and he had a slight growl in his throat as the man stood at the window. The gun was still on the end table. But John would see me if I moved, and I wasn't a match for a one-on-one fistfight. He'd win and I'd be dead and probably Homer as well.

Evie's apartment used to be my aunt's, and we'd upgraded the security. As long as the alarm had gone off when John had broken in, Greg and his men should be showing up any time now. And if Evie had understood even one of my hints, she might have called the station. I still had hope, but honestly, as soon as Evie showed up, he didn't need me or Homer anymore. I'm sure Evie would fight for both of us, but it might not be enough.

Maybe this was one of the times Greg had been right. I'm always in the wrong place at the wrong time. Except all I'd done today was go to work to get some stuff done while I waited to go deliver blankets. No good deed goes unpunished.

As I held my silent pity party, the front door to the apartment burst open and Toby entered with his gun drawn. I saw John move toward the table, but then the back door opened and Greg and Tim burst in. Greg had a gun aimed at John. I could see when Greg got close enough to press the barrel into John's back because that's when John stopped moving. His arms went up and behind his head like he'd done it before.

"You all right?" Greg stepped toward me after Tim put handcuffs on John.

I nodded, rubbing Homer's back. He'd stopped growling as soon as Toby and Greg entered the apartment. Apparently, he'd turned the protection duty over to them. Dogs knew who to trust. And John was not on that list.

"He killed Gentry." I stood and moved as far away from him as I could. "He wanted the clock money for himself."

"Yeah, his sister figured that out. I guess she still had part of a heart left. She just told us that John was the mastermind of this entire situation." He slowly holstered his gun as Toby and Tim led John Marshall out the back door.

"You can't believe anything that witch says," John screamed from the apartment deck.

Homer leaned into me and sighed as soon as he saw John leave the apartment. I rubbed the little guy's head. "You were amazing today."

Chapter 23

Evie showed up just as they were putting John into the back of the police car. She'd taken one look at him and turned to the building, running up the stairs to the apartment. At least that's what Toby said when he told the story. "She didn't care about John being held in the police car. No, she was worried about Homer."

I had to agree with his assessment. When Evie reached the apartment, her face lit up when she saw Homer in my arms. The little guy started wiggling in excitement and she ran to him. She took him from me, then went to the door to get his leash.

Evie turned to me and shrugged. "Sorry, he probably needs to go out. I don't want him to be too excited."

I didn't blame her. We had plenty of time to talk out what had happened. I turned and looked at Greg, who was leaning on the doorframe, watching me. "Look, this wasn't my fault. At all. I thought Evie was upstairs having problems with Homer when I kept hearing him running around the apartment. Well, I thought I was hearing Evie run around the apartment. Homer's too tiny to make much noise. Anyway, I went upstairs to help, and Homer ran out of the apartment directly to me. Then John appeared. I didn't have time to get away because he had a gun in his hand."

"I can't even let you go to work without you getting into trouble." He pulled me into his arms and squeezed me tightly. "I'm so glad you're okay."

"How did you know I was here?" I relaxed into his hug, but I didn't want him to let go, like ever.

"We had an alarm go off at the bookstore. When you didn't answer I walked over, but by then he had you in the apartment. I watched on the camera feed downstairs until Toby and Tim got here. And the best part: We have his confession on tape." He kissed me on the head, then let me go.

"I thought Becky told you he killed Gentry?" Now I was confused.

Greg picked up John's gun and put it in a baggie. "She did, but she didn't have any proof. So we needed something more. Now we have her testimony and his confession and, from what my CSI guys found in his hotel room, what looks like a murder weapon."

"He kept the knife?" It never failed to surprise me what stupid things people did. "There's a whole big ocean right there for him to dump it in. Never to be seen again."

"Hubris." Greg looked around the room. "I need to call to get the techs over here so we can get Evie and her pup back home before nightfall."

Crissy stood in the doorway and knocked on the wall. "Hey, sorry. I see things are happening here, but are you still going to Bakerstown with me?"

I glanced at Greg, who held his hands out in a go-ahead motion. "Sounds like I'm free here. I need to run down to the office to grab my tote. Meet you out front."

"Okay. And on the way there, you'll explain what's going on?" Crissy glanced back at the two police cruisers in the parking lot.

"Of course. See you in a couple of minutes." I reached my office before my legs started shaking so bad that I had to sit down for a bit. I bent down and let the tears come. I'd been close to death before, but this time I didn't know if I was going to get out of the jam. Maybe I'd just stay out of Greg's investigations from now on. And not try to help others so much. I wiped the tears away and laughed.

And that was like telling myself I wasn't going to eat sugar anymore. I picked up my tote and then stopped at the display case, grabbing two Iris cookies. I needed sugar, and it wasn't nice to eat in front of someone without offering them a cookie too.

Maybe we'd get milkshakes at the drive-in on the way home.

* * * *

Time had flown by since that afternoon sitting with Homer in Evie's apartment. Evie had sold the clock to Beth or, actually, Beth's LLC, which held the ownership of all her treasurers. John had been charged with the murder and a few other charges, like breaking and entering and holding me hostage. I guess there wasn't a charge for holding a dog hostage or Greg would have charged him with that as well.

Tonight I was at the South Cove Winery with Amy, Esmeralda, and Darla for a girls' night out. Darla had told her staff not to come to her with any questions. And Matt, her boyfriend, had told them not to let Darla do any work tonight. The band was playing soft rock and we were all a little tipsy when Deek came into the Winery for dinner.

"Deek! Come over here and sit down for a second." I waved my barista over. "How's moving going?"

"Fine. Evie left the apartment cleaner than I'm leaving the basement, that's for sure." He sat down, and Amy poured him a glass of beer from the pitcher.

She held out the beer. "Go ahead. The glass is clean. Apparently, Esmerelda doesn't drink beer. She's a gin and tonic person."

He took the glass and held it up. "Thank you. Here's to the four loveliest ladies of South Cove."

"Why, Deek, you're making me blush." Amy smiled. "Nice to know I'm still desirable even though I'm an old married lady."

"Now hold on, you're going to get me in trouble." He sipped his beer. "Anyway, my mom said to thank you for renting me the apartment. I seriously think she thought I'd never move out."

"And how old are you really?" I teased, and the mark hit home. His face blushed into his blond roots. "Anyway, I should be thanking you for taking the apartment. I hate renting to someone I don't know. When Evie bought her house I thought it might just stay empty for a while. Especially after Toby turned the apartment down."

"He's a saving fool." Deek glanced over at the hostess, who had a bag she was holding up for him. The Winery didn't do anything but bar food, but the pizza was really good. He drained the glass as he stood. "There's my dinner. Thanks for the drink. I need to finish unpacking so I can spend Sunday writing. I'm close to getting this next book done, at least the first draft."

I watched him leave and then turned back to my friends. "He's a hard worker."

"Everyone in South Cove is chasing a dream." Esmeralda had been watching him leave too. "I'm seeing a bright future for him."

I picked up my glass. Esmeralda was right. We were all chasing a dream of some sort. Right now all my dreams were coming true. I had a man I loved. A home to shelter us. The best dog in the world. And a table filled with friends. "To bright futures. For all of us."

Recipe

Esmeralda's Creole Seafood Stew

I love starting a recipe with sautéed onions, peppers, and garlic. The kitchen takes on a smell that screams home and comfort to me. And when it's cold outside and I want a little bit of fancy, this fish stew does the trick. Especially if the Cowboy (my husband) has made a batch of fresh bread that day. Esmeralda grew up in New Orleans, so her version of this stew is probably a little spicier than mine, but you can always add a little tabasco to the mix.

Heat a large Dutch oven, then add:
 3 tbsp. olive oil
 1 cup chopped sweet onion
 1 tsp minced garlic
 1 chopped green pepper
 3 chopped celery stalks

Sauté until the veggies are translucent, then add:
 1 quart tomatoes (or one 28-oz. can)
 1 small can (6 oz) tomato paste
 3 cups chicken stock
 1/2 tsp thyme
 Salt
 Pepper
 1/2 tsp cayenne pepper

Simmer for 20–30 minutes to combine the flavors.

Add to the stew:
 1 lb. tilapia, cut into bite-size pieces
 1 lb. cleaned and shelled shrimp

Simmer another 5–10 minutes.

Serve with fresh baked bread or a green salad.

Can't get enough of Lynn Cahoon?

Don't miss the rest of the Tourist Trap series

and check out her newest series,

The Survivors' Book Club Mysteries.

THE TUESDAY NIGHT SURVIVORS' CLUB

is available now

from Lynn Cahoon

and

Lyrical Press

Printed in the United States
by Baker & Taylor Publisher Services

Printed in the United States
by Baker & Taylor Publisher Services